"So, you wish to become a nun then?" he asked, his voice almost a whisper, teasing her ear with his breath.

"No, not a nun," she stuttered. "But I could live a contemplative life there." Her claim was a bold one and one that would be refuted by most any person who knew her.

Suddenly, he stood behind her, grasping her shoulders and drawing her back against him. His body was like a stone wall, all hard with no softness to be felt anywhere. He leaned down and whispered again.

"Would you give up all that you have, Lady Sybilla? Would you be able to obey and live quietly?"

He moved one arm across her, holding her to him while he used the other to slip into her hair and move it to one side. His breath tickled her neck now and she tried to ease away. Instead, it opened the whole of her neck to him. Exposed, held securely against him, she was vulnerable in a way she'd never felt before. She should be crying out in fear, but her body reacted most strangely—her breasts swelled under the weight of his arm, her skin tingled yet ached for something more…

"Would you give up everything?"

* * *

His Enemy's Daughter
Harlequin® Historical #1034—March 2011

His Enemy's Daughter

TERRI BRISBIN

*Knights of
Brittany

Bk 3*

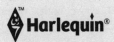 **Harlequin**®

4 ½ H

TORONTO NEW YORK LONDON
AMSTERDAM PARIS SYDNEY HAMBURG
STOCKHOLM ATHENS TOKYO MILAN MADRID
PRAGUE WARSAW BUDAPEST AUCKLAND

Recycling programs
for this product may
not exist in your area.

ISBN-13: 978-0-373-29634-7

HIS ENEMY'S DAUGHTER

Prologue

Thaxted Keep
north-eastern England—
June AD 1067

Bishop Obert pounded his fists on the thick wooden table in a most inappropriate gesture for a man of God. The muscles in his cheek began to twitch and he fought to keep control over his completely human temper. 'Twas times like these when he wished he'd never taken Holy Orders or represented the king. 'Twas times like these when he would like nothing more than to raise his fists and react to the words spoken to him. The scarred warrior came closer to the table, undeterred by his friends' furious whispered warnings. Obert could not help but flinch as he approached.

First, the man's size would give any man pause for he stood more than six feet tall and possessed the muscular build, power and menace of a man of war. But his face,

half-torn apart by an axe's blow and half still the one
that earned the man the title of the 'Beautiful Bastard',
gave him pause for another reason and drew some other
emotion from him.

Obert thought fear the likely cause, for no one but a
fool would look on Soren Fitzrobert and not offer up a
prayer for their own soul and his. And no one who knew
him before the fateful blow struck him down in the Battle
of Hastings would ever look on him now and not feel pity
for all he'd lost. But Obert had dealt with enough proud
men in his life to know that pity would make things
worse.

'These are the king's orders, my lord,' he said, using
the title he knew the man wanted and craved almost as
much as he craved a return of his appearance. 'Surely
you would oblige the king and carry out this one task
before taking your own lands?'

'Why can Brice not see to this task for the king?'
Soren demanded. 'Eoforwic was his kin by marriage,'
he offered, 'at the order of the king.' Obert observed
his glare and heard the sarcasm in his voice. The anger
was subsiding and acceptance had crept in, whether the
warrior recognised it yet or not.

'The king has asked this of you,' Obert said calmly.
'Since Alston sits in the north, you can travel by way
of Shildon and handle the matter. He does not wish for
the rebels to gain a stronghold while our attentions are
elsewhere.'

Lord Giles tugged his friend back from the table
and spoke to him quietly. Lord Brice stood silently, but
watched with grave regard for his friends. Finally, Soren
nodded to Obert.

'Very well, my lord bishop,' he forced through his teeth. 'I am ever the king's loyal subject.' Soren tilted his head in a bow that was neither respectful nor meant to be.

Obert watched as the warrior's friends offered their help in the endeavour and as the man begrudgingly warmed to the thought of fighting Saxon rebels. Though Soren accepted it, Obert knew that he was different, changed irreparably by the blow that had nearly killed him. Never again would he be the carefree, beautiful young man who drew women to his bed like a bee to honey. Never again would any man look at him without wincing in pain or in sympathy…or in pity at his condition.

God help the woman meant as his wife! The pity filling Obert's heart in that moment was for Sybilla of Alston. The king's declaration ordered Soren to marry her if she was alive, but gave him the discretion to marry elsewhere if she did not please him. Watching the three friends talk, he wondered if their advice would temper his anger.

Obert had overheard Soren's intentions to destroy anyone related to Durward of Alston, the man who'd wrought the terrible damage to his body long after the battle was called. Would his vengeance take the life of the innocent young Sybilla or could Soren be directed away from his path of darkness before she was destroyed? And before his soul was damned?

Offering up another prayer, Bishop Obert announced that he would present Soren with the king's charter after Mass. Leading Lord Giles and Lord Brice and their wives into the chapel, he noticed Soren's unease at being surrounded by so many people. As he prepared the altar and donned the garments necessary for celebrating the Mass, Obert prayed as he'd not done in many, many years.

Mayhap God could influence this knight when his friends and others had failed?

But, as he watched over the next weeks as Soren prepared to head north and saw the darkness in his spirit and in his heart, Obert doubted that anything, mayhap even God's intervention, would be strong enough to help in the knight's battle to become the man he should be.

Chapter One

Shildon Keep,
north-east England—
July AD 1067

The acrid stench of fire and death burned his nostrils and his eye. Soren Fitzrobert blinked quickly and surveyed the devastation before him.

Crops and outbuildings yet burned in the late daylight of midsummer, the smoke darkening the sky more effectively than the setting sun could. The dead lay in pools of their own blood as it seeped into the ground. The silence crushed him, for not a sound echoed across the yard or the land surrounding it now. Stephen approached—from his good side, he noticed—and waited for his orders.

'They are cowards,' Soren said as he lifted his helm off and rubbed his head. 'Look, they burn their fields, kill their own people and run.'

'For certain, these were Oremund's orders,' Stephen

answered, disdain for the man involved clear in his voice.

'If he was not dead, I would kill him again, slowly, for something like this,' Soren declared. Lord Oremund had been in league with the rebels who sought to overthrow the king's rule and return the old Saxon lords to their place in England. He'd been killed in the battle to secure his friend Brice's claim to Oremund's half-sister's lands.

Oh, vengeance ran hot in his own blood and this bit of sympathy for the slain did not cool it. He had cause to seek out and destroy those responsible for his condition, but these villagers—men, women, even children—deserved not the fate of being massacred by their lord's men. Soren even understood how innocents could be caught up in the throes of war, but this was not warfare.

This was slaughter.

'Seek any who live and gather the dead for burial,' he ordered. 'Burn the bodies of those who fought against us,' he added.

Stephen hesitated, but did not speak. Soren turned his good eye to gaze at him. The flinch in the man's gaze lasted less than a heartbeat of time, but it happened and Soren saw it. Worse, though, was the glint of pity that passed quickly through the battle-hardened warrior's eyes for him.

His stomach clenched in a way now familiar to him when faced with this constant and unfailing reaction to his face. Fear or horror or revulsion followed quickly by pity. By Christ, he was sick of it! Soren turned away and walked off, not waiting to see if his orders were obeyed or not.

His blood boiled with hatred then. He would seek out the get of Durward of Alston and destroy any of them who yet lived and wipe his very name from the earth. The skin over his eye and the ragged scar down his face and neck itched then, reminding him of the damage wrought by the coward Saxon after the battle had been called. Soren fought the urge to touch it, for there were too many watching him now.

Another of Brice's men called out to him and Soren nodded for him to approach. In tow, the halting shape of a priest walked behind, head bowed, prayers whispering under his breath. The priest did not look up and so he collided with Ansel and stumbled. It was as the priest raised his head that their gazes met and it happened.

The horror. The fear.

The priest instinctually made the sign of the cross and looked away as though unable to bear looking at him. Soren seethed with anger and hatred and lashed out.

'Get him out of here, Ansel!' he yelled. His voice echoed in the silence and everyone who was not watching, now did so. Soren did not care.

'Soren, he wants to bless the dead,' Ansel explained calmly, unaffected by his fury.

He sucked in a breath, trying to regain control, as the need to strike and hurt and destroy pulsed through his blood and nearly overwhelmed him. Clenching his fists and his teeth, Soren waited for the blinding rage to ease. The priest cowered and whispers rippled through the yard as the people there, both villeins and his men, waited to see his actions.

He could not speak, his throat clogged with anger; his arms and hands ached with the need to hurt someone, anyone. Soren simply nodded permission at Ansel as he strode off. The only thing that helped at times like these was labour—hard, physical toil that would tire his body and drain some of the hatred from his soul. So, he walked to where groups of the men cleared the bodies from the fields and wordlessly joined them.

Hours later, exhausted from days of hard riding and the battle this morn and even more from the digging and carrying, Soren barely made it to his blankets. It would take days to bury all the dead and get things in order here before he could head north to Alston. Days wasted when he should be taking control of his own lands and killing those related to Durward.

He had given his word to Obert and to Brice, so he had no choice but to see this through. And he would, though not happily. Once he had held the charter in his hands, spoken the words making him the king's man and received the bishop's blessing, the tension had grown within him. With every passing hour and day, the need to claim his own lands and make his place forced him forwards, like a hunger in his belly for a meal he could not or should not eat.

With every passing day, the gnawing fear that this dream would be snatched away from him grew. Held out like a choice bone to a hungry dog, the promise of these charters enticed them to dance to the king's tune, regardless of the dangers. Soren and his friends were bastards, never meant to inherit or rule over wealth or lands. This opportunity from the king was unheard of and the threat of failure dogged his every step, just as it had Giles and Brice.

No matter now, he told himself for the thousandth time since regaining consciousness and discovering the offer made by Bishop Obert. Soren's dreams and hopes for a life had ended on the battlefield and now he lived only for vengeance. Though he would pursue the king's gift, he had little planned once he actually claimed it.

As he fell asleep on his fifth day of 'handling' Shildon for Brice and the king, the guilt struck him. And the irony as well, for he had the same fate in mind for Alston as Oremund had done here—burn it to the ground and wipe the slate clean so he could make his own mark on it. He wondered if he would feel pity for the get of Durward when they were dead at his hand and whether it would wipe him clean as well.

Sleep claimed him before he could answer his own question.

Soren called out for his men to mount up and then did so himself. He fought to keep the smile from bursting forth on his face, for it would only make him appear more demonic than he was without it. After securing the lands and organising the people left alive, Soren was leaving one of Brice's men in command until Brice decided who would oversee these lands for him.

The thought of riding to the lands that would be his, cleansing it of the vermin now living there and the fighting that would be necessary to accomplish those tasks charged his blood with heat and made his muscles ache to draw his sword. There would be time and opportunity aplenty, so he bided his time now, waiting for his men to fall into line behind him.

His attention was drawn to watching as they formed in their battle-ready lines and he never noticed the small boy approaching from his side. The scrawny child's bleating scream made him turn just before the boy attacked.

Attacked? The boy did indeed have a dagger in his hand and he held it high as he ran towards Soren and his mount. It took little time or effort to stop the attack, for Soren simply leaned over and grabbed the pitiful thing from his feet by the clothes he wore and dangled him above the ground. Due to Soren's long reach and the boy's non-existent one, there was no hope for success or escape.

'What the hell do you do, boy?' he yelled, shaking the boy until he dropped the dagger. Pulling him in closer, Soren pushed his hood back and used the horror of his face to terrify him even more. 'Do you think to kill me?' Once his men realised there was no threat, they laughed at the boy's puny attempt and waited for Soren to handle him.

'You…you…' the boy sputtered, swinging his fists even though he could not reach Soren.

'Bastard?' Soren offered in a low voice.

'Aye,' the boy nodded and then spat at him. 'You bastard!'

That insult had stopped hurting some time ago. Soren had discovered the truth of his parentage at about the same age as this boy here and had learned the hard way not to let it goad him into anger or action.

Insults only had power when you let them control you, Lord Gautier's voice expressed a long-forgotten lesson of life.

'As is my king and yours now, boy,' Soren agreed.

His men laughed, having been taunted with the same words themselves since most of them were born out of the bonds of marriage. That was part of why they'd all banded together and why he was at ease with them. No high-born men in his ranks to belittle him. No legitimate sons of nobles served with him, for only Gautier's legitimate son Simon had ever befriended them. Bastards all, with excuses made to no one for it.

Soren dropped the boy onto the ground and waited to see what his next move would be. Strange, the boy was the first one here who did not flinch or wince at the sight of his face.

'What are you called?' he asked.

'I am called Raed,' the boy said as he stood and thrusted out his chin.

'Raed of Shildon, where are your parents?' Soren realised that the name did match the boy's colouring, even though his own did not. The boy glanced away from him, looking instead at the freshly dug graves along the road and nodded.

'I have no mother,' he answered in a low voice. 'My da lays there.'

An orphan. Soren glanced over at Guermont to determine if his men had killed the boy's father. Guermont's slight shake told him that it had been the work of Oremund's men.

'What skills do you claim?' Soren asked. Something about the boy touched him deeply, in a place Soren had not thought existed any longer. This Raed seemed to have about eight years and Soren remembered how strong pride had filled him at that age. The boy shrugged and shook his head.

'Foolish and fearless, then, for attacking an armed knight with but a puny dagger is asking for death.'

As the words escaped, a twinge pierced that place again—the one that recognised the truths one did not wish to know. Raed leaned over and picked up the dagger, shifting it from hand to hand, positioning it much as a warrior would. Clearly, the boy had used it before. In that moment, Soren made a decision that surprised even him and for reasons he could not understand fully.

'Fearless, I can use. Foolish, I can beat out of you,' he said, gruffly. The boy's face paled, but he did not run or turn away. 'I am in need of a squire, I think. Bring him, Larenz.'

The men laughed and Larenz approached the boy, grabbing hold of his shoulder and dragging him to the back of their troop. Not certain why he had just taken on the task of training the boy, Soren raised his hand and gave the signal to ride.

He never caught sight of the boy during the next four days' journey to Alston, but Larenz reported on him each day. Only the night before they reached Alston did the boy show himself and only for a moment before he tucked himself back into the shadows of the camp.

Soren's rest was fitful the night before the battle, as it always was—partly due to facing an unknown outcome and partly due to the thrill of battle. He woke from dozing and walked the camp, speaking to some of the men, yet in reality seeking out the boy he'd taken. He found him, curled in a ball far from the cooling ashes of a fire, shivering in the dawn's chill. Seeing an unused blanket nearby, Soren draped it over the scrawny form and began to walk away, stopped by the quiet whisper of the child.

'And what are you called?' Raed asked.

'Soren,' he said. 'Soren the Damned.'

For no matter what happened on the morrow, no matter the outcome of William's fight against the rebels plaguing his lands, no matter that the blood of his enemy would be spilled, Soren knew his soul was damned to the darkness in which it now lived.

Chapter Two

Sybilla, Lady of Alston, stood up straight and moaned as her back spasmed in response to the movement. Pressing her fists into her lower back, she tried to ease the pain caused by leaning over too much and by carrying too many large rocks to the wooden palisade. They must shore up the defences, said Gareth, the commander of those who yet defended her and the keep. So, she helped as much as she could. Lady or not, another pair of hands lightened the work of all and gave her the hope that the wall could be strengthened to protect the keep from the coming invader.

Sybilla accepted a cup of water from the servant girl passing by, tightened the leather ties around her braid and began anew. They had little time to finish this task before the invader king's pawn arrived at their gates. After receiving the message that he travelled there to claim the lands of her father, Sybilla and her late father's steward Algar decided to protect themselves from the devastation committed on their neighbours and kin when faced with the same situation. She did not believe they could hold out long, but if they presented their strength, she and they hoped to negotiate a peaceful transition— one that allowed her people to live and her to travel to her cousin's convent and live out her life there in peace and contemplation.

With her father and her brother dead, with no other Saxon kin able to come to her rescue or to stand against these invaders as they moved inexorably north towards her lands, Sybilla knew she and her people had few choices and little power.

They worked until nightfall, taking advantage of every moment of summer's daylight to build the wall as high and strong as they could. Gareth had nodded his approval of their efforts in that stern, serious manner of his, but Sybilla knew it was not enough. Still, they had two days, possibly three, before the invaders arrived and they would take every moment given to them to prepare.

The birds' song that heralded the dawn also brought terror to their doors, for the invaders crested the hill across from the keep and formed their lines to attack. Sybilla quickly gathered the children and took them to the back of the keep and carried out whatever Gareth ordered. Though she'd lived there for all her life, never once had they needed to defend it from outsiders. Even when her father and brother went off to fight alongside their king—her brother to Stamford Bridge and then her father to Hastings—their defences here were perfunctory and never needed.

Now, though, it meant the difference between life and death.

When things were settled in the keep, she climbed to the top of the wall to see what forces they faced. Gareth ordered her away, but Sybilla thought that meeting the enemy face to face might ease the situation. If Duke William of Normandy's man thought them no threat, he might not attack before they could negotiate. Holding her hand over her eyes to shade the growing light of the rising sun, she shivered when she saw him.

Black. Everything he wore was black, except for the slash of red on his shield, angling to the left that she understood spoke of his bastardy. Or his duke's? She knew not which, but once more her body trembled. His armour was black, not reflecting the rays of the sun above him. His horse, a huge, monstrous destrier, was the colour of midnight, without any markings to lighten his coat. And Sybilla felt as though death stood before her on the field.

Or the devil incarnate?

She shook herself from fear's control and walked to Gareth's side. His jaw clenched, he issued commands to his men in a low voice so that they would not carry across the open field in the silence. Sybilla noticed the silence then, and counted their numbers, at least the ones she could see.

Holy Mother in Heaven! They would never survive an attack from a force of this strength. She began to think they'd made a mistake when the giant's words confirmed it.

'I claim the lands and people of Durward the Traitor and order the gates open.'

Gareth shook his head and, though tempted to call out orders of her own, she acquiesced to his experience and knowledge in such matters. 'Twas a mistake.

'Prepare to die!' the warrior called out and he and his men launched their attack.

Gareth ordered her from the wall and Sybilla rushed down the steps, intending to get back inside the keep before the invaders reached the walls. The wall shuddered in that moment and Sybilla realised that the first line of attackers were using rams to knock down the wall! Worse, they did not approach the strongest part of the wall near the gate; they used their weapons on the newest section, the weakest part. She needed to get past the very place that they were battering down.

Rushing along the path, avoiding the soldiers running to take their places and listening to her people crying out in terror, Sybilla tried to focus on all that Gareth had told her. Instead, every time the walls shook, she paused. Then, her worst fear was realised as the ram did its horrible task and the section of the wall in front of her shattered and fell.

Until Sybilla regained consciousness, she did not know she'd lost it.

She struggled to get to her feet, but her head ached and dizziness made her nauseous. She reached up to push off the blinding bandage that covered her head and eyes and discovered it was not a bandage blocking her sight at all—she was blind.

'Here now, lady,' a familiar voice whispered to her. Aldys, her maid's mother, touched her face, drew the bandages back into place and eased her back down. 'You were injured, my lady. You must lie still,' she warned.

Sybilla tried to touch her face, her eyes, but Aldys brushed her hands aside. Panic filled her and she felt the very breath in her lungs being squeezed out. Then another woman took her hands and held them.

'Lady, they have broken in through the wall and are at the doors of the keep. Gareth said you must stay here,' Gytha, her maid, whispered. 'Some of the rock hit you on the head, on your eyes, and there is much bleeding.' The pressure on her head eased, but returned quickly. 'We are trying to stop the bleeding.'

'I cannot see,' she whispered. 'I cannot see!' Sybilla could feel her control slipping away and terror of a new kind filling her heart and soul.

'Hush now, lady,' Aldys soothed. 'We will see to your injury. All will be well.'

The pain grew and grew until she felt faint, but the sound of the keep's doors being destroyed shook her awake. Then the great wooden doors crashed apart and the sound of fighting spilled into the keep.

'Gytha,' she moaned out. 'You must get the children to safety now.'

''Tis too late, my lady,' her maid answered.

Suddenly, she was pulled to her feet and dragged along by some unseen hands. Women screamed and she was jostled as they struggled against the strong grasp of whoever had come into the keep. Then, just as suddenly, she was tossed to the floor. Clutching her head, she tried to sit up, but could not. Then Aldys gathered her in her arms and she heard Gytha on her other side.

Chaos and terror reigned and Sybilla screamed along

with them. She had seen the enemy and knew without doubt that he would slaughter them all. She suspected it might have been his intent all along, for he'd not paused or asked for a parley as others might have. Listening without being able to see only heightened the fear for her; hearing her people being tormented and harmed tore her heart apart, piece by piece.

Is that what he wanted here? To destroy everything her father had built and nurtured? What kind of man would do such a thing? Her unspoken question was answered moments later when a silence so deep she thought she must have fainted filled the hall.

She heard not a sound, not even the breathing of those around her in those tension-filled moments. Then, just when she thought she would scream out, the whispered prayers of the women at her sides reached her. They were praying for mercy!

'Bring those who survive before me.'

It had to be him! The dark giant who commanded the forces. The devil on horseback who had destroyed her home and killed her people. Before she could gather any shards of courage together, she was pulled to her feet once more and towards the voice. Aldys and Gytha protected her on each side, still whispering prayers for protection to any saint who would listen. She heard words like 'monster' and 'demon' and 'devil' whispered by those around her and she trembled, unable to mask her own terror. Soon, he called out for silence and everyone obeyed.

'I am Soren Fitzrobert, now lord of these lands.'

Those around her gasped at his words. The first surprise was that he spoke in their tongue and not the

Norman one, but it was his declaration that sliced her to the core. Her family had owned and ruled these lands for generations, one of the proud and mighty Saxon families who counselled the king and the Witan. Sybilla felt her body shake and she reached out to Aldys and Gytha for support.

'Do not beg for mercy, for I have none for those faithful to Durward the Traitor. Only those who swear allegiance to me will live.'

Shock ran through those listening. Sybilla shook her head. How could he demand such a thing? How could he execute those who owed their living to her father? His cold voice and emotionless commands chilled her soul and she knew she had no chance. Had he already killed Gareth and the others? Without being able to see, she did not know and that was in some ways worse.

'Aldys,' she whispered, 'is Gareth here?'

'Hush, lady. The warrior approaches.'

Sybilla could hear his heavy steps coming nearer, so she clutched Aldys and Gytha, her chest tight with fear. His words, spoken so close to her she could almost feel his breath, did nothing to ease her fears.

'I will, however, show mercy to any of you who tell me of Durward's get. Where is his daughter?'

Again, shocked whispers spread through the room, halted only by his angry voice.

'I will have you all killed unless someone tells me where she is.'

His voice spoke of his true intentions. Cold, without feeling or mercy, it revealed the truth of his words—he would kill them all. Would he stand by his word and not kill them if she stepped forwards? Was it simply a ploy on his part?

'Stay, lady,' Aldys warned under her breath.

'Your time is running out,' he called out. 'Guermont, bring the archers. It will be easier that way,' he coldly ordered.

Some of the women screamed then, children cried out and the crowd surged and stumbled as they were pushed back and back until they could not move any further. Sybilla realised they were being placed against the wall, easier targets for the demon's archers. Through it all, no one identified her as the lord's daughter. They would die for her, she knew it in her bones. She also knew that, even if it meant her death, she could not allow them to do so. Though Aldys and Gytha kept hold of her, she pulled free and stepped away from them.

'Soren Fitzrobert,' she said, her voice trembling even as she tried to steady it and herself.

Sybilla tried not to shake and the sounds of his spurs scraping on the stone floor approached. Remembering his size, she knew it would take only one blow to bring her death. The pounding pain in her head grew with each passing second and she knew she would not be able to stand much longer without help. The sound of his breathing came from above her head and she fought the urge to reach out to steady herself.

Straightening up as much as she could, wincing against the tightness of the bandage and the feel of her blood trickling down her neck from the wound on her head, she said the words that would save her people and damn herself.

'I am Sybilla of Alston, Lord Durward's daughter.'

Silence reigned as the sound of his sword as he drew it from its sheath met her declaration and she offered up a prayer for her soul as she waited to meet her fate.

Chapter Three

Hatred raced through his veins as she spoke her name. Months of waiting, months filled with nothing but pain and suffering, had brought him here and he pulled his sword free from its scabbard. The red haze of fury and anger filled his vision as he raised the weapon of her death above his head and savoured this moment he'd dreamed of and prayed for since the battle at Hastings. For a moment he was tempted to drop the sword and use his bare hands to wring the life from her body, knowing it would appease some primitive need within him for vengeance, but he gripped the sword's hilt tightly as he shouted out his hatred for all there to hear.

'Death to all who carry the blood of the traitor Durward!'

But, before he could swing his weapon and end the life of the last of them, his vision cleared and for a brief moment he saw only the woman kneeling before him. It was all the delay that the crowd needed for they took advantage and surged forwards and pulled her into its centre. She fought against them, trying to push herself forwards, but they did not allow it.

He took a step towards them and the entire throng backed away, finding themselves between his men and the corner of the hall. They could go no further and had no chance of surviving an attack by armed knights and archers, but they would not relinquish their lady to him.

'Soren,' Guermont whispered at his side. 'Mayhap this is not the way?'

Soren turned to him, unable to hear out of his right ear, and glared at him. In spite of his momentary hesitation, he had not come this far and got so close to his purpose to be defeated or delayed by some villagers and children. And that was all who defended her now. Her men were either dead or prisoners, and yet, the least of her people gathered around her as though they could indeed stop him. Still, Guermont's words of warning slowed his actions. Killing innocent peasants would damn him even more than he was already cursed by God.

He slid his sword back into its scabbard on his belt and strode towards the crowd, his men following behind as they formed a wedge that moved through to its center. When they'd pushed or pulled her free and dragged her from the rest, the crowd did not slow in its defence of her. First an old woman, one of those closest to the lady, fell to her knees and began to beg.

'Mercy, my lord! Mercy!' she called out loudly.

'Mercy! Mercy!' another called. Then another and another until the hall shook with their pleas for a mercy he did not have. Or he thought he did not have until the wench's hand touched his and she fell to her knees.

'Spare them, I beg you. They seek to only to protect me,' she implored. 'They are not to blame here.'

In spite of her condition, in spite of the bloody rags tied around her head and her torn and soiled gown, she looked every bit the proud daughter of the old lord. Her defence of her people, now his people, touched him regardless of how much he hated this moment of weakness in his hour of triumph.

'What happened to you?' he asked, not even trying to keep his anger from his voice.

'The wall…stones…' she began to say. 'My eyes…' She could say no more, for her body began to shake and tremble as though hearing the news herself for the first time.

'You are blind?' he asked.

A defect like this gave him complete absolution in disregarding the king's wishes for him to marry her. It could be grounds for an annulment of any betrothal. It was an impediment to a true marriage and could be…

She cannot see me!

Soren realised that it was the tiniest seed of hope that spoke those words inside his head. Blind, she would never see his deformity. She would never look on him in revulsion as his torn and mangled flesh was revealed. Blind, she would never gaze in fear or pity at him the way others did.

She could not see him.

'Take her,' he said quietly.

The hall erupted in screaming and lamenting as those present believed he would have her executed. The lady said nothing and did not resist his men as they led her forwards to the front of the hall and up the steps of the dais there. His warriors had to form a line between the people and the dais to keep them from pushing forwards to her side.

He climbed the steps there and walked to her side, glaring at those who would argue his power to do as he would. Her quiet voice forestalled any orders before he could call them.

'My lord?' she said, turning her head to gauge his position and proximity. 'My lord Soren?' she said again.

A flash of heat pierced his body as he imagined the sound of her sultry voice in his bed. She would whisper it over and over, acknowledging his power over her body and soul as he pleasured her for hour on hour. She would cry out his name as he entered her, thrusting deep within her flesh, making her his and his alone…

Soren shook himself from such a vision and glared at her. Realising the futility of it, he walked to her.

'Aye,' was the only word he could force out.

'Would you grant me a moment with a priest before…?' Her voice faltered for a moment. Only a moment. 'Before my death.'

He would have admired such bravery in anyone else, but he steeled himself against her. Angry at himself for even the fleeting thought of showing kindness, he turned away.

'You will have need of a priest, Sybilla of Alston,' he barked out, 'but I do not intend to kill you this day.'

'My lord?' she asked. 'Am I to be your prisoner, then?' He watched as she tried to come closer and stumbled. Damn it! He fought the urge to reach out to help her.

'Prisoner of a sort, lady,' he said. 'You will be my wife.'

The hall erupted again; the people surged forwards, trying to free her from what they thought would be a fate worse than death. The lady remained silent and then crumpled to the floor.

Chapter Four

His head pounded. His eye burned. His throat grew hoarse from shouting. His hands yet itched to twist the wench's neck and end the line of Durward's seed, but his words had put a stop to the possibility of killing her quickly. Soren raised his arm and rubbed his hand across his brow, trying to ease the pain there. A moment of weakness and he would now be responsible for her. A weakness he thought crushed out of him by the relentless suffering and pain of his ordeal and by the humiliation and torment of his condition and the loss of everything he valued in life.

The object of both his hatred and his newest pledge now sat silent and unmoving in a wooden chair he'd called for when she collapsed before him at the news of not her impending death, but her impending marriage to him. Soren only knew that her reaction was far less hysterical than if she could look upon his face and see him as he was now. Shaking off any regrets and trying to accept his path now that he'd stated it for all to hear, he searched the hall and the doorway out to the corridor for any sign of the priest. He yelled out the priest's name once more, hoping that someone would find him and hasten his steps.

The silence that filled the chamber allowed him to hear the approach of a small number of people and he let out his breath as the portly priest and his clerk stumbled in through the doorway and blessed his way through the stunned mob that now awaited his word and deed. The cleric reached the dais just as Soren's meagre stores of patience wore out. At least the horror did not show on his face when their gazes met, though he could see the narrowing of his eyes and the restraint the priest exerted on his reactions. All those hours on his knees in prayer and fasting had apparently taught the priest some measure of self-control. Soren crossed his arms over his chest and nodded at the pair as they climbed the few steps and approached him.

'Tell her to ready herself for marriage,' he growled to the priest with a nod at the wench. He needed to get this done before he changed his mind.

'My lord...' the priest began to stutter. 'She is...'

'I said to see to her now, Father.'

He watched as the priest started towards her and then stopped. After glancing between the two of them—his lord and his lord's intended—Father Medwyn slowly turned from her and returned to stand before Soren.

'My lord, she is blind,' he whispered.

With malice aforethought, Soren exaggerated his motions and turned his good eye, his only eye, towards her. 'Aye, Father, she is blinded.' Narrowing his eye's gaze on the defiant, hesitating priest, Soren waited for him to decide to defy or obey.

'My lord, if you will allow,' the priest petitioned, leaning closer to speak only to him. 'This is a clear impediment to marriage. You can find another, mayhap?'

The priest did not realise the boon her blindness was, and of certain, he would never speak of it if he did, but Soren had in that instant of insight. Now, her blindness would cause her to live as his wife and breed him sons.

'I need not her eyes for a true marriage, Father. I only have need of her womb to consummate the words spoken.'

Since everyone in the hall had stopped speaking at once, Soren heard his words echo into the air around them. He stood close enough to hear her gasp and see her body stiffen as the insult and sentence struck. In truth, he cared less for her than he did the last mount he had purchased, nay, earned, and had paid more attention to that horse's physical qualities and potential. A wife would lie with him and give him children, sons who inherit that for which his flesh and blood had paid a steep price. And though it would pain him, the man once known as the 'Beautiful Bastard', Soren knew he would rather pay for comfort of the other sort when he needed it and keep it an honest exchange of coin for service rather than see the horror in a woman's gaze.

In his wife's eyes.

She cannot see me.

It was settled.

'Bring her,' he ordered and he waited for his word to be obeyed.

Though some of his men openly scowled, they did as

they'd been told to and soon, with a man at each side, Durward's daughter stood next to him as they faced the priest. She'd not spoken a word yet, but he could hear the sound of her shallow breathing as dead silence reigned once more. What she could not see, but her people could, was the soldier standing behind her with his sword drawn and aimed for the wench. Any disturbance, any outcry, they knew would be met with her death. He saw mutiny in some gazes, frank terror in others, but underlying it all was something more frightening to him in that moment— they loved their lady and would do anything, even acqui- esce to him, in exchange for her safety.

He would later tell himself otherwise, but he nearly lost his nerve in the face of such devotion and pure affec- tion. Watching her as she stood tall in spite of the hold laid on her by his men, he realised that she bore the same love for her people in return.

A sense of longing so strong that it almost took him out at the knees tore a path through him, tearing his heart and soul in two. Soren found it difficult, nigh to impossible, to breathe in that second. He shook his head as though to clear his thoughts, then the second emotion pierced him—the one that reminded him of his true pur- pose. The one that had sustained him through the pain and suffering since that September afternoon and every single, tortuous one that followed.

Anger.

Fury in its strongest form.

Righteous and purifying and fortifying.

It gave him the chance to regain his control and banish any mercy that might be creeping into his heart or soul for her. Straightening to his full height, he glared at those around them who might give any indication of arguing or disagreeing with his decision to proceed—both in marrying her and in marrying her now—and watched in satisfaction as they capitulated. Turning his gaze on the priest, Soren waited for him to begin.

The delay was hardly noticeable, but he noticed and he would hold the priest accountable for it later. Once he began, Father Medwyn accomplished the joining quickly, and if the bride's vows were not loud and if the groom's were not enthusiastic, no one dared comment on it. Once they were pronounced wed, Soren glanced at the windows to gauge the amount of daylight still remaining and estimated the amount of work yet ahead of them before any could seek their rest.

Calling out orders, he strode from the dais, mindful of so many things and yet forgetting one until his man brought his attention back to…her.

'Soren?' Guermont yelled over the growing din of soldiers and villeins and the general mayhem and confusion of those conquered. 'My lord?'

Soren paused as he replaced the leather hood he wore on his head and tugged his mail coif over it into place. He shook his head, refusing his helmet from one of the younger men and turned to see what Guermont wanted. Guermont simply nodded his head and Soren realised he'd left her…his wife…standing in the hold of the soldiers awaiting his word.

'Take her…' he began, then realised he did not yet know the layout and accoutrements of this manor and keep and could offer no direction in which to send her. He turned to those still huddling along the wall.

'Where are her chambers?' he called out, aiming his

question at the woman who had fallen to her knees first, crying out for mercy for Durward's daughter. When neither she nor the others answered, he shrugged. Turning back to Guermont, he shook his head.

'Tie her there—' he pointed at the chair where she'd been sitting '—and you can find a place for her later.' Just as he thought would happen, the old woman called out then, emboldened by his threat.

'My lord?' she said, not waiting for his permission to approach. 'I served her mother before her and serve Lady Sybilla now. I would see to her care.'

As he'd suspected, they would dare much for their lady. This old woman did not grovel or beg, she did not even look away from him when he met her gaze. Not willing nor able to give in before all of his men and those newly vanquished, Soren rose to his full height and strode over to the woman…who had the good sense to bow her head at his approach.

'And you will continue to serve her at my pleasure,' he said, watching her face for signs of rebellion. But she schooled her expression in respect and obedience and if it hurt to say the words, he could not see it on her face.

'As you say, my lord. At your pleasure.'

Appeased for the moment, Soren nodded. 'Show them where to take her and prepare her for me.'

'My lord?' the woman asked before he could turn away.

'What part of my words do you not comprehend? I made no secret of the only use I have for the traitor's daughter. Once I have secured the land, I will consummate our vows.'

Lord Gautier would have taken a cane to his back for

such flagrant words of disrespect, but Soren could not help it. And, as usually happened with such ill-spoken words, the bitterness of them burned his tongue before they even left his mouth. Still, he would not, could not, relent in this, so he glared at the woman until she nodded her understanding.

'See to it,' he ordered as he strode from the hall into the yard to sort out a different kind of chaos than the one that now made his gut clench.

Sybilla barely heard a word or sound around her. The pain pulsed through her head and burned her eyes, making it difficult to even remain standing. Instead of fighting the strong grip of the men holding her, she let their strength keep her on her feet. It was wrong, so wrong, to speak vows before a priest to a man she had no intention of marrying, but the shock and sorrow of the day crushed her into compliance.

To his will and not her own.

One day she would need to answer for her failure to object when asked by the priest if she consented to this marriage, but now she felt too overwhelmed to dwell on it much. And Sybilla found she had not the strength of body or will to focus her efforts on anything but not being dragged like a sack of flour through her own hall.

The soldiers said nothing as they followed Aldys to the stairs and then up to the second floor where her chambers were in the corner tower. When she tripped for the third time, unable to judge the height of the steps and to adjust her pace to those hauling her along, the tears began. This was her home, the place she knew better than anyone, yet she could not tell how many steps there were or how steep they were. By the time they reached her chambers, the fear about her fate and her injury and the possibility of being blind for the rest of her life took control and she collapsed in a crying heap when the soldiers released her.

Nothing had intervened in her despair for what could have been minutes or hours and then she drifted back to an awareness of herself and her surroundings.

To the sound of her maid and Aldys both praying for her!

Sybilla tried to raise her hand to her face and the source of her pain and found she could not move.

'My lady,' Gytha whispered. 'You are awake!'

Sybilla nodded, but tears threatened again so she did not even try to speak. A hand behind her head supported her as a cup was placed at her mouth and she took a few sips. Watered wine eased the dry tightness in her throat.

'We feared you would not wake,' Gytha whispered again. From the sound and tone of the maid's voice it was clear that there was a need to remain quiet.

'Where am I?' she asked. Without sight, everything felt different to her. Unable to see her surroundings, even her bed, if it was hers, did not seem familiar at all. 'Are we alone?'

There was a pause before Gytha answered and Sybilla could almost imagine the two women exchanging glances between them before speaking. It was something they did frequently now that they both served her needs and when they felt the need to soften the coming blow. Sybilla had seen it when the news of her brother's death at Stamford

Bridge came, then when her father's fate further south at Hastings arrived here months later. Their wordless exchange was so filled with sympathy, she could almost feel it now. Sybilla tried to push herself up to sit, but her arms and body did not obey her.

'Hush now, lady,' Aldys soothed. 'We cleaned the wound and there is a new dressing in place. The bleeding is almost ceased.' Sybilla felt the soft touch of a hand across the bandages now in place. 'We are in your chambers.' Then Aldys's voice came from closer to her ears. 'We are alone, but his lackeys check often and watch everything we do. They probably listen for our words, so have a care.' Sybilla tried to nod her understanding of their situation.

'Where is he?' she whispered, knowing he would have to come here sooner or later now that their marriage had happened. She swallowed against the fear of what would follow.

'He left the keep after…after…' Sybilla nodded—she knew when he had left. 'He can be heard calling out his orders in the yard and even beyond the wall.'

A strong shudder passed through her then, remembering the sound of his voice as he called for Alston's surrender. And as he'd demanded she step forwards to face his death sentence. She shook again. Not death now, but something she imagined he would make worse than death. As a vision of him in his black armour flashed in her memory, she trembled as the thought of what she would suffer at his hands became clear to her.

'I…cannot…' she stuttered without thinking. Shaking her head, Sybilla felt the fear take hold of her. 'I cannot do this.'

Aldys and Gytha leaned in close, each taking her hand and squeezing it. 'Hush now, lady,' Aldys repeated. 'Rest and gain your strength.'

Because you will need it later were the unspoken words in her warning. But later came much too soon.

'Lady?' a voice called from the hallway. Sybilla could not identify the person behind the call.

'What do you want, boy?' Aldys asked.

'Lord Soren sends me to bid you make ready for him.'

'He sends a boy to tell you such things?' Gytha whispered.

'Monsters such as him will use anyone they can to do their bidding—women, children, whoever!' Aldys's anger made her voice low and almost unrecognisable.

'Lady?' the boy asked.

'Aye, lad. I heard your message.' Sybilla nearly could not get the words out, but she asked one question. 'Are you of Alston?'

'Nay, lady. I am Raed of Shildon.'

'Shildon?' she asked. A village some days' journey to the east from Alston.

'Aye, lady. My lord Soren took me from there to serve him.'

Sybilla sank deeper onto the pallet, her head pounding now from the injury and from all that faced her. Dear God in Heaven, he was a monster! He stole children from their families and forced them into his service? She shook her head, unable to say or think anything more.

Agitated by this news of how Soren acted, Sybilla could find no rest. She tossed and shifted on the pallet, for both comfort and ease escaped her. Nothing eased the pain in her head or in her heart. She felt the tenuous control she'd managed begin to wane as the hours passed. When she heard the sound of heavy footsteps approaching down the corridor outside her doorway, she wished she could have fainted and not faced what would follow his arrival.

But the saints above and even the Almighty seemed to ignore her prayers and kept her from sinking into oblivion. Sybilla hoped only not to disgrace herself and her name when he touched her, but from the way the fear took hold, she knew any control she had would end the first moment he came close.

Chapter Five

Soren had tried not to think much on the coming night, he just wanted to accomplish as much as possible before the sun set. So, he'd focused his thoughts on how to hold so many prisoners, and how many of his own men had been killed, and how many villeins had fled his approach and how many yet remained to tend the fields, and other matters as weighty as those. It was only as he climbed the steps leading to the second floor of the corner tower of the keep that he realised he'd thought about her more than he wanted to admit…even to himself.

The scorn and scolding he saw in the gazes of his soldiers who stood guard stopped him in his steps. He was about to address their insubordination when Stephen called out his name. Since the man stopped at the end of the corridor and did not come to him, Soren walked back to hear his concerns.

'Soren, is this wise?' Stephen asked in a low voice.

'What do you speak of?'

'I know that a man's blood runs hot after battle, but is this wise?'

Coming from this man, someone who had learned the hard lesson of misplaced lust after a battle, gave Soren pause. But, this was not of his concern.

'If I was caught in the throes of bloodlust, you would be lying unconscious on the floor for asking such a thing and I would already be lying between the wench's thighs halfway to satisfaction,' he said. Soren glared at his friend. 'So, ask me not such things and we will both be the better for it.' Soren turned away, but was stopped by Stephen's grasp on his arm. He shrugged it off easily.

'She is your wife now, Soren.'

'She is Durward's get.' The men who fought with him knew, had heard, his plans for any who carried the blood of Durward of Alston and who came under his control. In all the dark and painful detail. The change in her circumstances mattered not.

'And now your wife. Different than what you had planned on. A different matter completely now.'

'And my concern alone, Stephen. Do not make me regret accepting you into my service.'

The warrior looked as though he wanted to argue, but he controlled that urge and nodded. With only one more glance over his shoulder at Soren, Stephen left. Soren continued his path down to the doorway to her chamber. The guards stepped aside and waited for his orders.

'Stay down there. I will call you if you are needed,' he said, directing them to the place where he'd just spoken to Stephen. 'No one comes further until I say so.'

He noticed the sweat on his palms as he reached for the latch and lifted it. He swore he felt no nervousness, but his heart raced and his chest tightened as he faced the next step in seeking vengeance against the man who had destroyed his life…and his body and soul. Soren pushed open the door and stepped inside.

Her servants, both the older, stout-figured one and the younger, lithe-bodied one, stood like statues next to the pallet. The wench lay nearly motionless on its surface—motionless but for the quick and shallow rise and fall of her chest and the curling of her fingers as though she tried to take hold of the bedcover and could not find purchase of it.

'Can she see?' he asked. The injury to her head did not necessarily mean blindness. 'When the bandages were removed?'

With a stiff shake of her head, the older woman confirmed her condition and he let out his breath.

'I told you to prepare her,' he said, moving then and making his way slowly across the chamber. 'Undress her and get out.'

'My…lord…' the younger one stuttered, bowing her head now in an unsuccessful attempt to placate him. 'Twas too late for that.

He hesitated in spite of his intentions and watched as they helped her to stand next to the bed. Now in a clean gown and tunic—what did they call those, *syrce* and *cyrtel*?—with her injury tended to, Soren could see her loveliness. And he could see the terror that drained her face of any colour and made her body tremble with fear.

Her pale hair fell in waves over her shoulders, but it was her hands that caught his eye. Fine and graceful, like the curve of her neck as she whispered to her servants.

Any trace of the earlier bravery she'd displayed had fled her and he could see that she was younger than he first thought...more beautiful as well. But it was her delicate features that struck him now. She was a well-born lady and he was...

He shook his head to clear his thoughts and to focus his intentions. 'Either you undress her or I will see to it,' he said, harsher than he needed to, but he made his point.

Soren turned away then, trying to ignore them, hearing them move to do his bidding rather than allow him to do it. Soren busied himself with removing his heavy leather belt and scabbard, and lifting the chain coif from his head and loosening the leather helm. Turning away, he positioned the leather patch to make certain it hid the stitched flesh that covered the place where his eye should be. When it grew silent behind him, he turned back to find the wench lying under the bedcovers and her garments in the hands of her maids.

Good. He let out a breath he did not realise he'd held. His task here would be done quickly and he could see to more important matters. If his seed did not take, he could visit her until it did and then not see her until the birth of his heir.

As he'd realised during his hours of toiling to make this place his, apathy would be a more fitting punishment than the hatred that simmered just below his skin, waiting to tear free of his control and wreak havoc on his enemies...on her. Though vengeance was key in his plans for her, he would make this woman nothing but a vessel that would bear his seed and fulfil his needs.

Soren smiled grimly, glad that success felt so close at

hand. With a nod, he ordered them from the room and when the door closed he took in and released a deep breath. But the smile remained. Only when he was within an arm's length of the bed did he notice her trembling once more. The curling mass of her pale hair outlined her head and shoulders and distracted him again from his contemplation of vengeance sought and found. Though the bandages had been removed, she lay with her face turned away from him as though she did not wish to look upon him.

The humiliation he'd felt when others had turned from the carnage that used to be his face returned in an instant, pouring bile into his stomach. But, one glance at her empty gaze and he remembered that she could not see him at all. Relief flooded his senses in that moment and the tension evaporated within him.

She cannot see me.

He allowed himself to revel in that realisation and he felt lighter than he had in all the months since that September day. Standing over her now, Soren noticed the creaminess of her skin and wanted to caress those graceful lines of her neck, the fullness of her lips and the fragile daintiness of her slender figure. It would, he realised, take little effort to tug the linens out of his way and see the rest of her feminine curves and skin laid bare. With just this small hint of her comeliness, his body warmed and readied for the task ahead. Soren reached over to lift the sheet away when she startled so suddenly that he jumped back.

'Sybilla,' he said, realising he should offer her some words of explanation. He did not doubt she came to this ill-gotten marriage a virgin.

The sound of her name on his tongue for the first time felt rough and ill-fitting. He swallowed and cleared his throat. Before he could move closer or do anything, she tossed the covers back and pushed herself off the bed, sliding away from him. He reached over to grab her, but slipped and landed across the bed, with an empty hand. Leaning up, he watched as she tried, like a trapped, wild animal, to run with nowhere to go.

Her bare feet skidded on the wooden planks of the floor and her momentum carried her as she stumbled across the chamber. Soren climbed over the bed and reached for her just as she got to her feet and dashed away. Like a madwoman, one too caught up in escaping to remember she could not see. Confused and probably still dazed from her injury, he watched as she pressed herself up against the wall, whispering and shaking her head.

Soren spoke her name several times, but clearly she was incapable of hearing him. He approached her as he would a high-strung mare, trying to gentle her with a calm voice.

'Sybilla,' he said, sliding off the bed and trying to get to her before she caused more damage to herself. 'You must stop.'

She stood motionless, but only for a deceiving second, and then she bolted as soon as he moved towards her. He almost got hold of her when she knocked over a small table that held a jug and cups. Soren managed to take hold of her shoulders and stop her from further injury, but she began to wail as soon as his hands touched her skin. It was a pitiful sound that he hated hearing, both for what it made him want to do and what it made him

feel. Sybilla would have backed away from him but for
his hold on her and she surprised him again when she
collapsed to the floor.

Soren told himself that she simply sought to avoid the
inevitable and that he had every right to claim her body
this night, but something deep within him refused to let
him take that step. Instead, he whispered her name and
tried to calm the devastated woman he had forced into
marriage. Somehow he guided her over to the bed and
settled her under the bedcovers.

He ran his hands through his hair as he gazed around
the chamber and wondered how he had so mismanaged
this situation that had seemed completely under his control just minutes before. His plan to bed her regardless
of her feelings on the matter fell apart in the face of her
pitiful condition. Some remnant of his old self ate at him
as he witnessed the fall he'd planned for so long. But only
for a scant moment as he realised he could not, would
not, bed her this night.

Acknowledging it, acknowledging that he could not
take her against her will, no matter his will or his desire
on the matter, seemed to let loose all the anger he'd held
inside for so long.

She'd won again.

Her father had defeated him yet again.

Soren felt the rage seething and turned away from
the bed and her. He struck out in blind anger, at the
only thing he could, grabbing a nearby wooden loom and
throwing it frame first against the wall, then crashing it
to the floor. He heard Sybilla scream out, but ignored it
this time. He'd given up much this night and could give
no more.

Unfortunately, the loom had landed partially against the door, blocking the path of his retreat, his exit, so he had to call out for the guards. When they opened the door immediately, Soren knew they'd been right outside and not down the hall.

'Get this damned thing out of here!'

Only as they began to collect the wooden beams did she react, sobbing and sliding from the bed where he'd placed her. He blocked the guards' view of her and wrapped a blanket around her as she scrambled towards the remnants of the loom. He shook his head in confusion and disbelief.

Was she mad as well as blind?

As he watched, Sybilla tried to gather and touch the pieces of the frame in her arms, all the time rocking to and fro and sobbing. Stephen arrived at the doorway and frowned as he watched the strange scene before him.

'What happened, Soren?'

Soren shrugged. At first he thought fear had taken hold of her. Fear of consummating their vows would be something he could understand since she was a maid and was his bitterest enemy. But then, she seemed to have lost her wits and her way. Now, the heart-wrenching sobs that seem to come from her soul confused him. Damn it! Why did Stephen have to be right in his warning?

'The loom fell,' he explained, leaving out the part about his unleashed anger causing it. Incomplete. Inaccurate. It was as much as he was willing to explain.

'She does not seem well, Soren,' Stephen said as the wench continued grasping and crying. 'Should I summon her maid?'

What else could he do at this point? There would be no

consummation this night and he wondered if he'd made a mistake by taking her as his wife. He looked around the chamber at the damage caused and shrugged. Mayhap the women could calm her and even explain this to him.

'Aye, get them and seek the healer.'

Stephen left and Soren observed her from where he stood. She had not moved from her place on the floor and did not appear to even feel or hear anything as she rocked and cried. When he heard the sounds of the women's approach, he stepped slowly out the door, continuing to face and watch her. With a motion of his hand, he stopped them several paces from the door.

'Stop,' he ordered in a whisper. 'You, you come here quietly,' he directed to the older woman. When she walked to where he stood, he nodded. 'Tell me of your lady's behaviour.'

The older one leaned over and peeked in the chamber, gasping at the scene before her. When she moved to enter, he held her back with his arm.

'Tell me why she acts as a madwoman.'

'What did you do to her?' the maid demanded.

Soren reached over and grabbed the woman by her garb, hauling her up close to him. 'I do not explain my actions to a servant,' he growled through clenched jaws. Pushing her away, he nodded at the lady in question. 'Has she lost her wits?'

Her answer was interrupted by the healer, a man brought with them who understood how to treat injuries and heal with herbs. Brice's wife had spoken highly of his treatments and Soren was pleased to find him still alive after the slaughter and brought him here to Alston for the time being.

'My lord?'

'Teyen, have you treated the lady for her injuries?'

'Nay, my lord. Her maids saw to her while I saw to those more in need,' he explained. 'Should I now?'

Soren rubbed his forehead, trying to ease the shattering pain growing there in the face of this absurd situation. 'What happened to her?' Soren asked. 'You, there…' he nodded at the younger servant '…what are you called?'

'Gytha,' she stammered out.

'Gytha,' he said, 'tell me how was your lady blinded?'

'When you…the attack began, she was running to collect the children into the keep as Gareth directed. The wall shattered in front of her and struck her down.'

'So she lost consciousness?' he asked. Gytha nodded. 'For how long?'

'Until you…you broke into the keep. She'd just awakened then.'

He'd seen many men who became dazed and confused after head injuries in battle. Some forgot themselves for a time. Some believed they were other people and some even became violent or attacked others. Some never recovered. A head wound would explain much.

'Teyen, see to her. A calming brew might—' Teyen's shaking head stopped his suggestion.

'It is better not to let her sleep deeply, my lord. Some do not awaken after such an injury if left to sleep too long.'

'Whatever is necessary. Let her maid go in first and see to her condition, then follow.'

'Aye, my lord.' Teyen stepped back to allow Gytha entrance.

When the girl gasped at seeing her lady huddled on

the floor, clutching pieces of the broken loom, Soren grabbed her arm and shook his head. 'If you cannot be calm, you cannot go in,' he ordered. Soren waited for her to accept his words and then released her. He did not miss that Stephen stepped closer as he'd grabbed the girl and watched the exchange with an intensity that spoke of more than a casual interest.

The older woman approached as Gytha touched her lady's shoulder and began to whisper in a soothing voice to her. Though she seemed too nervous to do it, the maid had the wench off the floor and walking to the bed within moments. She, Sybilla, now limped, he noticed, favouring her left leg and foot as she moved slowly. Just when Gytha guided her to the side of the bed and began to help her in, Sybilla began to shake her head and became agitated. Gytha quickly took her to a chair that remained standing and sat her there.

'You asked if she has lost her wits, my lord?'

The older woman's voice surprised him. Soren turned to face her.

'The lady has lost everything but her wits, my lord. Her father, her brother, both lost in battle. Her mother lost years before that. Her future lost today. And now, worst of all, her sight.' The woman took a breath before continuing. 'Such loss cannot help but overwhelm a person of such kind spirit and good heart as my mistress.'

He watched as Gytha began to evaluate the lady's injuries and tended to them. The older woman's words brought a feeling into his heart he did not recognise at first. Many times the target of it himself, it took him some moments to accept that it pulsed through him now.

Pity.

He pitied his wife.

Worse, he pitied the daughter of the man who had destroyed his life and his future.

Faced with this emotion, one he did not wish to feel for anyone who carried the blood of Durward within them, Soren did what he needed to do before it could take hold and ruin his plans for vengeance—he fought it and walked away the winner.

'What are you called?' he asked, backing out of the room and crossing his arms over his chest. If it was a defensive stance, he would never admit it.

'I am Aldys,' she said, with a bow of her head.

'I am holding you responsible for your lady's care,' Soren said. 'See to it.' If she questioned or doubted or misunderstood his command, he knew not, for he was down the steps before she could open her mouth and get words out.

Chapter Six

Although the darkness of Sybilla's heart never lifted, the confusion of her mind eased as the pain in her head did over the next several days. Or, at least, she thought several days had passed. Without the ability to see the sun's passage through the sky or the falling of dusk and night and without the regular duties of her life before his arrival, Sybilla did not know for certain.

She gave herself over to the grief that festered unreleased in her heart and soul and could do little more than sob or sleep the hours away. Truly, there was little else to do now. She could not see and she could do nothing for herself. She had nothing now that this invader had destroyed her home, imprisoned those set to the duty of protecting her and finished the task his king and other foolish men in power had begun by taking everything and everyone that mattered away from her. The worst moments were those she somehow remembered through the haze of pain and loss—the exact one when she lost control over her grief and her actions.

The loom.

Blind, with her thoughts muddled and with her only plan being escape, she'd stumbled in a panic around her chamber without being able to see her route. Though she'd lived in that same room for years now, without sight it became like a foreign terrain with no path to follow. She lost more self-control with each misstep until he dragged her to the bed. But when he destroyed the loom in the corner of her room, the only remaining remnants of her world came crashing down along with the wooden structure.

It was the last thing that connected her with her father and her brother, for they'd built it for her after her mother's death in an attempt to assuage her grief and draw her back to the daily life in their household. It had been successful; working on the loom soothed her heart and kept her busy.

Now it and every other trace of her family was gone, save her. And from the sounds of his threats floating in the air, her life was also in danger from the man to whom she was now wed.

Her appetite fled with each passing day and the only sustenance she took was what her maids forced into her in a cup. Why bother sustaining herself when there was little to live for now? And her survival meant nothing to anyone here any longer?

Any hope, any tiny flare of it, had been dowsed when Teyen had removed the bandages and she'd managed to open her swollen eyes…and faced an obliterating black-ness. Nothing.

No hint of light or movement.

Nothing.

She was truly blind and time would not restore her sight to her as her faithful servants had persuaded her to believe. So she let herself sink into that darkness a little more with each passing day. She hid from all those she'd sworn to serve and to protect, unable to face them as she was. Unable to offer them anything now that she'd lost everything. Then, just when she believed she could do no more than content herself to exist in this dark oblivion, he invaded once more, using the boy to bring his commands to her.

Her maids were more nervous than her—flitting around her chambers, arranging and rearranging her hair and clothing several times and fussing over her more than ever before. As though her appearance mattered when nothing truly did.

Sybilla sat in silent darkness, waiting for his arrival. The sound of his footsteps rumbled like thunder moving closer, but she could not seem to rouse much fear or any other feeling at all. These last days had emptied her of her grief and every other emotion. Like the husks left strewn on the ground after harvest, there was nothing left within her.

She heard the door open on hinges that clearly needed to be oiled and then silence filled the chamber. The shallow breathing of those waiting by her side sounded like the horses in the stables when she sneaked in on a cold winter's morn to visit them. Laboured, low and fast, they grew more erratic as the seconds passed.

'Out!' he ordered in a gruff bark.

One word and her loyal servants abandoned her to him. Whatever he did to engender such obedience did not go unrecognised by her. Fear. Deep, abiding fear.

They'd described his horrible injuries in specific gory details to her, clucking over her marriage to him and alternately praying for her deliverance. They whispered rumours of his black deeds—the innocent crushed under his heels without mercy. They exposed their fears to her without regard for her own. But it mattered not, for she felt nothing.

He closed the door with no effort to be quiet and then strode around the chamber, his steps tracing a loud path until he stood at her side. She knew because she could now hear his breathing very close to her. Standing before him in the hall, she'd felt tiny, but sitting while he stood made her feel like a dog at his feet. Sybilla would have stood, but she was as yet unsteady on her feet, her balance thrown off by the lack of sight and her injuries.

'Lady,' he said in a tone more respectful than she thought possible from their last encounters, 'are you well?'

'What does your healer report to you?' she asked in a voice unused to speaking. She'd had little to say over these last days.

'Teyen said your wound no longer bleeds and the dizziness is lifting. Is that true?'

Although his words seemed to show an interest in her condition, there was no concern underlying them. She could hear that much. Strange, how she noticed that now. Without sight, she had only hearing to provide her with information about the world, and people, around her. Sighing, she nodded in reply.

'And the pain?' he asked. Sybilla noticed a slight

inflection in his voice, one she might not have if forced to look upon him.

''Tis not the worst I have ever suffered through,' she said.

He grunted instead of answering then. She listened as he moved from her side and walked to the other side of the room.

Into that corner. It stood as empty now as she was.

'There are things we must discuss, lady.'

Sybilla tried to feel something, anything—even fear would have been welcomed to show she yet lived—but nothing was there inside. Even a fool would have been afraid of what was to come.

'Such as?' she asked, simply to make this audience end sooner…so that she could return to her silent, dark world.

'Your men will not answer my questions. I tried to… encourage them to do so, but they will not betray you.'

Dark threats swirled in his voice. Her men were alive? She clutched the arms of the wooden chair, curious for the first time in days.

'Who yet lives?' A tiny thread of hope to hear the names of those who'd done so much to protect her tingled deep within her heart.

'Only a handful of your men were killed in the battle,' he answered, with a tinge of insult echoing in his words. 'It took little time or effort to breach the puny defences of this manor and keep.'

At another time she might herself bristle at the insult offered to her as lady of this manor and keep, but none of her past pride rose to fuel her ire.

'How do you ask them to betray me?'

* * *

If he clenched his jaws any tighter, his teeth were sure to break. Soren held his anger in check and let out a breath. Did she know she tried his scant patience with every word she spoke?

He stepped away from her, walked a few paces and turned to observe her with a bit of space between them. Teyen's reports over the last sennight seemed accurate—the lady did not appear ill, though the bruises on her forehead and face retained the dark purple shades and swelling of a still-fresh injury. He could not see her eyes, for clean bandages covered them. Even uncovered, her eyes did not see. Now, she gripped the wooden arms of the chair in which she sat and he noticed her fingers relaxing and tightening when he'd mentioned her men. It was the only sign of interest in anything he'd witnessed from her in days.

Oh, she might not know it, but he'd watched her many times since his arrival and since that terrible outpouring of grief had happened. She sat as she did now or remained abed for hours at a time—moving hardly at all, asking for or about nothing. The spirit he'd witnessed in the hall when she tried to protect her people from him had been extinguished like the flame of a candle in the wind.

But, correctly, he'd guessed that her people would be her weakness as much as she was theirs. With a few well-placed and timed threats, he'd forced their co-operation in repairing the damage done to the walls and in organising the stores of the manor. Soren needed more information, though, information that only the lady seemed to possess.

'I need the rolls of the manor, to find how many owe service here and how many belong to the land. You know their location.' He would have missed the slight nod if he'd not been watching her. 'Where have you hidden them?'

'Is Algar dead, then?' she asked in a soft voice.

Part of him urged him to lie to her—not to add to the burden of guilt she must carry—but he tamped it down. The daughter of Durward deserved no such consideration, he told himself again.

'Aye, he is dead. We found his body in the rubble of the wall, along with four others.'

He could have told her that they were following her with orders to get her to safety, but those words would not flow from his tongue. Unwilling to dwell on that small measure of courtesy granted to a woman he came here prepared to hate, he repeated his demand.

'Where did he hide the rolls? Or did you accomplish the deed?'

The silence went on for several minutes with no sign of an answer in the offing from her. Soren used his leverage then.

'You put their lives in danger, lady, with your refusals. How many more must die because of you?'

Her indrawn breath told him of his success in piercing the lady's apparent lack of concern.

'You would kill them for something not in their control?'

'If it will gain me that which I need, aye,' he said, using her inability to see in this battle of wills. Clearly, she could not hear his lack of resolve and now had no visual cues to use to decide whether he bluffed or not.

Memories of his own days spent blinded by his injury threatened, but he gathered his control and prevented them from flaring.

'Tell me the names of those who died and I will take you to that which you demand.'

He laughed aloud at her attempt to bargain with him. A bit of spirit yet remained within the woman and it pleased him somehow. He preferred to face a strong enemy, to sharpen and hone his skills against a worthy adversary, than against a frightened woman with nothing to risk or lose. Soren also knew the value of timing in a battle, and this was nothing less, so he turned without another word and left. Let her sit and worry over his choice for a bit.

He strode down the stairs, having a care for the steepness of the steps. His eye could not discern the depth of something, especially a thing cloaked in the shadows, well enough yet, so he braced his hand on the wall as he moved downwards to the landing. Such a limitation served as a constant reminder of all he'd lost with Durward's blow and served to strengthen his resolve to overcome it as well. He'd learnt to adjust the aim of his bow quickly to sharpen the accuracy of his arrows' flight. But, simple things like staircases thwarted his attempts to appear as he once was—confident, accomplished and skilled. Guermont, who now stood as his second-in-command here at Alston, met him at the bottom.

'This encounter would seem better than your last one with the lady,' Guermont said, walking at his side through the hall to the door that led out to the yard. 'The guards have reported no outbursts from her since the first one.'

'Has she asked to leave her chambers? Have her maids asked?' Soren asked.

Guermont oversaw everything and everyone within the keep for Soren, so that he could see to the defences and the outlying buildings and lands. Soren had toiled alongside his men, the villeins of Alston and the prisoners he'd taken during his attack. Once the entire manor was under control and rebuilt to withstand attacks from the rebels who yet gathered to fight off the rule of King William, he would have time to better organise those who served him.

Though he'd initially planned to tear the place apart, plank by plank, stone by stone, he would have to wait on that, for the rebels were active once more in the north of England. Soren and his troops would be pivotal in controlling this area and they needed Alston, for now, as their base. Once the area was secured, Soren would be able to destroy the home of Durward and begin anew with his own plans.

'Nothing. Her maids remain at her side every moment, leaving rarely and never allowing her to be alone in her chambers. If one runs some errand, the other remains there.'

'Send to me if she asks to leave her room, Guermont,' Soren ordered, stopping a few paces outside the keep. 'Keep her maids with her for now.'

'Is she a prisoner, then?' Guermont asked.

'Nay, not a prisoner. All she has to do is ask and she has my permission to leave that room. But, she must ask it of me.' Soren nodded and turned to leave. A question in his mind stopped him.

'Is she eating?' he asked. The woman looked gaunt, more so than when he'd seen her last in the light of day.

Guermont shook his head. 'She eats little. I hear her maids cajoling her to take some porridge or broth.'

A memory of those first days after waking from his weeks of pain and herb-induced sleep shot through him then. Once he knew the extent of his injuries and the profound change it had wrought to his life and his body, he cared little if he ate or did not. He cared little if the sun rose or set. Sybilla of Alston was going through the exact same pattern that he had, but she could not even see around her to know if it was day or night. At least he'd been spared one eye to make his way in the world, such as it was.

Shaking off a growing sense of some emotion he neither understood nor appreciated, Soren left Guermont to his duties and sought out the place in the wall where the prisoners worked to repair it. He watched the men all defer to one man when given orders. They waited and watched him before obeying, a pattern repeated over and over. Stephen walked to his side.

'Is there a problem, Soren?'

'Nay. I am just watching that one,' he said, nodding in the direction of the older man. 'Was he the commander of Durward's guards? The one on the walls next to the lady?'

'I cannot tell,' Stephen replied.

Without delay Stephen walked to where the man walked and pulled him out of the line of prisoners, dragging him to where Soren stood. The length of chain attached to his ankles served to keep his strides short and prevented his escape. When he stood before him, Soren crossed his arms over his chest and studied the man.

'You commanded the manor's defences,' he asked, not doubting it for a moment. 'What is your name?'

'Gareth,' the man answered, meeting his gaze and not flinching or looking away. Clearly, this warrior had seen many battles and the results on human flesh.

Soren motioned for Stephen to release him and then, without hesitation or warning, he swung his fist, landing his punch on Gareth's jaw, knocking him to the ground.

'That is for closing your gates when you could not hope to keep me out.'

The Saxons watched now, ignoring their work and trying to get closer. His men stopped them, forming a wall between the prisoners and him, shoving them back to their places. Soren watched as Gareth climbed to his feet, wiped the blood from his mouth and stood straight before him, as though ready for the next blow. Soren had no intention of more, he simply wanted to make his point that the man's actions were foolhardy. In a battle when outnumbered by overwhelming numbers, antagonising one's opponent was not the smartest course of action.

'Come,' he directed and he walked away, expecting Gareth to follow. Soren strode a short distance away from the others and stopped, turning to face Gareth.

'How long have you served as commander of the guard here in Alston?' he asked.

'For nigh on ten years,' Gareth answered.

'Have you received word or instructions from kith or kin about the forces of William and the war?'

'Nothing until your message arrived last week, not since before the battles in the south.'

'All of England is now under William's control. Those Saxons who yet resist are being run to ground and exterminated like the vermin they are,' Soren explained, trying to make the man understand that resistance was futile.

'Even your boy-king has sworn allegiance to William and been shown lenience and respect.' He watched the man listen to his words, but his eyes did not show acceptance. 'Make peace with that or you and those who support the rebels will be crushed.'

Gareth neither accepted nor rejected his words, he just narrowed his gaze and then blinked. Soren's outriders had found traces of rebel camps not far from the edges of his lands and Soren would do everything in his power to wipe them out. No urge within would force him to allow the rebel leader Edmund Haroldson to escape, if sighted or encountered again. Not like his friends had done— allowing softer feelings towards their wives to interfere with their duty to eradicate the enemies of William from the face of the earth. Soren had hardened his heart and would never let a woman stand between him and his duty.

'Stephen, take him to Father Medwyn's clerk and have him make a list of all who died due to his foolhardy attempts to keep me from my lands.'

Gareth fought against Stephen's hold, shaking his head at Soren's commands.

'I will not betray my lady,' he said boldly.

Soren laid him out with one blow.

'Do not think to naysay my orders,' he said loud enough for all to hear and so that none could mistake his claim. He shook out his fist, relaxing the hand that had delivered the punch. 'I am lord here now and answer to no one, save my king. You are but a prisoner whose life and death I hold within my grasp.' Soren turned and walked away, leaving Gareth to consider his decision. His patience was at an end.

Chapter Seven

$Sybilla$ tried to allow the silence to swallow her, but her mind began to spin out questions now that *he* had left. Why did he have to ask her to think or to care when she just wanted to be sucked down into the quiet darkness that threatened all around her? Why had she even asked about the dead? Sybilla knew it had been a mistake and that was confirmed only minutes later.

Just when she thought she might finally banish those questions, his voice carried through an open window into her chamber. When those in the yard quieted, as they did now, his deep, strong voice rumbled as though he stood next to her.

He raged and threatened again. There in the yard, he enforced his will on those unable to resist it. Her head pounded with pain and she rubbed her forehead, trying to ease it.

'Here, my lady,' Aldys offered. 'Some ale for you.'

The maid plied her with the drink, but Sybilla shook

her head, not wishing anything to drink. This time Aldys did not argue with her, and Sybilla heard the *plunk* of the cup being placed on the table at her side and her servant's footsteps walking away. Whispers passed between Aldys and Gytha and grew in volume, becoming a strident argument and one too loud for Sybilla to ignore. She would blame it on his questions earlier for they'd spurred on more and more thoughts in her mind.

Unwelcomed thoughts.

Unnecessary ones.

Uncomfortable interest.

Thoughts led to words, which led to questions, questions she tried to contain within her, but they burst out without warning.

'What is happening that has you both clucking like hens?'

Their indrawn breath made her realise that she'd not spoken of her own accord to them since the day…since the day *he* arrived in Alston.

'Lady, he has taken—' Gytha began. But Aldys cut off her words.

'Girl!'

She sighed. They were ever like this. 'Aldys, tell me.'

Another pause followed and Sybilla could almost see the exchanged glances again before Aldys spoke.

'The new lord beat Gareth and had him taken away, lady.'

Gareth yet lived?

Sybilla felt the tug of concern growing within her heart. Gareth had somehow survived the battle and now would die because she would not give *him* what he demanded. This conqueror was carrying out his threat because she would not obey him. Sybilla gripped the arms of the chair, not believing that she would or could stop him from his atrocious act but, for the first time in days and days, wanting to intervene.

'Take me to him,' she ordered in a calm voice that did not reveal the tumultuous roiling in her stomach.

After days of living in a purgatory, empty of all feelings or concerns, Sybilla was shocked at how quickly those lost emotions came flooding back into her heart and soul.

The two maids began to argue between themselves, so Sybilla pushed herself up from the chair and took a tentative step towards the door. And then another. Within moments, they were at her side, guiding her steps while they warned her against such action. Walking, even in her own chambers, without being able to see her path, was terrifying! The palms of her hands grew sweaty and her heart pounded with each step.

Worse, fear of confronting the man who had killed so many in his efforts to claim Alston dogged her every move forwards. With his size and strength and with the ever-present anger and hatred for her and her family, he would kill her with one blow—if he chose to strike her. She shivered as she remembered the moment she heard him draw his sword and knew he would not delay or hold back his anger once he'd decided on her death.

Would it be today? Would dying be easier than trying to live, blind and at the mercy of a man who clearly had none? She swallowed back the fear and reached out to touch the door, searching for the latch.

The shuffling of feet before her alerted her to their

presence. One of the guards spoke, though both now stood close enough to her that their feet touched as she tried to move forwards.

'My lady?'

'I wish to speak to your lord. Take me to him now,' she said, trying to speak in a calm manner that belied the lack of nerves she felt inside her.

'I cannot do that, my lady,' he said. Before he could explain, she offered another choice to him.

'Aldys, seek out the new lord and bring him here,' she said, hoping her voice exuded the calm of one in charge of a situation.

'She cannot leave either, lady.'

Her temper, one that had laid dormant for days and days, flared. Amazing how quickly an unused thing could come back to life.

'My servants have had leave to see to my needs since your lord arrived. By what right do you stop them now?'

A moment of silence met her question and the shifting and scuffing of heavy feet on the wooden floor outside her doorway as the guards considered how to answer her.

'By Lord Soren's command and their duty to him, lady,' answered another voice from further down the corridor.

Sybilla turned and listened as this new man strode towards her chamber. Clenching her hands together, she took a deep breath and then another and another, gaining a bit of control with each exhalation, until the man arrived at her door. Sybilla stood her ground and swallowed deeply.

'Lady Sybilla, are you well?'

'I need to speak to your lord,' she repeated. She took a step forwards, unsure of how close the guards were, or where this man stood. 'You are called…?'

'I am Guermont, serving now as Lord Soren's steward.' She now felt his foot in front of hers, telling her that he was close indeed. But his introduction reminded her of her failings.

Guermont served as steward because Algar was dead.

'Take me to your lord,' she repeated. 'Now.'

One of the guards coughed and the other cleared his throat, drawing her attention to one side and then the other. From the sounds, she could tell that Guermont stood directly before her and the guards must stand close at his side. With Aldys and Gytha at her side, she was blocked in tight with nowhere to move.

'Please return to your chambers and I will send a message to him that you would speak with him,' the man offered. It was not enough and Gareth could be dead before his lord deigned to seek her out.

'It is important that I speak to him now, Guermont.' Her hands began to shake at the thought that he might refuse her. 'A man's life is at stake in this matter.'

A stalemate. Whether in battle or in controlling villeins, power and uncertainty vied for dominance and in this case, she knew Guermont weighed his options. Moments passed before she heard his sigh—he would relent.

But the loud voice, arguing and shouting, that echoed down the corridor between her chambers and the stairway to the main hall told her differently. Lord Soren returned, full of anger, full of threats, full of force, and she stood there unable to move out of his path. Sybilla shook now, expecting at any moment to hear the news of Gareth's death at his hands.

Worse, she knew that by her own timidity and inaction and by existing in a haze of sorrow for her own condition, she'd caused it when she could have stopped it with but a word earlier. Sybilla stumbled back, away from the door, away from him. Her maids shuffled back, trying to guide her to no avail.

Guermont spoke in low tones to him, explaining, she could hear, her request to speak to him and he grunted in reply. Then, with that one word that seemed to be his favorite, he cleared the room and area of everyone.

'Out.'

Sybilla waited, barely breathing, as he strode with bold loud steps into her chambers and approached her. The door slammed, distracting her for a moment, but Sybilla could swear she could feel the heat of his body moving closer to hers before he spoke another word. Now that her heart and soul had awakened from their slumber, Sybilla braced herself for this new, terrible world he would bring.

Instead, he pressed a small piece of parchment into her hand, uncurling her fingers and letting them grasp it. She tried to understand what it was, but could not. Lifting it between them, she shook her head.

'You know I cannot see,' she said. 'Do you do this to make certain I know my limitations?' Though she did not doubt his hatred of her for a moment, this belittling action seemed low of him to do.

'This,' he said, encircling her hand and the parchment

with his larger hand, 'is what you demanded from me in order to comply with my request.' His voice, deep and rumbling even when almost a whisper, caused tingling to race up and down her skin and her spine.

'My demand?' Did this mean…?

'You demanded a list of your dead. It lies on that parchment in your hand.'

She grasped it tightly, crumpling the precious sheet before she relaxed her grip. This did not excuse Gareth's death, though. How would she atone for her inaction that had added another's name to this tally of her sins, her failures?

'And you had to kill another to prove that you now rule here? To make certain I know you will enforce your commands and demands?' Bold words, but her heart pounded so loudly she was certain it could be heard by him.

'Kill another? Of whom do you speak now, lady? Other than those who took up arms against me and were killed in the battle, I have sent no others to their deaths here.'

After spending only a sennight or so in the dark world of blindness, Sybilla was beginning to pick up on other signals of danger. The tone of his voice was one such clue and every part of her prepared for the onslaught of his anger now. Clearly, she'd insulted him somehow and she would pay. When he grabbed her shoulders and hauled her up closer, with only the tips of her toes touching the ground, she felt the danger in his hands.

'I fulfilled my part—now, Lady Sybilla, tell me where the records and rolls are hidden.'

She swallowed hard against her fear and told him. 'In

the small chamber next to the kitchen. A small storage closet dug into the stone wall holds the important records of Alston and my family.'

'Who else knows its location?' he asked, giving her a slight shake.

'Only my family and Algar.'

'Your father's man Gareth knows not?'

'Gareth? No.' Terror struck her heart then. 'Did you try to torture it from him before he died?' she asked.

Each encounter with her engendered a new response within him and he never knew if it would be anger, hatred, pity, ambivalence or even good, plain, unmitigated lust. Not knowing meant being unprepared, as he was in this moment, and left him ill at ease, without a way to effectively deal with her. One look at the pained expression on what he could see of her heart-shaped face when she thought he'd executed her father's man and Soren nearly lost his resolve not to soften towards her.

The only thing that brought him back from the brink of losing his control was the knowledge that she could not see him. Placing her back on her feet, he stepped away from her.

He would not explain his actions, especially not to her, even if the words sat on the edge of his tongue and wanted to vindicate him in her opinion. So much of his recent life had been driven by his quest for vengeance and for Alston that he'd given little thought to the wisdom he'd learned from Lord Gautier of Rennes. Now, as he gazed down at the woman who personified his obsession for revenge, he heard the older man's words in his mind.

Hatred is the perfect weapon for it gives your enemy

power over you that you would never otherwise put in their hands.

Had he not done exactly that?

He watched as Sybilla tried to regain her balance, her hands flaring out as she wobbled on her feet. Soren waited, but then did reach out when she stumbled once more and would have fallen.

It seemed that now people believed the worst of him based on his appearance just as they had previously always thought the best. A prisoner of his anger and his torn flesh, Soren waited for her to regain her balance and then turned to leave. Well, he was in no mood to disabuse her of the wrongness of her judgements or to enlighten her of his true actions here.

'You are not a prisoner here, lady,' he said. 'You and your women can go and come as you please.'

'Twas time for him to move along and get his plans underway and she was, regardless of his original intent, a part of that. The surrounding lands must be secured, the keep and walls repaired and strengthened against attack and stores replenished. Now, with the information he knew would be in the manor's records, he would know who owed service, who owed crops, and who owed other goods to the lord.

He glanced back as he reached the door and noticed the forlorn look of her face. Even with the bandage in place, the downturn of her mouth was in view. Damn! Soren did not know why he did so, but as he left he offered her the words of comfort he knew she needed to hear.

'Gareth is not dead.'

He did not delay or hesitate in leaving her chambers,

but he sought out his men to help him find the storage closet and the needed rolls of the manor.

'Enough.'

Stephen waved him off and pulled off his helm. With his surrender, Soren had no other opponent to fight. He'd fought every other man standing in the area that they'd used as a practice yard. Outside the walls, yet within clear sight of the keep and its gates, it was a level plain back to the treeline and perfect now for the needed exercise and practice of fighting skills. Usually this was something he enjoyed—pushing his muscles, his body and his mind to their limits and then a bit more to improve his already formidable abilities on the field of war.

Though the others began to loosen and remove layers of heavy mail and thick quilted hauberks, he remained clothed. Sweat poured down his head and neck and over his body, but he would not undress before them. Not like before when his body was a thing of male beauty and when it was admired by others—men for its strength and women for the pleasures it promised.

Now, a tangle of criss-crossing scars marred his skin from head to hip, all marking the path of an axe's blade and resulting in torn and yet-mangled flesh. Healing irregularly as they had, the skin lay tight and twisted and never lost its sting. Peering off to the woods at the edge of the field, he remembered a stream they'd crossed on their way here. That would fit his needs perfectly.

Soren told Stephen of his plans and then whistled to his mount. Climbing on the black monster's back, he pointed him in the direction of the trees and touched the horse's sides with his boots. Within minutes, they had crossed from the sunny field into the shadows of the woods and Soren guided the horse deeper and further until the sound of the rushing water could be heard ahead of them.

When they reached the nearest part of it, Soren jumped from the horse and tossed the reins around a branch to keep him there. Then Soren waited and listened for any sounds that would reveal others nearby. After a few minutes of silence but for the birds and other small creatures that lived within the wood, Soren walked to the edge of the rushing flow and began to peel off the layers of protection and clothing he wore.

Once naked, he stretched this way and that, trying to ease the tight, scarred flesh. He stepped into the rushing water and nearly lost his breath at the chill of it. This land was so much colder than his homeland of Brittany. There, the lands were warmed by mild breezes off the sea and the sun dominated the days. Here, *merde*, it was enough to freeze a man's balls from his body!

He did not let the cold stop him, striding in until the water reached his waist and throwing his head under it. The sweat washed away and his body immediately cooled from his exertions of the day. Soren scrubbed his skin and rubbed his scalp with the water. He'd not planned this so he'd not brought along any soap. Next time…

Hell! Next time he would bathe in heated water *inside*! Surely Sybilla would allow him the privacy of her chamber to do so.

Soren walked to the edge of the stream and sluiced most of the water off him as he left the current. Turning, he leaned over, grabbed the length of his hair and twisted it, allowing the worst of it to drip back into the stream.

As he did so, he noticed the reflection of himself in the calmer edge of the stream. He could not help but stare at the monster there, the one everyone saw now when they beheld Soren, the Beautiful Bastard.

If he turned to one side, his face barely looked touched, but it was the other side that bore the brunt of the blow that had nearly killed him in battle. It was that side, his right, that made others cringe in horror or turn away in fear or revulsion. Caught up in the vision reflecting off the water's calm surface there, he nearly missed the sound of leaves crunching beneath someone's feet.

Nearly.

Soren crouched and reached for his sword and dagger, ready to face danger. He turned his face so that the unscarred side was forwards and he could see better into the shadows.

'Who goes there?' he called out.

'Raed,' said a voice to his right side in the bushes.

'Return to the keep and I will be there anon,' he ordered, keeping the worst of his injuries hidden from view. The boy would have nightmares for days if he saw the extent of it. And he'd be worthless as a squire if he saw the results of battle now before trained.

'Aye, Lord Soren,' the boy called, never showing himself.

Soren took up his clothing and put on only what would cover him for the ride back to the keep. But what bothered him throughout that ride was the realisation that softer emotions were creeping back into his soul. Emotions like sympathy for the boy…and admiration for the woman.

When she haunted his dreams over the next several

nights, in spite of her keeping to her chambers regardless of his leave to do otherwise, he knew changes were coming. He just prayed his soul would survive them.

Chapter Eight

Though things were settling back into a routine in Alston, one she could hear through the portal her window provided, Sybilla remained in her chambers. The parchment he'd provided yet remained rolled and in her grasp most of the time. Instead of finding someone to read it to her, she simply spent her empty hours offering up prayers for the souls of those listed there.

The souls of those who'd died for her.

The worst part of this was she lacked the courage to go out among her people now. Blind, she could not serve them as she should as lady. All of her duties, ones she'd performed for her father after her mother's death, had been lifted from her control, much as her keep and hands had, with the arrival of Lord Soren and his men. Now, others ruled, others oversaw, others supervised every aspect of life here in Alston. So, she sat here in her chambers, hiding from all she'd had before and even from the people she should be serving.

She could not sew or embroider now. She could not weave and that was something she always did when troubled or unable to sleep. It soothed her restlessness and helped her to concentrate. Moving the threads over the loom aided her in seeing other patterns around her. Now, with nothing to do to be useful, she sat praying.

And wondering.

He'd not touched her since that disastrous first night and had never spoken of exercising his marital rights to her bed and her body. Had he decided against consummation? Did he plan to put her aside? Sybilla shifted in the chair, her body exhausted from doing nothing at all and her mind now teased with this possibility.

She'd planned to ask him for leave to go to her cousin's convent before he attacked. With no one there to lay claim, or argue his, to Alston, Sybilla had hoped that his anger against her people would dissipate. Mayhap he would allow it now if she did not contest the annulment of their ill-timed, ill-fated marriage?

She'd managed to sew some gold coins into the hem of her cloak that would be enough to donate to the convent for her entrance there. Certainly in these hard and trying times, there would be a place made for her.

As though her very thoughts had conjured his interest, Sybilla heard the light, running steps of the boy he used to bring messages. He stopped before her chambers and spoke to the guard, only one now there on duty as the lord had granted her permission to leave her chambers at any time. Then he knocked on the door and opened it.

'Lady,' he said quietly. Then, 'I mean good day to you, my lady.' Clearly he was working on his manners and being instructed by someone on how to do it.

'Raed of Shildon,' she acknowledged. 'Good morrow to you as well,' she replied in a lighter tone than she felt. Why should the boy be taken to task because she was feeling low?

'My lord Soren said to expect a bath to be sent here to your chambers this day.' He said the words carefully, as though he'd spent hours memorising them. Just so, for he missed the importance of those words to her and to her life.

Her maids gasped, understanding the meaning of the words delivered by the boy. Then they began to whisper between themselves. Sybilla's body shuddered from deep within at the realisation that he, Lord Soren, did intend to claim his marital rights…and this very night!

'Lady?' The boy cleared his throat and then spoke again. 'Is aught wrong?'

'Nay,' she said, shaking her head. 'Twould be unseemly for him to return to his lord with a report that included her screaming or fainting at the words he delivered. No matter that she felt like doing both at this moment. 'Nay,' she repeated louder to convince both herself and the boy. 'Is there anything else?'

He thought about it for a moment and then spoke. She could almost imagine a furrowed brow as he tried to remember any other words he was supposed to deliver to her. 'Nay, my lady. That was the message.'

The shuffling feet told her he was leaving. 'Raed?'

'Aye, my lady.'

'How many years have you?' If she could have seen him, she could have judged by the milk teeth still remaining in his mouth and his size, but blind she had no clue.

'Almost nine, my lady,' he said. 'I was born nearer to winter than summer.'

She nodded, unable to think of anything else to say. He left without another word to her, pausing at the door, she heard him stop, and then leave. He said nothing to the guard this time and she listened as his steps moved away down the corridor.

'Twas strange how she'd never noticed the echo of feet on wood outside her door until now. She'd never noticed most of the sounds of the keep except the crowing of the cocks in the morn or the occasional song of the night birds as the sun set. Now, sound was all she had to tell her of the world moving around her. The activities outside her chamber and her window were the only indication to her that life was moving on with or without her. It took but a moment or two for her maids to begin their assault.

'He sends a bath to you?' Gytha exclaimed. 'A bath, lady?'

'His message is clear, lady,' Aldys said. Always the practical one, she continued, ''Twould seem clear he plans to make you a wife in more than name only.'

What could she say in reply? Sybilla nodded her head in agreement and felt a tremor of both dread and excitement deep in the pit of her belly. All of her conjecture about her future changed with this simple message, one carried by a boy who had no inkling of its significance to her or her life. Any plans to offer him an alternative vanished in that moment and a life completely contrary to the one she'd hoped to present to him in unemotional words and sensible terms opened up before her.

A wife.

A wife? Married to a man who had less consideration

for her than he did for the men who served him. A man who she knew only by his violence and shouting. A man…who would claim her body with his and claim her life and future.

Sybilla swallowed against the fear that tightened her throat. Heat billowed in her cheeks at the thought of lying with such a man as the one she'd seen across the field, sitting like the devil's own on his monstrous steed. She remembered his height and his strength and even, in that moment, how large he'd felt next to her on the bed that strange night.

'Is there aught I can tell you, lady?' Aldys asked quietly, now close by her side. 'You were very young when your mother passed and mayhap—' Sybilla did not give her time to go into any details.

'I am prepared for what I must do, Aldys,' she said. 'Better this night than the first one when shock and terror ruled my mind.' Whether or not that was the truth, Sybilla spoke those words, trying to convince both her maids and herself of it. 'I think the chamber should be cleaned out before this night,' she said, giving the two women something to think of other than her. 'Will you see to it, Aldys?'

At first she thought they would be insulted that she questioned the neatness of her room, but instead they seized upon the task as she'd hoped they would. Only a passing comment, whispered low yet still heard, gave her pause about the coming night. Gytha, thinking her words would not be heard, allowed her concerns to be voiced and Sybilla trembled upon hearing them.

'The blindness might be a godsend,' Gytha whispered

to Aldys. 'At least the lady will not have to look upon his face when he beds her.'

Try as she might, those words sunk into her soul and Sybilla added herself to the litany of prayers spoken in the next hours.

Raed liked the lady. Back at Shildon, there was no lady present, only the lord, and he was a tyrant. At least that's what his mother and father had whispered when they thought him asleep or not listening. But he had listened and learned about his parents' fears of the one who ruled over them on old lord Eoforwic's estate in the north.

Now, returning to his duties outside, he worried that he'd not carried the message as well as he'd wanted to. The words, repeated over and over until he could recite them back, had caused her face to pale and her hands to shake. His stomach ached, remembering the sight of it. And of the fear in the gazes of the other women who served her.

Running down the stairs and then pausing to make sure no one had seen him do that, Raed thought back on Lord Soren's command and realised his error. Still, it puzzled him why the lady would be so afeared of a bath.

He made his way back out to the yard, where the prisoners worked to rebuild the wall surrounding the keep. It was smaller than the one at Shildon, but larger than many here in England, according to Larenz, who'd come across the sea with the invader king's army. Larenz watched out for him now and gave him his tasks each day. Raed was pleased that he would some day be squire to Lord Soren, if he learned his duties, and mayhap even a knight when grown.

'What's the matter, boy?' Larenz asked as he approached.

At first Raed hesitated to admit his mistake, but Larenz always seemed patient with him, like his father had been. And even though Lord Soren had threatened to beat him, he'd not yet done so. Instead, a warm place to sleep and enough food to fill his belly was his each day. Larenz told him that everyone made mistakes and, so long as you learned a lesson from it, 'twere fine. When he got closer to the man, Larenz grabbed his hair and rubbed his head almost like Raed did to the miller's hound when he was allowed to play with the dog.

'Is all well?' Larenz and the others spoke a different tongue, but most managed to say their English words clear enough to be understood. Only a few of Lord Soren's men did not, but he'd ordered them to learn quickly.

'I took the message to the lady as Lord Soren commanded.'

'And?' Larenz asked. 'What happened? Did she refuse him the use of her chambers?'

'Nay,' he said, shaking his head. 'Why would she? He is lord here and all belongs to him.' It seemed clear to Raed, so why would the lady not have realised it?

Larenz laughed aloud, shaking his head at Raed. 'Boy, you know not the way of things between men and women. Ladies sometimes believe themselves to be in charge.' Larenz knelt down on one knee, bringing himself down so that Raed could meet his eyes. 'Tell me what happened.'

Raed's hands sweated then and he worried more about

what he'd forgotten to tell the lady. What would Lord Soren do for this failure at his duties?

'I told the lady Lord Soren would be sending a bath to her chambers this evening.' Raed swallowed and tried to be calm. 'I forgot to tell Lady Sybilla that it was for him.'

Larenz laughed louder then, gaining attention from others nearby. Raed wanted to believe his laughter signalled no need to fear about his error.

'Should I go back to the lady? Should I tell Lord Soren of this?'

He would bear the beating as punishment for his mistake and he would learn from it, as Larenz had said he must. Larenz stood then and mussed his hair again, grabbing the back of his cloak and guiding him along at his side.

'Nay, boy. A bigger mistake would be to get between the lord and his lady. Let them sort this all out themselves.'

Raed smiled and tried to accept Larenz's words, but something was wrong between Lord Soren and Lady Sybilla. If they were married, as his parents had been, should they not share their chambers? For as long as they'd been in Alston, Lord Soren sought his rest outside or in that small room near the kitchen and ate with his men or alone. The lady, injured grievously, remained in her room. Neither one seemed happy and neither spoke much to the other.

How strange these nobles were—married yet not. Not like the rest of the people whom married meant living together and working together.

Raed thought that maybe her fear was like his had

been—based on the horrible way Lord Soren looked. He'd admit that his looks took some time to get accustomed to. It had taken Raed days and days, but now the scars that covered one side of Lord Soren's face did not bother him much at all.

Had the lady seen Lord Soren before she was blinded? Or mayhap the others had spoken ill of him to her? She did not seem the silly, easily frightened type to him, but he was only a boy and she the lady of a great family here in the north. Even he knew that.

'Raed, seek out the stable master and see to Lord Soren's mount,' Larenz ordered.

His mistake could not have been too bad or Larenz would never send him to his favourite place in all of Alston. Surely not? Raed loved working with the horses and taking care of Lord Soren's mighty beast of a horse was something he would never tire of.

'You are certain?' he asked just one time to make sure his error was not a grave one.

'Aye, boy, go now,' Larenz said and Raed followed his orders, not even looking back when Larenz let out another burst of loud laughter as he ran off.

Larenz could not contain it and he laughed again as the English boy ran off. He was a good sort, doing whatever was asked of him, trying to please Soren and find a new life here at Alston. Not even the worst Soren offered scared the boy off, much to his credit, since many men better, older and wiser than him had trembled time and time again. But this boy stood his ground and 'twas plain to see that Soren liked that.

Larenz liked him, too, for he had a strong spirit and

a good heart in spite of losing everything and everyone he'd had when Oremund destroyed the village of Shildon rather than letting it fall into Norman hands. Watching the boy run to the stables, such as they were, Larenz was reminded of Soren at the same age. Older by almost a score of years, Larenz had guided some of Soren's training, too, and then served with him in William of Normandy's quest for the throne of England.

He saw Soren walking off with Stephen and Guermont and was, for a moment, tempted to inform him of the boy's gaffe, but decided against it. They'd all watched as Soren and the lady avoided each other—Soren did it a-purpose, the lady for other reasons—but it needed to be brought to a halt. Unless they made their peace, Alston would remain a place of battle—Saxons against the Normans and Bretons, men against women, common folk against their rulers. All hinged on the relationship between Soren and Sybilla, even if those two did not know or realise it.

Mayhap this misstep, done with no ill intentions by the boy, would be just the thing to bring the two together? Clearly, they had much in common and much they could learn from each other—if they were together.

Oh, there would be problems, but how better to solve them than together and, if there were two more kindred souls who needed to be together, he'd never seen them. Laughing once more, he strode off to his own duties, determined to keep his tongue firmly planted inside his mouth and to let the two sort this thing out between them.

God have mercy on all of them if they failed.

Chapter Nine

Sybilla could not help the sigh that escaped as she sank into the steaming water. She'd bathed from a basin since the battle and had not washed her hair thoroughly because of the wound, but now she surrendered to the heat and the feeling of washing away all the grime and sweat of this week. Several extra buckets sat along the wall to be used if needed and she considered sitting here until the water went cold. But this day she did not have the time to waste sitting here, avoiding what was to come.

She shivered in spite of the heat of the water and the chamber, for a fire blazing in the hearth warmed the room. She listened to Gytha and Aldys walking around the tub, Aldys in charge of washing her and Gytha preparing the bed. The linens had been laundered and the bed made fresh for this night. Everything was ready for his arrival, as she would be shortly.

Sinking back into the water, she waited and listened for any sign of his approach. Since the meal was just ending in the hall below, Sybilla thought she would still have time, more time, to accustom herself to the idea of what would happen between them this night. So, when he came, without the usual heavy footsteps or yelling, it surprised both her and her maids.

'Lord Soren!' Aldys said sharply as she dropped the bucket with which she was rinsing Sybilla's hair. Her voice moved around the tub, taking what could only be considered a defensive stance between the door and the tub in the corner. 'Gytha!' she said. The scurrying of feet meant Gytha joined Aldys between her and her lord and husband.

'Lady Sybilla is not yet done, my lord,' Aldys explained.

The door slammed and Sybilla felt it rattle the tub. Her natural inclination was to stand, but instead, she sank lower beneath the water and the sides of the tub.

'Done?' he asked, not stopping at the door. His voice grew closer and she sank lower. 'Done what?'

'Her bath, Lord Soren. The one you ordered for her,' Aldys said slowly as though speaking to a babe.

'I ordered no bath for her, woman. The bath was for me.'

Sybilla did not know whether to be relieved or insulted in that moment. Was this a reprieve from him claiming his marital rights, then? No one moved, she certainly not, and the silence continued on for what seemed like for ever.

She heard him approach and heard the swift intake of his breath. Surely the shadows of the chamber's corner and the water did nothing to hide her flesh from his view. His shallow breathing spoke of arousal. Sybilla found her own breathing just as shallow at the realisation that he saw her nakedness.

'Finish your bath, lady,' he said in a husky voice. 'I will call for more hot water and return for mine.'

'Here?' she asked. 'You want to bathe here?'

At first she was confused and then understanding struck her—he wished for privacy and this was the only private chamber in the keep. But if she thought he would explain, she was wrong.

'I will return later.'

And with that simple declaration, he was gone, walking swiftly to the door and closing it with the same strong slam that he'd done when first he'd entered her chambers. She let a moment or two pass by and then she moved, shifting in the tub and grabbing hold of the sides.

'Aldys, help me get out,' she said, already twisting her hair to rid it of most of the water. 'Gytha, a drying cloth. Pray thee move quickly, I wish not to be caught unclothed again.'

'The bath was for him?' Aldys asked as she guided Sybilla from the tub. 'The boy never mentioned that.'

'I do not fault young Raed for this misunderstanding. He must live in constant fear of being beaten and punished for every little misstep or error,' Gytha whispered. 'I hear the new lord threatens him daily.'

Sybilla allowed their help and tried to ignore their chatter. They'd all assumed something that now seemed quite different than what Lord Soren's message had been. Did he mean only to use her chambers to bathe, then? Had this not been about consummating their marriage after all? Did he after all plan to set her aside?

Her women moved efficiently and quietly and soon she

was seated in front of the hearth, letting her hair dry in its heat. Aldys was careful with the strokes of the brush, avoiding the place where her scalp was torn and easing it gently through the tangles until it moved smoothly down its length. Sybilla found it soothing to her frayed nerves and the slow strokes relaxed the tension in her body. With her eyes closed, she could almost ignore the world around her and fall asleep.

The knock, softer than she could have imagined him capable of, woke her from her lethargy. She gathered the bedrobe closer around her and nodded to whichever of the women would notice. Aldys opened the door and allowed him entrance.

Soren had never felt out of place in a woman's bed-chamber in his life until this moment. He'd been in many, from the most common to the noble-born, and knew his place in each—lover, confidante, companion in passion—until he crossed over the entranceway to Sybilla's room. Her maids watched him, scrutinising every step he took and every expression he made as he walked in, and closed the door behind him.

Though he would never have admitted it, he did not want to share this intimate vision of his...wife with the other men who stood guard in the corridor. And though he wanted to continue to blame her for all the sins of her father, the sight of her naked in that tub had undone all his resolve to remain aloof and unaffected by her. He'd made that oath to himself when he'd felt pity for her creeping into his heart, but he'd had no idea that the emotion he would have to battle with would be lust.

One glance at her creamy flesh, her pert, rose-tipped breasts and womanly form, and his body had hardened in preparation for bedding her. Not that he'd arrived at her door with that intent, but years of it meaning exactly that had trained his body to ready itself…and to do it quickly, for there was no telling how much time he would have to enjoy the lady involved.

Now, she sat on a stool near the fire, unmoving but enticing him again with the curves of her body that pressed against the soft folds of her robe and shift. The Saxon garb she usually wore hid most of her figure from his sight, so seeing her without the layers and veiling tempted him more than even that first night and his first sight of her in the bed.

Soren wanted no witnesses to his bath, so he pushed the door open wider and nodded his head to them. Although the older one looked as though she would argue, wisely she kept her words to herself. The younger one had no such sense.

'Lady Sybilla?' she asked. 'Should we go?'

'Aye, go,' he ordered, though he did not shout it as he wanted to.

For some reason, there was a feeling of calm in this chamber, even from the lady, and he did not wish to disturb it. 'Twas almost like he'd entered a refuge of some kind, a safe and restful place. Not what he would ever think a bedchamber to be and it did not make sense to him, but he accepted it and gave them another nod. He closed the door to find her standing.

'Do you wish me to leave?' she asked. 'I suspect you want the privacy this chamber offers and will give you that.' She took a step, an unsteady one, towards him and the door.

'Nay,' he said, imagining what the men in the corridor

would see and think as the lady proceeded down past them. He shook his head before remembering that she could not see him. 'Nay, there is no need.'

The lady stepped back and sat down once more, turning her back to him and giving the illusion of choosing not to look. Soren walked to the tub and dipped his fingers in the water. Warm, but not hot. He noticed the buckets along the wall and poured them in. Now steam rose from the surface and he smiled. It would feel wonderful to soak in this.

Unable to break his habit, he walked into the darker shadows in the corner of the room and peeled off all the layers of clothing he wore. With the worst of his injuries hidden by the darkness, Soren stepped into the tub and sank below the water's surface. He might have moaned and was not certain he had until her soft laughter echoed across the chamber to him.

Soft yet nervous laughter.

'I confess—a hot bath is a weakness of mine, lady.'

Had he said too much? He did not expect to converse with her, but to ignore her completely while using her chamber and while she sat but yards away seemed ridiculous. Soren had always like being clean and baths with the help of a willing woman usually led to other pleasures, but since his injury a hot bath helped to ease the tightness in the skin now stretched tautly to cover the gaping wound he had suffered.

He opened his eye and watched as she lifted the brush she held and ran it through the length of her hair. Soren shifted in the water as his cock hardened and rose. He'd seen it loosened and lying around her shoulders in the bed and he'd seen it braided and arranged. Now, clean and shiny from the brush strokes, he fought the urge to go and tangle his hands in it. When he moved too fast, trying to look away and focus on his…feet, the water sloshed over the side and on to the floor.

Then it was his curse that echoed across the room. Soren settled back in the water and cursed again, this time under his breath. He noticed she'd stopped in the middle of a movement and sat with her arms raised.

Mayhap this was not the good idea it seemed to be when he planned it? The boy must have mixed up the message he'd sent to Sybilla to inform her. What had Raed told her? Soren reached over the side and dipped his hand into the bowl of soft soap. Scooping some into his palm, first he lathered his hair and then spread more over his arms and chest, massaging the scars and rough patches of skin until they softened and eased.

'What did the boy tell you earlier?' he asked as he reached for more.

At first she paused, then she stood and took a few steps in the direction of the tub…and him. Her eyes were open, the swelling that had closed them gone now, but she remained sightless. The lady held her hands out before her, trying to feel her way across the chamber. Uncertainty covered her face and soon she stopped and remained still.

'He truly is not at fault, Lord Soren.' She clutched her hands together now, her hair swinging about her body and reaching all the way to her hips. 'Pray thee do not beat him for this.'

She thought he would punish the boy over this? He felt the anger rising, but tamped it down. By judging him in this manner, she did nothing that others, even his own men, did not do. Still…though he'd raged at the boy, he'd not touched him in anger even once. And in spite of that raging and in spite of the fact that Soren was convinced the boy had seen him clearly at the stream, Raed never seemed afraid of him. The boy never ran from him or failed to meet his gaze when speaking. Yet the lady thought he would suffer for this misstep.

'What did the boy tell you?' Now he truly was curious about the message carried here.

'He said you were sending a bath here.'

'And?'

She shook her head. 'That was all he said.'

Soren was beginning to see what had happened. 'And you thought the bath was meant for you?'

'Aye,' she said. Did she realise she blushed now? A becoming bit of pink crept into her cheeks, erasing the pallor of this last week and replacing it with something more attractive.

'I do not mind sharing my bath with you, lady,' he said, purposely misunderstanding her.

Sharing a bath could be a pleasurable few hours while sharing bath water was usually a necessity. Filling a bath tub of this size took considerable work and would not be for only one person in most situations. It would be set up in the kitchen area near the hearth so the water did not need to be carried far from the fire. Having one here today was a luxury, an indulgence, one not to be repeated often.

'Share your bath? Surely not,' she said, a bit too breathlessly for his own comfort.

An innocent who had no idea of the possibilities in pleasure between a man and a woman. Well, he did and his body did, too, reacting to the thoughts racing through his mind now that involved this tub, hot water, soap and the woman standing before him. So much for his finding a refuge of peace and quiet. He needed to change the direction of this conversation and his thoughts before all his control was lost and he was pulling her into the tub or tumbling her onto the bed and taking the wife he was still not certain he wanted.

Soren understood that what had happened to her, with her, that first day and night, had given him a reprieve of a sort. Time to sort things out once the haze of his rage eased and time to avoid mistakes that would haunt him for the rest of his life.

One such mistake was taking her as wife.

He'd done it in the heat of battle, in spite of his words to Stephen to the contrary. Now, he knew that consummating their vows would have bound her to him, leaving no way out. Once he'd made that decision, though, the thoughts of her and the images that seemed to occupy his mind were all of the passionate kind. As she'd begun to heal a bit and come around, evidenced by her plucky resistance to his demands for the location of the manor rolls, Soren found her occupying his thoughts much more than he wanted to admit. Now she stood before him, dressed in only the thinnest of bedrobes, blushing and breathing in a manner that spoke of arousal…or at least interest.

'So what did you think this bath meant, if not to share it with me? Did you think I was being kind, then?'

Would he never learn, or rather unlearn, his damned attraction to women? When would he realise that this was going in a dangerous direction? But years of flirting with and enjoying the company of women, beautiful and plain, high-born and common, had taught him habits that were nigh impossible to forget. And even the recent scorn and fearful reactions of women to his new appearance had apparently not burned it out of him either. She stammered at first, then shook her head as though refusing to answer, but she closed her eyes, tilted her head up as though offering a prayer of some kind and then spoke.

'We…I…I thought you meant to claim your marital rights,' she proclaimed, looking none too happy over the possibility of it.

This explained much. Soren's men had been staring at him all afternoon in a strange way. Smiling at him, too, in an unexplained manner and for no reason. But now he understood what they thought, what they all thought, thanks to one untrained boy's misspoken message—they believed he was here to bed her. Part of him wanted to laugh over this and part wanted to get out of the tub, peel off her robe and claim those marital rights.

He could almost hear Lord Gautier laughing at him in that moment. And as he searched for the right way to handle this, he knew that mayhap he was not as far gone as he and many others had thought him to be. A bit of the man he used to be crept into his soul.

'And is that what you want me to do, Lady Sybilla?'

Chapter Ten

Why had she foolishly admitted the truth to him?

She should have remained quiet and not spoken and not engaged him in this conversation that was now mired down in a dangerous place. If he'd only wanted a bath, that was all right with her, but talking about sharing a bath had caused such strange feelings to rush through her body. Then one word led to another, a question to an answer and so on until now she'd unwisely shown him that she had thought he was here to share her bed!

Sybilla reached up and pushed her hair away from her face. Loosened from its braid and freshly washed, it was an unruly mass that surrounded her shoulders and face with a mass of curls. She realised that no man had looked on her hair this way. Why was she thinking such frivolous things when he waited for an answer from her?

He'd stopped washing, for she could hear no sound of water splashing or movements in the tub. Did he stare at her now? She swallowed once and then again, but her throat grew tight in nervousness. What did he look like naked if he looked so formidable across a field of battle?

She shivered at the very thought of such a thing. He cleared his throat, reminding her that he was awaiting her response. Sybilla squared her shoulders and shook her head.

'Nay.'

She heard him move then, the water sloshing and splashing as he must be standing and stepping out of the tub. Sybilla wrapped her arms around her and tried not to shake too much. His steps moved closer until she could feel the heat of his body near hers. But he'd given her an opportunity to speak her mind, so she decided to be bold, much bolder than she felt.

'I had planned to ask your leave to go to my cousin's convent.'

'When were you planning to ask that, lady?' he asked, his voice coming from just above her and to her right. She turned to face him and lifted her face.

'The day you attacked. I was going to relinquish my claim to these lands and retire to my cousin's convent in order to save my people from harm.' She shrugged. 'You gave me no opportunity to do so.'

The silence, broken only by his breathing, made her uneasy. Sybilla took a breath and released it, trying to calm the racing of her heart. Did he truly stand so close with nothing between them? She could smell the scent of the soap he'd used when she inhaled and could imagine him smoothing it over his skin. She shivered again.

'So, you wish to become a nun, then?' he asked, his voice almost a whisper, teasing her ear with his breath.

Oh, dear Lord in heaven, he was *that* close!

She desperately wanted to move away, but dared not. Was he giving her the chance now that he'd not done before? Would he let her go?

'No, not a nun,' she stuttered. 'But I could live a contemplative life there.' Her claim was a bold one and one that would be refuted by almost any person who knew her.

Suddenly, he stood behind her, grasping her shoulders and drawing her back against him. His body was like a stone wall, all hard with no softness to be felt anywhere. Sybilla knew enough about how men and women joined in carnal knowledge to know what part of him pressed against her back now, but she tried not to think of that. Then he leaned down and whispered again.

'Would you give up all that you have, Lady Sybilla? Would you be able to obey and live quietly?'

He moved one arm across her, holding her to him while he used the other to slip into her hair and move it to one side. His breath tickled her neck now and she tried to ease away. Instead it opened the whole of her neck to him. Exposed, held securely against him, she was vulnerable in a way she'd never felt before. She should be crying out in fear, but her body reacted most strangely—her breasts swelled under the weight of his arm, her skin tingled yet ached for something more and the place between her thighs grew moist and heated.

'Would you give up everything?'

The touch of his tongue on her skin made her jump. Then he kissed the same spot. Over and over he placed his mouth on the sensitive place and kissed it. She could not help the gasp that escaped when his teeth nipped her skin, not enough to hurt but enough to send icy hot tremors through her whole body.

Enough to make her come to her senses!

'And what, Lord Soren, do I give up?' she asked, straightening her head and tugging free. 'Lands and people that are no longer mine? A husband who came within seconds of killing me and now plans to use me only as a brood mare? A life lived blind, unable to see or do anything that gave me pleasure or satisfaction? What exactly do I stand to lose by entering the convent?'

Time spun out between them as she stood in the darkness that was now her world, awaiting his response. Sybilla half-expected him to strike her now for her insolence, just as her father would have if she'd spoken to him in this manner. The touch of his mouth to hers was not what she expected.

This time he did not hold her in place. He simply placed his lips on hers and kissed her. She gasped at the feel of it and then felt his tongue slipping inside her mouth. Stunned, shocked and completely inexperienced in such things, Sybilla did not know what to do. She'd been kissed before—her parents, family, even her father's overlord—but never by someone in this intimate manner. When his tongue touched hers, swirling around it, and pressing more firmly against her mouth, Sybilla forgot about everything else.

He recognised his mistake as soon as he got close to her. Old habits died hard and his enjoyment of taking pleasure where he could came roaring back at him. This was his wife, after all—he could take her to bed and pleasure her and no one could naysay him. It was right…

his right. But her words took him out of his need for pleasure and to the heart of the matter.

He had come here to kill her.

He had taken her lands and everything and everyone she held dear, to what extent she still did not know.

He had stolen her sight and whatever life she could have had.

Sybilla had spoken the truth of it all, yet her mouth beckoned to him anyway. The urge to touch those full lips and silence her with pleasure overwhelmed his control. He would show her what she would miss if he had their marriage annulled and let her go to the convent.

So, he stole but one kiss.

Only to show her the folly of her belief that she had nothing to lose. To demonstrate that she would miss *something*. Instead he taught himself a lesson, one that would be difficult to forget.

The woman he'd married might be blind and might be innocent, but he could feel her arousal, feel it against his mouth and taste it on her tongue. If he continued and deepened the kiss the way his body urged him to, her mouth would soften even more against his, her breasts would swell in his hands, the nipples would tighten into buds and he would suck…

Merde, he thought as he fought the passion that rose within him, he could have her beneath him in minutes, if not sooner, both of them panting and him kissing parts of her body she most likely had never considered having kissed… She would arch to his touch and call out his name…

Durward's voice, his laughter as he attacked from behind, echoed in Soren's head at that moment and he pulled back at almost the instant he was about to surrender to the need to have her. He stepped back, releasing her mouth.

Her expression showed her surprise and her confusion. Though her eyes could not see, she blinked as though waking from a slumber and frowned. Her mouth, the one that would tempt him again this night in his dreams, closed into a thin line. The flush of arousal still coloured her cheeks.

Soren pushed down the concern he felt growing even as the passion cooled. He ruthlessly ignored all the things he knew she needed to hear from him, from a man of his experience, from her husband, and walked away. Picking up the clean garments near the tub, he dressed hurriedly and turned to face the door.

He would not give in now to weakness when it was his inner strength that had kept him alive this long. He could not relent and let her in or even close to him. He had almost made his escape when her soft voice echoed across the chamber.

'Do you give me leave to go to the convent?'

It would be the easier of the possible paths to take. It would be almost the kindest thing to do rather than condemning her to the life he'd planned for her. It would make complete sense, considering her condition and her inability to carry out the duties expected of the lord's wife.

What had begun as teasing, as flirting, had turned deadly serious with only a kiss. Soren had plans, plans he'd paid for with his own flesh and blood, plans that he'd spent months making and refining and waiting to see come to fruition. Now, when everything was on the edge of success, could he step back and forget all he'd suffered because of a kiss? The heartless monster everyone thought he'd become battled with the better man he always wanted to be in that moment.

As it turned out, it was a tie. Or a stalemate, depending on how he looked at it.

'No, Lady Sybilla, you do not have my permission.'

He lifted the latch on the door and pulled it open. Stepping into the corridor without looking back, Soren breathed in and out. The coolness of the air there eased his way out and made it possible to breathe. At his direction, the guard had remained belowstairs, keeping the lady's maids there, too, so no one witnessed his hurried exit of her chambers.

Soren positioned the patch across the sunken area of flesh, then he placed the leather hood over his head and adjusted it. With those ready, he walked down the steps. Durward's laughter still tasked him, making him realise that he had lost the battle after all. The irony of wanting the woman he'd sworn to destroy was not lost on him, but neither did he forget that she almost gave herself over to him in that one moment of the kiss they shared.

And he wanted to keep her. He wanted the opportunity that she offered without even having knowledge of it herself. He wanted to be with a woman who shuddered in passion and not in horror. Damn if some needful place in his heart did not realise it and want her even more for it. Convent? His arse! Unfortunately, another part of his body seemed to be controlling his actions and it was not his head.

He passed by the guard whose duty it was to watch over Sybilla and her maids, who both stood with hands clutched and twisting their garb as though expecting him to announce he'd killed her. Then Soren remembered what the entire keep seemed to suspect his reasons were for sending a bath to Sybilla's chambers and shook his head in disbelief. As he began to walk to the small chamber off the kitchen where he usually slept, he spoke to the one called Aldys.

'Has she eaten today?' he asked. He suspected the answer, but wanted it confirmed or denied.

'She was quite nervous, Lord Soren,' she began to explain. He waved off the rest of it.

'On the morrow, she leaves that room. The weather has broken a bit and it should be pleasant at some time. When the sun is up, get her dressed and get her out.'

'But, Lord Soren,' the woman pleaded, 'she cannot see!'

'She does not need sight to walk. Guide her. Both of you!' he said sharply. 'You do your lady no service keeping her shut away in her room. It ends on the morrow.'

He nodded his head in the direction of the stairs, sending them to her now. He added one thing. 'Do not offer her food or drink. Serve her if she asks, but do not mention it otherwise.'

The horror on their faces told him immediately that they mistook his instructions and they believed him planning to starve her into submission. He let out a frustrated breath and explained further. 'Speak not of food to her. I will have the evening meal sent to her chambers and eat with her.'

It did not go well. Clearly the thought of eating with him turned their stomachs. 'Do not question my orders, nor tell her of them. Do your duty or I will re-assign you to ones you can perform adequately. Call on Guermont if you need assistance, but *get her out of that room.*'

The horror in their expressions did not ease. So be it. He cared not if they agreed or not. Soren understood better than most what the lady was going through. He'd survived the shock and numbness after regaining consciousness and then faced the permanence of his injuries and the changes they meant to his life. The worst time was when he'd prayed for death rather than wanting to live…like this.

She would reach that time of purgatory for her soul and her spirit. For now, Sybilla probably believed her sight would return. He was certain that she'd convinced herself even now that this was simply a temporary condition, that Teyen was wrong in his assessment of the severity of the injuries she suffered. But until she accepted her blindness would not go away, her soul would have no peace.

Soren had learned much in his own struggles, but never had he expected to be the one watching someone else experience what he had. Or expected to be the cause of it. For the first time in the months since he'd decided that he would live for vengeance, he now questioned whether or not he could keep up the pursuit of it.

Lord Gautier had taught him well that vengeance ate a man's soul bit by bit and now Soren wondered if that wasn't the truth of the matter. Though it had given him the strength to survive his dark night of purgatory, he considered that mayhap he would need something more to give him the strength to live.

He reached the room and closed the door. His meal sat waiting as he'd ordered and Soren sat on the stool to eat.

Removing the hood, he stretched his neck and shoulder, easing the ever-present tightness. As he sat alone eating, he realised that his desire for a bath alone had caused this chain of events. Later, as he lay unable to sleep, he thought he heard Lord Gautier's laughter again.

For the first time in months, he missed his friends Giles and Brice, who'd trained and fostered with him in Rennes. Bastards all three, they had somehow met and befriended Simon, Gautier's son and heir, and found themselves being tutored and raised by that wise man. After the battle at Hastings and once his friends knew he lived, they'd ridden off at the king's orders to claim their lands. He yearned to be fighting at their sides, as they'd always done, but it had taken months for him to recover and he'd joined them in battle just in time to help Brice chase the rebels from his lands.

They'd promised to be at his back when he needed them and he had pushed them and their advice away when they'd tried to offer it to him. Now he wished they were here, for they would understand his dilemma—neither of them had wanted the woman they married, yet each now was happy in his marriage. *Certainement* neither had planned to kill the woman as he had, but he had his reasons. Valid reasons, or so they seemed to be until this night and that kiss.

Confused more than he wished to admit even to himself, Soren tossed and turned all through the night, plagued—as he knew he would be—by thoughts and memories of the tender kiss he'd shared with Sybilla.

By morning he knew two, nay, three, things: first, he still did not know if he would or could keep her as his wife; second, the worst of her journey towards survival was yet to come. The third was the hardest to accept of all—it had been easier existing in the blinding haze of vengeance than trying to live as the man he'd always wanted to be.

Chapter Eleven

'I do not understand, Aldys.'

'Lord Soren ordered it so,' her maid explained.

It made no sense to her. She could do nothing outside this chamber and very little in it. She had no wish to disgrace herself before those who had served her and her family for years and she especially did not want to be with people when she could not tell who or how many were there around her.

'I cannot do this,' she finally admitted.

'My lady, you must. I fear what will happen if you remain here.'

Sybilla was trying to ascertain the reason for this need to leave her chambers when a knock came at her door. Both maids gasped loudly and she trembled at the sound. What did they fear would happen to her? She heard Aldys greet whoever stood outside in a very quiet voice and usher them in.

'Good morrow to you, Lady Sybilla. 'Tis I, Guermont,'

he added, to let her know who stood before her. Tactful and discreet, as was his way it seemed.

'Guermont,' she greeted him with a nod.

'Lord Soren bids you come out into the yard and enjoy the warmth of the sun while the day is clear,' he invited.

'I cannot, sir. Please inform your lord so,' she said calmly, or in what she hoped was a calm voice. Her hands began to shake then, and the parchment she held crinkled in her grasp.

'Lady, I fear I cannot go to him without bringing you with me,' he explained quietly. 'Those are my orders.'

'Aldys, please explain to Guermont why it is not possible to do as he says. I cannot see. I cannot make my way down the steps or outside this room.' She could hear the desperation in her own voice—did they? 'Ask your lord to allow me to remain here until my vision returns.'

The silence around her told her more than words could have. None of those present believed her sight would return. She could not, indeed, would not, think about such a possibility. Shaking her head, she refused to budge.

'Lady, I would ask you to walk at my side and let me guide you on the steps. But if you refuse, I will carry you down, whether silent or screaming. The choice is yours.' The quiet tone belied the serious intent of his words.

Sybilla was terrified into wordlessness. Why did Lord Soren want to humiliate her in this way? Was it his punishment for daring to ask to leave him? Was he so disgusted by her zealous reaction to his kiss that he would now disgrace her in public?

'Here, Lady Sybilla,' Guermont said as he took the

parchment from her shaking hands and placed them around his arm. 'Let me escort you.'

The chainmail dug into her skin as she clutched him tightly. He wore his protection even now when the battle was long finished. Did Lord Soren as well? She lost track of their path until Guermont brought her to a stop.

'Lady, we will go down only one step at a time. If I am going too quickly, just give the word and I will slow our pace,' he offered.

The steps that had never slowed her down now loomed as an abyss before her. Sybilla felt as though she were suspended over a black well, waiting to fall into its depths. Then, all at once, he took the first step, dragging her at his side.

'Mayhap we should count as we descend so that you know how many steps there are?' he asked quietly.

'The lady has lived here her entire life!' Aldys snapped at him from behind them. 'Think you she knows not how many steps there are?'

But Sybilla had never needed to know how many steps separated her chambers from the main hall before. Unable to speak, for fear had clogged her throat, she nodded, hoping Guermont was watching. When he began counting to her with each one, she knew he had been. He had counted out a score and they stopped. Out of breath from both the exertion and the fear of walking into the blackness before her without being able to see, Sybilla drew in a ragged breath, waiting for the next step.

'The hall has been cleaned of rushes and the tables moved aside to form a straight pathway to the door, my lady,' Guermont reported. 'There were twenty steps on the stairs, but I suspect it will take us twice that many paces to reach it from here.' He was giving her clues about their path and the layout of the hall now, alerting her to changes made since the Normans' arrival. 'We will walk slowly as you gain your bearings, my lady.'

And then they were off. Guermont placed his hand over hers on his arm and guided her, counting out their paces under his breath so that she, but no others, could hear them. They had only taken a pace or two when it began.

First, a collective gasp went up from those in the hall as they saw her. Then, her name was murmured through the room, echoing as it got louder. She stumbled as she listened to it.

'They are pleased to see you, Lady Sybilla,' Guermont said.

'Do they…do they know I cannot see them?' she asked. Aldys and Gytha never mentioned what had been told about her to the people. She did not know if they thought her a prisoner, dead or something else.

'Aye, my lady. They know of the extent of your injuries. Indeed, many have been offering prayers in the chapel for your recovery.'

Her breath caught then, her unseeing eyes filled with tears. She had feared they would blame her for their situation. If she had not stupidly allowed Gareth to resist the Norman lord, they might not be mourning their dead. Sybilla blinked, trying to stop them, but she felt the first of many trickle down her cheeks. When someone touched her gown, then another touched her arm, whispering her name as they walked by, she let them flow freely. Guermont yet counted out their paces and when he called off forty-and-three, they stopped.

'A few more than forty, my lady, and we are at the doorway to the yard. Do you need to catch your breath before going further?'

She brushed the tears off her cheeks and cleared her throat. Sybilla had never expected this reaction—from her or from her people. Her heart ached inside her chest and she shook her head.

'Nay, Guermont, I am ready. Lead on,' she said.

'Just so, my lady.'

The door creaked on its hinges as it was swung open and she stepped outside for the first time since the attack. Summer had blossomed in full and she felt the warmth of the now-midday sun on her face.

Sybilla paused there, waiting, praying, hoping, begging God to allow her to see the sun's light as she left the shadows of the hall. To let her notice any difference in the darkness in which she now lived. Even a flicker of some change in the unrelenting blackness would satisfy her.

'My lady?' Guermont asked gently, as though he understood the reason for her pause. But he could not know.

Nothing.

Nothing spread out before her.

No light. No change. Nothing.

Sybilla let him lead her forwards into the yard. People were there; she could hear the voices of men, women and even children, as they worked around her. The smell of blooming honeysuckles filled the air and she inhaled, trying not to think about her disappointment. The earth beneath her feet and the trees and flowers all added to the wonderful cacophony of scents that filled her lungs with the fresh air.

'There is a bench under the tree near the wall,' Guermont said. 'You can feel the warmth of the sun there, but be shaded by the tree, my lady. It looks to be another forty or so paces.'

He guided her well, making their walk appear smooth. A soft word when the ground grew uneven. Another when they needed to avoid a puddle of mud, and so on until they reached the place he'd mentioned. Guermont lifted her hand from his arm, turned from her side and helped her to sit. Aldys spoke from behind her, letting her know of the maid's presence.

Sybilla tried to catch her breath again, surprised by how quickly she'd lost it during their walk here. She usually traversed this path and more many times a day, never feeling winded at all. But she'd sat unmoving in her chambers for so long that this small activity tired her. Though getting here had been a struggle, Sybilla tried to prepare herself for the next challenge—facing Lord Soren after last evening's débâcle.

Hoping he would not humiliate her where everyone could witness it, she accepted a linen from Aldys and wiped her face with it. For the first time in many days, she grew thirsty and realised her maid had not pressed food or drink on her this day. She would have asked for something, but a disturbance began on the other side of the yard. It grew in volume and strength and Sybilla knew Lord Soren must be approaching.

Orders were called. Soldiers moved to obey. People screamed and called out her name. 'Twas like reliving the day of the attack, only worse, for now Sybilla could see nothing.

'Is it Lord Soren?' she asked. When no one answered, she asked again in a louder voice, 'Pray thee tell me what goes there?'

'Some of the prisoners are trying to break free and come here,' Guermont said. 'The guards are trying to keep them contained.'

'Prisoners?' she asked before realising he spoke of her men, her soldiers, her people. 'Aldys! You must tell them to cease before he—' She did not finish the words, for *his* voice interrupted.

'Stephen!' Soren called out. 'Let them go to her.'

He capitulated again in her presence, something becoming a habit, it seemed. Soren nodded to Stephen, who ordered the guards to release the prisoners. At first they hesitated, probably fearing retribution for their acts of disobedience, but then Gareth led them across the yard to where Sybilla sat. Within moments, a crowd surrounded her, speaking her name and trying to touch the hem of her gown or her hand.

Guermont stood at her side, never moving from it, so he feared not for her safety. Not that he worried about her at all, but men held prisoner could not be trusted in their actions if it meant their freedom from chains. Gareth, he noticed, knelt before her, never moving as others came, gave greetings and moved aside for others to come closer. Soren continued to watch from his place near the stables.

'A wise exercise of power,' Larenz said as he walked closer. 'And a good one.'

Surprised by his approach and by his comment, Soren

turned to look at him. Larenz had trained him in many skills a knight needed to fight and win on the field of battle. Simon, now Count of Rennes, had allowed him the freedom to swear allegiance to one of the three in honour of his many years of service to the House of Rennes. For some reason, Larenz had chosen him.

The old man had remained with him after the battle and through his terrible ordeal. Larenz had seen him at his best, at his worst and now at some crossroads Soren did not yet understand completely. Uncomfortable at such realisations, Soren changed their topic of discussion.

'How is the boy?' he asked.

'He's a good one, Soren,' Larenz answered, turning to face the ongoing scene at the other side of the yard. 'Another of your good decisions.'

'Where is he? I have not seen him since yestermorn.' Larenz laughed and Soren faced another moment of truth. 'You knew he gave the wrong message to her?'

'Aye, Soren. I knew.' Larenz glanced over towards the stables and nodded in that direction. 'He hides from your wrath.'

Soren let out a breath and glared at Larenz. Did everyone believe he would torture a child?

'You have not been known for showing or being interested in mercy these last few months, Soren. Everyone who now serves you is aware of your plans and your methods of carrying them out.'

'You dare much, old man, if you believe your own words,' Soren threatened. He clenched his fists, angry that this man knew and allowed the situation to happen without warning him. 'Why did you not tell me?'

'It was time, Soren,' Larenz said quietly. 'It is time for you to make her your wife.'

In anything else, he would take this man's counsel, but in a matter so personal and so important, he wanted it not. Torn between striking out and walking away, Soren stared at the woman sitting in the midst of an adoring crowd. He hardened at even the thought of her now and as much as he'd like to blame the months of abstinence for it, Soren knew that had little or nothing to do with it. But simply because his body agreed, did not make it the right thing to do.

'Look past the vengeance you seek against her father. Look back to the young man who took the field with William that day. Think of the plans you three had and the futures you fought for. Is this to be the way of it for you instead?'

'You risk much, Larenz,' Soren said through clenched teeth.

'Nay, not much at all,' Larenz replied. 'Gautier would haunt me if I did not speak my piece to you at a time such as this.'

Being reminded of his foster father, a man they both held in high esteem, took the anger out of him. Facing Larenz, Soren saw a likeness he'd never noticed before. 'You sounded just like him then.'

'It should not surprise you, Soren. He was my brother.'

Surprise did not describe how Soren felt after this revelation. Never had he suspected such a thing. And if it was not something spoken of openly, it meant one thing.

'We shared a father, though many years apart.'

That explained much to Soren—Larenz's request to serve with them and his willingness to train three bastards with claims to nothing. Before he could reply, Soren was called to by Stephen and nodded his consent.

Stephen and the men began herding the people away from Sybilla and back to their duties and tasks or work. All but one followed the orders. Gareth remained on his knees in front of her as she bid farewell to those with her. Stephen took hold of him and began to drag him back to work, but he fought against leaving. Soren watched as Guermont stepped forwards and then the two of them looked to him.

'Do they seek to plot against you, Soren?' Larenz asked.

'Nay, I think not,' he said, shaking his head.

He suspected that Sybilla had not yet been able to have someone read the list that Gareth provided and she would ask him about it. But she would not ask him for leave for such a thing. This gave her the opportunity to find out the truth without having to lose too much pride to do it.

'Leave him,' Soren called out.

Stephen dropped his hold of Gareth and Guermont stepped away, leaving the lady with the former commander of her guards to talk in private. Gareth never approached her, speaking from his place before her, but Soren could tell the moment he revealed the names of those who had died in the attack.

'I am back to my duties, Soren,' Larenz said. 'Should I tell the men you will join us soon?'

'Damn you, old man,' Soren grumbled. 'You know I will not.'

Larenz laughed as he walked off, but Soren said nothing. He could only watch as sorrow enveloped Sybilla like a fog that had descended from the sky in a storm. Gareth never moved closer, even when Sybilla's shoulders began to shake. Everyone, even her maids, kept their distance in spite of her distress.

His feet moved before he'd made the conscious decision to do anything and his mind tried to think of something he could do for her. Seeing the bucket sitting on the edge of the well, Soren went to it and dipped it to fill it. Then, scooping up a ladleful, he walked slowly towards Sybilla, stopping just yards from where she sat.

'Have you finished your business with the lady?' he asked Gareth. The man climbed to his feet and nodded to him. 'Then return to your work.'

'Be at peace, Lady Sybilla,' her man said quietly as he walked away.

She sat with her head lowered, saying nothing. He could see the tears still leaving tracks down her cheeks. Soren looked off in the distance for a moment and took a deep breath. He did not want to feel the pity that pierced his heart in that moment.

'Hold out your hands, Sybilla.'

She held them out, but they shook so badly he feared she would spill all the water in the ladle before it got to her lips.

'Steady, now,' he advised. It made no difference, for they shook even more now. So he placed one of his hands beneath hers before he placed the ladle in her palms.

'Wha…what is this?' she asked, lifting her face now in his direction.

'The day is warming and I thought mayhap you would like some water.'

Something hung in the air between them, some moment of time that could be felt as it moved past, marking a second when everything changed and nothing would be the same again. To Sybilla, though inexperienced and not worldly at all, this moment felt like that, as the man who came here intending to kill her and destroy everything of her father left in the world showed her an unexpected kindness.

Another kindness, in truth, for he had allowed her to speak to Gareth and the others.

Sybilla lifted the ladle to her lips, his hand guiding hers from beneath. She sipped the cool water and allowed it to soothe her tight throat. Even knowing that this man did everything for his own reasons did not stop her from enjoying the water and the consideration, though she sensed he would not want to even acknowledge it as that. She had been thirsty, for she finished it in two mouthfuls. Sybilla lowered the ladle and handed it back to him.

'My thanks, Lord Soren,' she said softly.

Though she could hear others in the distance, she heard no clues to tell her others were nearby. The summer breezes rustled the branches of the tree above her and she could almost imagine herself there in the best of times instead of the worst.

Her curiosity grew though about his intentions now. As last evening, he did things for a reason and she wondered if she was misinterpreting his actions once more. Could he simply be kind or was this some sort of prelude? To what, she knew not. Listening closely, she could not tell if he was near or had left to go to the well.

'Lord Soren?'

'Aye, Sybilla.'

How had she never noticed the appealing deep voice he had before? Thinking back, she realised she usually heard him yelling or grunting and rarely had they just simply spoken to each other. Except for last evening when they had spoken and she had said too much. Still, she wanted to know.

'Why did you allow that?'

'You to speak to Gareth and the others? 'Twas simply the time for it to happen, Sybilla.'

'I do not understand. Time for what?' she asked. She thought she might, but wanted to hear his explanation and try to understand the reasons behind his actions. They were married for now and unless or until he gave her permission to seek the convent, they remained wedded.

'You needed to leave your chambers and they needed to see their lady. There has been too much talk among your people about not knowing your whereabouts or your conditions. So, I got you out here and eased their concerns. And…' He paused.

'And?'

'If they see you alive and well cared for by the monster now sitting in Durward's chair, they will believe they are safe from him as well.'

'Ah,' she said, nodding. 'You have found another use for your blinded wife after all, then. Brood mare and figurehead.'

He did not respond, most likely because it was the truth of the matter. His kindness was a sham, an act done for its impact. A burst of anger shot through her, giving her the courage to ask the question at the heart of all of this. The one question she'd thought of but had not dared to ask before.

'Why, Lord Soren? Tell me why you hated my father so much? Why did you come here seeking to destroy my family or what was left of him?'

'Sybilla, do not push me,' he growled a warning to her, his voice now hard and angry.

She heard the ground crunch beneath his boots as he began to walk away without answering her. Sybilla stood and took a step in the direction he moved in. 'Lord Soren, I must know!'

Sybilla heard him turn towards her. His breath was fast and shallow as he approached her. She braced herself, knowing in that moment that she would not like, nay, she would hate the words he would say. Oh, why had she asked?

'Because your father made me into the monster I am now, Sybilla.' She gasped, never dreaming that was the reason. But he was not yet finished tearing her heart and soul apart.

'Your father struck me down with a cowardly blow from behind, tearing my flesh asunder and taking everything but my life.'

Sybilla felt herself stumbling, light-headed and weakened by such news. He grabbed her by her cloak to hold her on her feet, while he completed the horrible tale he'd begun at her request.

'And now, just as he did to me, I have done and will do to you. Everything you had or valued will be mine.'

Never noticing that she was sitting down, Sybilla was only stopped by the hard surface of the bench. Her head spun from what he'd said and the fury within his words.

Her father could never have done such a thing. He would never have acted so cowardly. He…

Dozens of questions formed in her thoughts, but she could voice none in the face of his anger. She heard him inhale a deep breath and waited for his next act.

The sounds of his footsteps as he strode away shocked her.

Sybilla waited for his return or his voice to call out orders about her, but nothing happened. She sat in stunned silence for some time before gathering her wits and standing to make her way back to her chambers.

Chapter Twelve

War arriving at your door had a way of bringing clarity to a situation, Soren thought as the Saxons approached the gates. Word of their arrival spread quickly and his men moved into position along the wall after the prisoners were secured and the women and children locked inside the keep for their protection. Now, watching as the armed troops moved ever closer, Soren assessed their strengths and weaknesses. After deciding that they were more nuisance than real threat, Soren called out to them as they sat below.

'Who are you and what do you want here?'

'I am Maurin de Caen. My lands are a day's ride to the south and west, just over the hills,' the first man said. Of Norman heritage, it would seem.

'And I am Wilfrid of Brougham, Lord Soren. My lands are two days' ride in the same direction. We received letters from the king about the rebels and are here to discuss the matter with you.'

Soren looked to Stephen and Guermont, who, dressed in armour and sword, appeared more the warrior he was than the steward he'd become for a time. When both nodded, Soren climbed down the steps and went to the gates to allow them entrance. His men knew not to let down their guard for a moment and he would speak to these two in the yard, under the scrutiny and view of all. More importantly, within the range of his bowman, aiming from their positions along the wall.

He watched as the two dismounted and walked to him, waiting for the inevitable reaction. When neither gave his face more than a passing glance, he knew they must have been warned. He pulled off his metal gauntlets and held out his arm in greeting. One, then the other, clasped it. He motioned for them to follow him to a table set near the keep.

They talked about the situation in the surrounding areas and of the king's wish not to have the northern borders of the lands of England fall to the Scottish king while William's attentions were drawn further south. They spoke of the former earls of Mercia and Northumbria, Morcar and Edwin, whose lands surrounded Alston and who were currently the guests of William in Normandy along with the Saxon claimant to William's throne. Soren called for ale and food and asked Stephen and Guermont to join them in the discussions, for they would learn much. For more than an hour they conferred about every issue Soren could think of, save one. He dismissed his men and sat down to ask the questions he truly wanted answers to, for the rest of it was known to him already.

'Tell me of Durward of Alston,' he said.

The two exchanged glances and then Maurin began, though it was clear he measured the words in his response.

'Though much of these lands is claimed by the king of the Scots, Durward held this manor from King Edward and then by Harold's charter,' Maurin began. 'Harold had his doubts about Morcar and Edwin, even though related by marriage to their sister, and used Durward to secure this vital holding.'

'Did he owe any fealty to Mercia or Northumbria at all?'

Alston lay at the crossroads of several ancient kingdoms, all of which were highly sought after and whose ownership was highly contested, generation upon generation. As Soren waited for an answer, he witnessed another exchange of glances.

'Not fealty, Lord Soren, but a bond of another kind,' Wilfrid replied. 'Although a betrothal between Durward's son and a niece of Godwinson had been arranged, the boy's death and then Hastings ended hope of linking those houses.'

Wilfrid did not say the word, so Soren did.

'But…?'

'Morcar had already offered a marriage of his son to Durward's daughter.'

'Sybilla?' Soren asked. They nodded. 'Did she know?'

'Most likely not. Durward had not decided the matter when the call to march on the Norse at York came. As a vassal to Harold, he had to send men, so his son led them. Unfortunately, he met Morcar and Edwin before Harold arrived from the south…'

Soren knew the disastrous results, for that battle had been lost, with the English taking heavy casualties. He'd heard reports of it while recuperating near London. But this attempt to join the two houses was news to him and could play into finding the rebels who clearly had support here in the north from powerful people. Brice had sent word that Edmund Haroldson had been sighted near Shildon and was moving north. They suspected he was planning to seek support from Malcolm in Scotland, passing through this area to get there.

Soren understood the truth now of Giles's and Brice's words—the lands promised to them were some of the most dangerous in William's new kingdom and they would risk their lives and futures just trying to claim and hold them. With enemies on so many sides and few allies he could trust, Soren wondered at the probability he could succeed and live to have sons.

'They are still conversing in the yard, lady,' Gytha reported from her place by the window in her chambers.

Apparently deemed safe enough for entrance into the yard, Lord Soren spoke to his guests outside, not allowing them in the keep. Once he'd let them through the gates, she and her women had been permitted to leave the kitchens and return to her room above. It seemed a good plan, truly, but Sybilla dreaded walking the steps and being in the midst of so many she could not see.

Now, Gytha or Aldys stood at the window, telling her every step taken in the yard, whether she wished to know or not. She'd thought she'd met both Lord Maurin and Lord Wilfrid before and could have vouched for their identities, but *he*'d not asked her. In truth, they'd not spoken another word since the incident in the yard a few days before. She'd sought refuge in her chambers and had not been ordered out again, though her door was not barred, nor had she been commanded to remain within.

However, the taste of fresh air and the sun's warmth tempted her to try it again. Sybilla worried that the end of the perfect scene he'd staged for the benefit of her people had been ruined when she learned the source of his hatred for her father and for her. She tried to remember that war was war—it was vicious and cruel and took its toll where it could find it in lives and flesh. Yet Sybilla could never imagine her father striking such a cowardly blow from behind.

Since all the men here were sworn to Lord Soren and would never naysay him, she thought that speaking to Wilfrid or Maurin might give her more insight into battle. But dare she speak of such things to them? She'd not even shared the news with her maids.

'Is Lord Soren there?' she asked. 'Guermont or Stephen?'

Gytha sighed—one that Sybilla was coming to recognize, for it signified the girl's infatuation with the Norman knight Stephen. 'Lord Soren, aye. The others have left.'

'Seek out Guermont, Aldys. Bring him here if it is possible.' Aldys left quickly to seek out the steward belowstairs.

'Stephen told me that Lord Soren was called the "Beautiful Bastard" in their homeland,' Gytha shared. Then, as though realising the inappropriateness of the comment, she gasped. 'Pardon my loose words, lady,' she begged.

Sybilla realised she'd been going about this in the wrong way—the servants always knew more than they said and could be counted on to gain information within any household.

'Nay, Gytha, tell me what else Stephen said,' she urged. She understood the obvious reasons for his hatred, to be left looking as he did, and the constant scorn and fear he encountered, was reason enough, but she had sensed in him a different man from time to time and wondered if she'd only imagined it.

'Lady, mayhap I should not speak of such things to you?'

Sybilla knew Gytha well—if she knew something, she wanted to share it. A gossip, though not mean-spirited at all, the news could barely remain quiet within her for minutes, so Sybilla thought Aldys must have warned her from telling it.

'The "Beautiful Bastard"?' she asked quietly, waiting for the words to spill.

'Aye, lady,' she said, walking closer as she did. 'He is from Brittany and not Norman as most of them are. And he is of low birth, only raised by his king after… after…'

'Aye, Gytha, after the battle near Hastings.'

'He and two others were fostered by a nobleman in Rennes, their birthplace. The three of them and the nobleman's heir were raised together. Strange, that,' she commented.

Very strange. Though natural sons and daughters had many uses, this was unusual. 'And?' she prodded.

'They were trained to be knights.'

Sybilla wanted to grab and shake the girl until she told her the meat of this story, but she took and released a breath, praying for patience.

'Stephen said that they were known for their fighting abilities and for their way with women and that he, Lord Soren, was known to have a different woman in his bed each night—married, unwed, pretty or plain-faced, it mattered not to him. His looks, handsomer than all the rest, drew them like bees to sweet, he said.' Gytha sighed. 'Now though, Stephen said he is almost unrecognisable from what he looked like back then.'

There was the heart of the matter—as Soren had said, her father's blow had torn his body and his life apart.

'Stephen chatters like an old woman.'

Sybilla and Gytha gasped at the interruption and the invasion of their private discussion. Guermont had heard at least part of it.

'Guermont, my thanks for coming at my call,' Sybilla said, ignoring the rest and standing as she did. 'Am I permitted to leave my chambers now?'

'Aye, my lady,' he said from closer now. 'May I escort you somewhere?'

Sybilla held out her hand, waiting for him to take it.

'To the yard, if you please? I would like to speak to Maurin and Wilfrid.' She tried to say their names with the ease of familiarity, as though old acquaintances.

Guermont did not answer immediately, but paused as though considering this request. Then he took her hand and placed it on his arm, his heavily armoured arm. The coolness of the metal startled her at first, but then she grew accustomed to it.

'Remember that there are a score of steps, my lady.'

His easy manner and subtle guidance made it easy to forget that this was only her third time traversing the stairway and hall. When they reached the landing and she did not have to worry over falling headlong down to her probable death, she decided to seek more information from him as well. Being blind, she needed to know as much as she could that sight usually provided.

'How long have you served Lord Soren, Guermont?' she began. An innocuous question, certainly.

'We have fought together for the last six years, in various skirmishes in our homeland of Brittany when we served Gautier of Rennes and then here in England under the flag of Alain Fergeant, distant cousin to Gautier. I have only sworn service to Soren these last two months.'

Since he received his grant from his king to her lands.

Sybilla tried to think up another question, when Guermont stopped her with his own.

'Why do you not ask Lord Soren if you would like to know about his homeland?' He drew to a stop just before, if she'd estimated correctly, the door leading out to the yard. 'Do not rely on Stephen for the truth about Soren.'

'I doubt Lord Soren can even speak to me now that he has revealed the truth of my father's actions to me, Guermont. I wonder how I stand here alive and married to him rather than dead or in chains, considering what happened.'

Guermont cursed under his breath then and Sybilla

was glad she did not understand his language when spoken so quickly. 'He told you?' he asked.

'Aye. I asked and he answered.'

Another whispered curse followed and an equally quiet apology. Someone in front of them opened the door then, for she could feel the soft breeze flow over her. He moved his arm as a warning and then took the first step into the yard. They walked in silence now and she could tell that Guermont was surprised that Lord Soren had spoken of such things as he had. Sybilla heard his voice, even and deep, as they grew closer, then he stopped speaking and they stopped walking.

'Lady Sybilla, may I make you known to Lord Maurin de Caen and Lord Wilfrid of Brougham?' Lord Soren said as though this was simply a gathering of friends rather than the council of war it must be.

'My lords,' she said, bowing her head in the direction of the voices.

'My lady,' one said, coming closer and taking her hand. 'I have not seen you since you were but a child.' He lifted her hand to his lips and she felt the slight kiss on her knuckles.

'I have not had the pleasure of meeting you yet, but let me offer my felicitations on your marriage to Lord Soren,' the second one said as he repeated the actions of the first.

Sybilla could not tell which one was which. She did not remember either of them, from her father's discussions or her brother's. But something about their voices, the underlying tone, gave her pause. All was not right here. Guermont yet stood at her back, which made her feel safe.

There was a pause then, no one spoke and Sybilla tried to think of something to say. Soren did first.

'Lady Sybilla suffered an injury to her eyes, my lords. She cannot see,' Soren explained quietly. She began to wonder why he would expose her in this way, but then remembered his promise to her—he would take everything from her, even, it seemed, her dignity before strangers.

'My lady!' one exclaimed. 'How terrible!'

'I am certain it is only temporary, my lords. I expect my injury to heal completely and my vision will be restored to me,' she responded with much more confidence than she felt.

'We can only pray so, lady,' Lord Soren added, though his tone did not share her confidence at all. Truly, he seemed to be saying he 'thought not'.

Would she ever understand him? Was he ever speaking the truth to her or was it all just part of his plan to destroy her for her father's actions? Now uncertain of the path she should take, or whether or not she even wanted to, Sybilla waited on Lord Soren.

'Was there something you wanted, lady? Or did you seek to find if I've treated our guests well and shared our hospitality with them?' If someone, if she, did not know the truth of the matters between them, they would believe him to be a kind and caring husband. Instead, his words hit her as though he had struck her. Retreat was the only move possible for her now.

'Just that, Lord Soren,' she replied, smiling as sincerely as she could force herself to do.

'Guermont, escort the lady back to her chambers,' Lord Soren said.

Guermont stepped to her side and lifted her hand onto his arm, without a word. She bowed towards them and turned to go back inside. Confused and angry over his treatment of her, she walked without saying a word, all the way back to her room. Guermont said only a few words, as they approached the doors, the stairs, her doorway.

As he left her, she realised that he was angry also. She could feel it in the tension of his arm beneath her hand and in the way he walked beside her. And she could hear the words, spoken very softly, as he muttered to himself along the way. Clearly, he did not understand or agree with his lord's actions.

Well, that made at least two of them.

'He told her,' Guermont said as he approached. Larenz looked back to where Soren still met with the two Saxon lords and nodded.

''Twas only a matter of time, Guermont,' Larenz said. 'The truth will out eventually.'

Guermont and Stephen and several others had been friends with Soren, Brice and Giles for many years, fighting at their side, defending their backs, even through Hastings. He'd watched most of them grow to manhood while serving Gautier in Rennes.

Though all of them wished to help Soren, none had known the best way to approach him, so none had. The result was that Soren had sunk further into his own world of vengeance and anger and become even more distant from them all. The frustration was beginning to fray the edges of their loyalty and their bond to each other.

'He also told them…' Guermont indicated the two

guests with a nod '…that she is blind.' He shrugged. 'Why would he expose and shame her like that to outsiders?'

Guermont had clearly fallen under the spell of Lady Sybilla. 'Twas not a difficult thing to do, considering all these circumstances, but a dangerous thing if left to develop. She was a beautiful woman, and one of remarkable spirit, too. If only Soren would…

'Soren is an intelligent man and a better warrior. He has his reasons,' Larenz answered, believing his own words to be true. Guermont snorted his disbelief. Before he could reply, Larenz placed his hand on Guermont's arm to stop him.

'The man Soren was is buried deep now, under layers of hatred and vengeance and pain. But he is there, even now questioning his path. We must have his back in this, Guermont.'

'And the lady?' he asked.

'The lady is walking much the same path that Soren has. I think she will be the one to call forth the true Soren from within this damaged one.'

Guermont shook his head. 'But she is blind, Larenz.'

'Ah, aye, she is blind. But in this it will be the blind leading the blind.'

'If you say so, Larenz.' Though he clearly did not agree or understand, Guermont nodded. 'You ever were able to see the good in people. Lord Gautier said you would make a good priest for you could see into men's souls.'

'I love women too much to ever make a good priest, Guermont! Doubt it not!' Larenz smacked him on the shoulder and Guermont returned to his duties.

As Guermont walked away, Larenz could not help

smiling. His ability to read men's souls came not as something special or different, it came from years of watching those around him and noticing the details of their actions and studying the patterns they created. A good memory and a keen curiosity was how he had developed the skill and Gautier had recognised the talent and brought him into his service.

His brother had repented of some long-ago sins and Larenz had helped him in his quest. They never spoke of the reasons, only the actions Gautier wanted to carry out and the boys involved. Now, the smartest of the three stood before him, damaged and searching for his soul and for the man he should become and, out of respect and love for his brother, Larenz would continue his work until Soren found his way.

Chapter Thirteen

The visitors had left long ago, but Soren did not let down his defences yet. He called Stephen to him and gave him orders to follow them. Something was not right, but Soren did not know what. He was suspect of their loyalties for many reasons, but their comments after Lady Sybilla left had made him most suspicious.

Though they offered their sympathies and promised Masses would be prayed for her complete recovery, their thinly veiled advice about her being flawed and mentions of other wives being put aside for lesser flaws pushed the limits of their new acquaintance. Soren wished he'd had Larenz at table with them, for no one could see people's true motives as the old man could.

As he thought about the man, Larenz walked through the yard, with Raed in tow, heading towards the keep. The boy saw him and tucked himself closer to Larenz as though using him as a shield. He wanted to be angry, but there was no man better than Larenz to teach the boy what he needed to learn.

Except one thing, and that one needed to be taught to him by his lord. Soren called out to Larenz.

'Larenz,' he yelled. He noticed that everyone within sight or hearing stopped and watched him now. 'Send the boy to me now.'

Larenz spoke to the boy and then pushed him towards Soren. Hesitation was clear in every movement Raed made, from his head hung low to the slowness of his steps. Soren waved Larenz off and waited for Raed to arrive. When he did, Soren took him by the shoulder and guided him to the fence. They stood silently watching the horses within this makeshift corral for a few minutes. Then Soren crouched down, bringing him down to Raed's height.

'Did you see those men?' he asked. Raed glanced at him and then looked down again. He nodded. 'I do not know if I can trust them. So I sent someone I trusted after them to find out more about them. I trust Stephen,' he said.

Raed still watched his feet, but Soren continued, 'I need to trust those who serve me, Raed. I need to know that they will carry out my orders or watch my back.' He paused, fighting the smile that pulled at the untorn corner of his mouth. 'I need to know they will tell me if they cannot. Me, Raed, not Larenz or one of the others.'

Raed now shifted from foot to foot in front of him. Soren lifted the boy's head with his finger and marvelled that this child could meet his gaze without being struck by the horror of his face. 'Do I have your loyalty, Raed? Can I trust you to guard my back?'

The boy's lower lip began to quiver and Soren suspected he was scared close to tears, but Raed nodded. 'You can trust me, Lord Soren.'

'Good, then, we understand what is required between a lord and his man,' Soren said, standing back up. 'Never lie to me, Raed, and own up to your actions, good or bad, and you will make a good squire for me.'

'Aye, my lord,' the boy agreed.

'Seek out Larenz and finish your duties then,' he directed and watched as the boy began skipping away. Raed stopped after a few paces and turned back to him.

'Lord Soren, who watches the lady's back if we are all sworn to you?'

Soren looked around, for he would swear Gautier laughed at him. A child instructing him where others had failed—Gautier would find that humourous. He waved Raed back to his duties and leaned on the fence, watching the horses in the enclosure.

He could survive on vengeance, but he could not live on it, he knew that now. Though the need for vengeance yet flowed strongly within his veins, he wanted more than that now. After finding this place and working here these last weeks, he knew that this was the kind of life he wanted. 'Twas the life he'd always dreamt of when planning battles and hoping to win enough to finance a peaceful future. 'Twas the life that had brought him and Giles and Brice to these lands and that had enticed them to fight for William's claim here.

And the others, too. Stephen and others who would come to fight with him from Brice and Giles would want to stay on, find wives, protect and defend this land. They had plotted and planned and promised it time and time again in their youth and when the call from William had arrived in Brittany.

Now it was time to fulfil that dream.

First, though, he needed to consult the priest. He had questions about his marriage and the possibility of ending it. Then he would speak—not yell, not curse—to her and come to an understanding. Just as he had told Raed to take responsibility for his actions, Soren knew he must as well and Sybilla was his responsibility.

With a clarity in thought and purpose he had not felt in a long, long time, Soren went off to find Father Medwyn.

Sybilla nodded to allow Guermont entrance to her chambers. A day had passed since the visitors had been here and work around the manor seemed to be getting back to the usual pace of it. At least she thought so from the sounds out in the yard and the descriptions her maids provided of the height and width of the wall.

'My lady, will you accompany me to the chapel? Father Medwyn wishes to speak to you.'

Sybilla hesitated.

'The chapel? Can he not come here to speak on whatever matter concerns him?'

'I am but carrying out orders, my lady. I do not know the subject he wishes to speak about, or the reason for bringing you to him.'

Guermont sounded aggrieved. And why not, since he carried out many duties and did not have the time to stand here arguing with her. He sighed then.

'Your pardon, my lady,' he began. 'I did not mean to take out my ill temper on you.'

'It matters not, Guermont. You but surprised me,' she said, rising and holding out her hand to him. 'I am ready. Aldys, you need not accompany me.'

She did not know Father Medwyn at all, but she did not want her maid milling about if he needed to speak of private matters. All she knew of the priest was that he had arrived with Lord Soren and stayed. He was Saxon, from the west, in Wessex where the Godwinsons' centre of power lay. But other than that and the fact that he'd performed their wedding, she knew him not.

Guermont continued his practice of counting each pace they took and he stopped to allow her a moment before they began the terrifying climb down the stairs. This time there was something else.

'Lady, reach out your right hand to the wall next to you,' he said. 'Nay, lower.' Sybilla touched a rope there, hung from a post in the stone wall.

'What is it?' She slid her hand along it and noticed it descended with the stairs.

'Something to give you support. Lord Soren thought if you gripped it, you would feel more at ease walking down these steps.'

Startled by his actions, Sybilla tried holding the rope as Guermont guided her down. It did help. Their journey down seemed smoother and quicker than previous ones. When they reached the bottom, Sybilla could not help but smile over such an aid. Though she knew not the reasons behind this action, she was pleased by it. Guermont paused then as though they would stop, but they continued on after but a brief hesitation. It took little time to walk to the chapel, for the path had been smoothed and a stone walkway now led to it rather than the one made of packed earth. Guermont led her inside when they arrived.

'Lady Sybilla, welcome,' a man said. 'I am Father Medwyn, late of Shildon, but now serving Lord Soren and the people here.' She heard some piece of furniture scraping along the stone floor towards her as he spoke.

'Here now, lady,' he continued. 'Sit here and be comfortable.' Guermont guided her to the chair, placed it behind her and helped her to sit down.

'Lady, Father Medwyn will call for me when you are ready to return to the keep.'

With that, she could hear his steps along the stone floor as he left her there with the priest. Sybilla tried not to fidget, but it was difficult not to in such circumstances. She had no way of knowing if they were alone or if others were with them. So she asked, 'Father, are we alone?'

'Aye, lady, 'tis but the two of us.'

'Did you bring me here to hear my confession?' It had been many weeks since she'd sought that sacrament.

The priest laughed—he had a wonderful, warm laugh and she smiled. 'Nay, lady. But if you wish me to, I will. When we finish.'

She swallowed deeply. If not for confession, then why?

'Lord Soren has asked me to speak to you about your marriage.'

Of all the things she thought she might hear, this was not one of them. So, he had realised she was correct in wanting to go to the convent.

'What would he have you discuss with me, Father?

Has he decided to contest it?' An annulment would not take too long, if his king backed him in his request. She could move to the convent now and wait for it there. She felt the priest's hand on hers, as though trying to comfort her.

'He is offering you the chance to do so. He told me you wish to retire to the convent.'

She was startled at his words. Lord Soren would allow it? Now that she knew the cause of his hatred and how deeply it ran in him, mayhap he'd realised he would never be able to accept her as his wife?

'Aye, Father. 'Twas my plan on the day he arrived.' She could not believe it would be this easy to end it. 'He has agreed to this? Truly?'

'Aye, my lady. And he will provide a donation to the convent to allow your entrance there.'

All of this sounded too good to her. He did not seem to be the kind of man who allowed a woman to walk away from him. From what Gytha had revealed, he had been used to women coming to him. There had to be…

'What is the price for my freedom, Father? What does Lord Soren expect in return?'

'Truly, lady, he mentioned no such thing to me. He came here with questions about the validity of your marriage and the basis and conditions on which it could be annulled. Then he asked me to speak to you to explain the same to you. And to make certain you know that he will not obstruct you if you choose to pursue such a proceeding.'

She sat back against the chair and thought about this strange situation. She needed to know more. 'So, pray thee, Father, explain to me what you explained to Lord Soren.'

'Because of the nature of your impediment, your blindness, the marriage can, in fact, be nullified. Your condition, if permanent, will prevent you from carrying out your legal and marital duties and could harm any children produced during a marriage.' She gasped at his words, but he was not finished.

'Although Lord Soren did accomplish the taking of vows, even with knowledge of this impediment, it could be argued that he had no knowledge of the permanence of the condition. So, he can file for an annulment at any time without prejudice.'

'Are you saying that at any time during our marriage, so long as we do not consummate our vows, he can ask to set me aside?'

'Consummation will matter not in this situation, my lady. Once he decides that your sight will not return, he can proceed to end it.'

'And if it proves temporary, as I believe it to be?'

Sybilla did not care who told her sight was gone for ever, she would not believe it so. It could not be. When the swelling in her head and around her eyes healed, her vision would return.

It would.

It must.

It had to return.

She took in a ragged breath, not wanting to think of such things as remaining in this dark, hellish existence for her whole life. The priest patted her hand once more, but said nothing. He might not believe it, but she did. She would see again.

'If the annulment has been granted before your sight returns, you would be free to marry as you wish, as he will be. If your sight returns before any proceedings, then you remain married in the sight of God and his Church.'

'And he knows this?' she asked to be certain.

'Aye, lady. Do you have any other questions of me?'

'What does he want, Father?'

The loud sigh echoed through the stone building. She could almost see the lovely window her father had made in memory of her mother on the west side of it if she thought about it. Her brother's betrothal ceremony had taken place here as would her own have if death had not claimed her father. He'd spoken of a possible marriage contract on her behalf before Cerdic's departure at Harold's call, but she knew nothing more than that.

'Lord Soren did not discuss his preferences with me, only possibilities. I am sure he will speak to you about the details of your situation.' She heard the priest moving about and realised their interview must be at an end. 'I will call for Guermont to escort you back to the keep,' he added.

'Father, pray thee, may I have a few minutes here before you call for him? I have much to think about,' she said truthfully. She did not want to face her maids or anyone else until she'd pondered on this development. Or be around anyone until she'd sorted things through in her own mind. If she had to speak to him, she needed to understand her own thoughts on the matter first.

'Certainly, lady. I have to finish my prayers, so remain as long as you'd like and just tell me when you are ready to return.' He started to walk away, but stopped. 'You are facing the altar, if you wondered about that.'

She smiled then, for he noticed the small details for her. Sybilla made the Sign of the Cross and then offered up her normal litany of prayers for the souls of the dead, for her family, for her people. When she ran out of prayers, it was time to face the matter at hand.

But she found she could not do it. Lord Soren held this in his power as her husband and, until she knew his plans, nothing she decided mattered. She would give this a few days and then ask to speak to him. If he had smoothed the way by speaking to Father Medwyn, then he must want it as much as she did. There was no reason to remain here. When she heard a pause in the priest's murmured prayers, she asked him to call for Guermont.

The walk back was almost pleasant now with the weight of her future lifted from her shoulders. The air smelled of fresh rain and she inhaled deeply, enjoying the scent of it. The day was warm now that midday had come and gone, but it would cool quickly as the sun set later. So far to the north in England, Alston's weather was pleasant enough, though quite wet during the spring. Now, as summer waned down and the autumn would begin, they should have a good harvest, as long as war did not visit them again.

She drew to a halt as the truth hit her—she would not be here to work to bring the harvest in again. Sybilla would never toil to store the grains and vegetables, nor to oversee butchering the stock to use through the winter. She would not be here to celebrate Christ's Mass nor the New Year. Nor would she be here when spring brought colour and scent to the hillsides and the air.

'Lady?' Guermont asked. 'Are you ill?'

Sybilla had been so intent on escaping *him* that she'd never considered that she would be leaving *here*. Though she knew when her father spoke of a betrothal that she would eventually travel to her new husband's lands and live there, her brother's death had left her as heiress and now that arrangement would change. Guermont touched her hand to draw her attention.

'Lady? You have become very pale. Was this too much exertion for you?' He placed his arm around her waist, supporting her as they walked. Sybilla shook to clear her head. What a time for such a realisation to happen.

'Give me a moment, Guermont,' she said.

Sybilla waited for that attack of panic to pass and then let Guermont guide her back inside. The rope along the stairs aided her climbing them and soon they stood before her chambers. She thanked Guermont and was prepared to enter her chambers alone, when the door opened from within.

'Soren,' Guermont said.

'Come in, lady,' he greeted her, inviting her into her own room.

As she took the first steps inside, the smell of some of her favorite foods greeted her, making her mouth water in anticipation. Roasted quail? Could it be? Venison? Even the cakes the cook made for special occasions? How could it be? Lord Soren clasped her hand in his and drew her into the chamber and closed the door behind her.

'What is this?' she asked.

He guided her to a chair and helped her to sit…at a table. She felt in front of her, rubbing her hands around the surface and bumping into plates and bowls of various sizes. Lord Soren began calling out the contents of each as she did so.

She'd been correct—all of her favorite foods.

'This is supper. I thought that we could talk while we eat,' he explained.

To her, talking about ending their marriage and eating did not go together, but it did not seem to matter to him. She had eaten very little in the last weeks, mostly broths and stews that she could manage without being able to see them. A cup, a bowl with a spoon, she could do. More involved eating, she simply could not manage and had not tried.

'I am not hungry, Lord Soren,' she began, shaking her head. 'But I thank you for going through this effort.'

Her words were clear and decisive and would have persuaded him or anyone else of her uninterest had two things not happened: her stomach growled loud enough to echo across the chamber and he slipped a small piece of the roasted quail into her mouth.

It was juicy and well seasoned and succulent and delicious.

And the instant it touched her tongue, she wanted more.

'Good, is it not?' he asked, now at her side. She heard the scrape of a chair being brought closer. 'Here, I have more ready for you here,' he said, taking her hand and guiding her fingers to a metal plate in front of her. 'Try that.'

He did nothing else until she did as he directed. She slid her hand slowly to the plate and felt on its surface for the pieces of fowl he'd torn for her. Sybilla hesitated, fearing she would drop it on herself or the floor, but he urged her on in a tone she'd not heard from him before.

'Ah,' he said, 'I see the cause of your concern. You do not wish to wear the food or soil your clothing.' He moved away from her, walking around her to the other side of the table, before standing behind her. 'Let me fix this.'

Without another word of warning, he gently removed her veil and tossed it aside. Then he lifted each arm and tugged her sleeves up until they were tight against her forearms. Lastly, he encircled her neck with some cloth and she felt him tie it behind her. 'Your garments are now safely out of the way or covered, Lady Sybilla. Carry on.'

Playful. He was being playful with her. Mayhap now that he knew he could get an annulment, he felt that he could put aside the intense hatred he'd expressed? This was no Lord Soren she'd ever encountered before and she had no way of knowing how to approach him. Another growl from her empty belly took the decision from her.

'Here is more,' he said. She could smell a variety of aromas as he placed more foods on her plate. 'We can talk after you have eaten your fill. There is a cup of ale to the left of your plate when you need it.'

Once begun, it was difficult to stop. She had not realised how much she'd not eaten until she began to eat. He tore the meat and fowl into small pieces for her, refilling her plate numerous times as she consumed them.

'And you, Lord Soren? Do you not share this meal?'

Silence met her words. Had she said something wrong? Again?

'I must remove my hood to do so,' he explained. When

she shrugged, he went on, 'I wear a hood to cover…my injuries, lady. I care not to be gawked at for the way they appear.' His voice had changed then, back to the Lord Soren she knew. 'I cannot eat with it in place.'

Sybilla did not know what made her do it, but it felt right.

'Then remove it, Lord Soren. I will never notice and you will be at ease.'

After a pause, she heard fabric being untied, heard the rustling of clothing and the sound of something landing on the floor between them. And then, a most disconcerting sound—he released a moan that whispered of pleasure and relief. Though she knew the cause of it, it made her belly tighten deep within.

Then, without further words between them, he went back to sharing food with her, pouring more wine—watered, since she was unused to the strong type he'd brought for her—and offering tastes of all the dishes prepared for them. She tried to slow down, fearing a sore stomach from eating too much at one time, but each taste tempted her to another and another.

The final foods offered to her were some sweet wafers and small, flavoured cakes, both in a size that she could manage without any utensils. She ate only one of each before shaking her head to refuse more.

'My thanks, Lord Soren, for arranging that,' she said as she pushed the plate back away from her. Reaching down, she took hold of the linen napkin so that she could clean her hands and face. After she'd wiped her hands, it was taken from her.

'Here, let me do that since I can see what a mess you have made of yourself,' he teased.

'That badly?' she asked, as he dabbed the corners of her mouth and her chin and wiped across her lips. She slid the tip of her tongue out and licked her lips. Then she felt his thumb slide over it, retracing the path of her tongue. Her belly reacted again, feeling the light touch deep within her body. She shivered and he dropped his hand from her.

She decided it was time for that talk between them and not waiting for him to begin, Sybilla did.

'So tell me, Lord Soren, what has made you decide you do not want me any longer?'

Chapter Fourteen

God save him from innocents and fools! he thought as the words passed her lips. The lips that drove him to drink throughout the meal they'd shared. The lips he wanted to place his own on and taste. Not want her?

Right now, and with little more provocation than she'd already given him, he could lay her on that inviting bed near them, peel off the rest of the layers of clothing that covered her and kiss and lick and taste every possible inch of her skin. And once he was satisfied that no part of her had gone untouched by mouth and hands, he would place himself between her thighs and lay claim to the rest of her. His prick lengthened even now in anticipation and desire.

Not want her?

Soren leaned back in his chair and stared at her. If she ever had an idea of the amount of time and effort it had taken him to stay out of her bed and to speak to the priest about annulling their marriage, she would never think that. His mind understood her question, even if his body wanted to misunderstand it.

'The words of a child, lady.' He shifted in the chair to accommodate his erection, which she thankfully could not see, and continued. 'While instructing Raed on his duties to his lord, I was reminded of a lord's duties to his lady.' He must not think on *those* duties or he'd never get through this!

'I confess I do not understand, Lord Soren.' Her expression was one of puzzlement, disgruntled for some reason and puzzled for the obvious one.

'I told Raed that it was a man's duty to take responsibility for his actions and to admit when he erred. That is what this is about, Sybilla.'

'Lord Soren, forgive my impertinence, but why should you care what happens to me? You made yourself and your reasons for hating me very clear. I understand your hatred. I understand your need for vengeance. But this, this…' she motioned at the table and him with her hand '…I do not.'

He stood and pushed the chair back from the table. She tensed, preparing herself for whatever he would deliver to her. He'd seen her do it before.

'The blow from your father should have killed me, Sybilla. No one, not the healers, not the priests, not even William's physician himself, can explain how I survived. But I know how—I needed to live to seek vengeance on him. That alone kept me alive, through every excruciating hour, through every surgery to repair the damaged flesh of my body, through every time I tried to give up and die. Vengeance pulled me along and made me live.'

She shivered at his words and clutched the napkin in her hands. But it did not stop him from saying the rest.

'I came here to kill you and to destroy everything that belonged to Durward,' he said, not sparing her the truth.

Sybilla pushed back in the chair and tried to stand. He grabbed her by the shoulders and stopped her. Guiding her back to sit, he explained, 'You are safe from me now, lady.' But she shook as she sat there before him. He could see the terror return to her face.

'Alston and you were not what I expected,' he revealed. 'I forgot for a long time that my men fought with me, dreamed of a place of their own with me and accompanied me for that chance. I was quite ready to kill you until your people showed me what loyalty was. When they put themselves between you and me, it tore from me my resolve to kill you.'

He paused and watched a myriad of expressions move across her lovely face, each one exposing more about her to his scrutiny. The one that lasted was something he should recognize, for he wore it and felt it often enough—anger.

'So you married me instead?' she asked, tossing the linen aside now and clasping the arms of the wooden chair.

'It seemed the better choice at the time, lady.'

Then it happened for the first time since he'd met her—she laughed. Not a chuckle or smile this time. Sybilla laughed aloud and it was a sight to behold. 'Twas difficult to believe she was sightless, for her eyes sparkled and her cheeks flushed. Then the laughter softened and stopped and he missed it the moment it fled her face.

'And now, now you wish me to go?'

Soren had sidestepped explaining the real reason he'd married her, but now needed to reveal more about his plans than he wanted any one person to know. Could he trust her?

'Alston is a pivotal crossroads here in the north, Sybilla. It must be held to secure the entire border with the Scots and to keep Northumbria from absorbing William's lands.' He paused to let her absorb that part of it. 'William sent me here to take and hold these lands and to assess who was loyal and who sought to overthrow his rule, both here and in the south.'

Soren knew that Morcar and Edwin believed William would keep to the lands that belonged to the Godwinsons, but Soren knew differently—William intended to rule over as much of this isle as he could. Holding the western half of the north was only the beginning.

'And...?' Clever girl, she knew there was more.

'The traitors are closer at hand than even I imagined,' he said. 'I need Alston settled so that I can focus my efforts on the threats from the outside.'

'So, my seeking the convent will rid you of problems here at Alston?' she asked, a suspicious glint in her eyes now.

Soren ran his hands through his hair and shook his head. She really thought he wanted her gone. Apparently his plan made sense to no one but him.

'Nay, I need you here. Though once things are settled, I am willing to seek an annulment if that is what you wish.'

She shook her head at him. 'I do not understand. How does my staying help you at all?'

'I need to be able to concentrate on training and deploying my men and those who will arrive from Giles's and Brice's forces to help me. With the reports of rebels moving into and through this area, I must strengthen the defences of the manor and the keep and cut them off from their allies. With the harvest coming soon, I need someone who will work with Guermont and his men to oversee it all. Someone with experience, someone who knows the fields, the crops and the people here. You, Sybilla, I need your help.'

'I cannot oversee anything, my lord. I cannot see.'

The bitter words hung out there between them for several moments before he sweetened the offer.

'I will keep your people safe, Sybilla. Once the area is settled and the rebels scattered—no more than a six-month—I will honour your request to leave. Blind or sighted, you will be free to go as you please. Whether you choose the convent or another place, I will see to it.'

'A temporary marriage? An annulment even if I can see?' Sybilla wanted to be certain she understood this unusual bargain he sought with her.

'Aye. And if you decide you wish not to retire to the convent, I will make arrangements for you elsewhere. It will be as if this marriage never occurred.'

For some reason, the kiss they'd shared came to mind and Sybilla touched her lips, remembering the passion in such an innocent touch of mouths. 'Consummation? Will you seek to consummate this marriage?' She hesitated bringing the matter up if he'd not thought about it, but…

'Aye,' he said, his voice now husky and deep as he interrupted her. 'I will seek your bed.'

'Twas more a promise than an answer, she could feel it in his voice. Her body understood it as well and she felt a wave of heat rush through her veins as it responded to that promise. Still, she must be careful in this, for it was worse than facing the blackness of the stairs and waiting to fall down them. This was the chance to choose that which had never been hers before. There were enemies surrounding Alston, surrounding her, and she might be asked to help these invaders against her neighbours or other Saxons who had been loyal to their king.

But his last words, this promise of intimacy unlike anything she'd ever known, both tempted and terrified her. The results of joining with him could also cause more problems. Something he'd not mentioned yet…

'Children?' she blurted out. 'What if a child is created?' Though she might be willing to give up all interest in Alston—and she was losing her certainty in that more with each passing minute—was it fair to also do that for a child who should inherit it? If there was one?

'There will be no child, Sybilla. I will make certain of that,' he promised.

Men spilled their seed, children resulted. As a man of illegitimate birth, surely he knew that. How could he promise such a thing to her? Gytha's words came back to her about his past and his many lovers. Had no child resulted from such promiscuity?

'How can you be sure?' she asked. There were herbs rumoured to cause miscarriages and some to prevent conception, she knew of these from overheard conversations, but would they work?

She felt the heat of him as he stepped closer to her.

'There are ways, Sybilla,' he whispered into her ear, startling her and sending a wave of shivers along her spine. 'I know them.'

The touch of his mouth on her neck made her realise that he knew so much more than she about these matters of the flesh. As her resolve began to waver, as more questions raced through her mind in a now-haphazard manner, she voiced the one concern bred into her by generations before.

'Lord Soren, I will not betray my people. Even if I must give them up to you, I will not betray them.'

He did not reply, but she heard him there, still standing close, able to touch her wherever he would. She understood that he meant to consummate their agreement and their marriage as soon as she gave the word. Should she do this?

Doubt niggled at her in that last moment—she had nothing to prove this agreement existed. As the priest told her, at any time during their marriage he could call for an annulment, leaving her with no legal rights to her land or her people, with no income, nothing but her blindness. He'd sworn to destroy everything she had in order to complete his vengeance against her father. Might this not be part of it—to gain her co-operation, to use her skills and her body and then simply toss her aside when he had finished using her?

His hand sliding across her breasts nearly made her forget all of her doubts. His fingers played over them, caressing the tips of them until Sybilla felt them tighten. He kissed her neck then, moving along the skin, licking and then biting it until she gasped. All the time, his hand never paused its attention to her breasts. He cupped one, rubbing his thumb over the tip again and again, and, in spite of layers of *syrce* and *cyrtel*, she felt each movement as though it was skin against naked skin.

When she opened her mouth to voice her concerns, he covered it with his, tasting her and letting her taste him. His other hand crept up onto her head, sliding his fingers into her hair and loosening her braid. He held her to him, plundering her mouth as he caressed her breasts. She ached for something else, for something more, and she found her body arching against him.

His mouth never left hers, and Sybilla tasted more of him when he slipped his tongue inside to caress hers. He moved his hand and his tongue in the same motions at the same time and she was ready to surrender to him and agree to his devil's bargain if it meant more of this. Then he let his hand glide down, across her chest and on to her belly…and lower. It was a scandalous thing to be touched like this, but her body reacted despite her innocence. The place between her legs now tingled and grew wet as he placed his hand there and pressed. His long fingers sought the spot between her thighs and even with the layers of cloth, she could feel his intimate touch.

Sybilla lost the ability to think then. When he reached down, grasped the edge of her garments and began to slide them up, tickling and touching her legs, which were naked above her stockings, she gasped in shock and pleasure. She reached down and placed her hand on his arm, not sure if she should stop him or urge him on.

'Are you afraid, Sybilla?'

'Aye,' she whispered. In truth, she was terrified by

the step they were about to take and the claim he would make on her body and her life.

'Trust me,' he urged in a compelling and sensuous voice. 'I will have a care for you,' he promised. 'I can teach you how to survive the injuries you have.'

For some unknown reason, his words were like a bucket of water tossed on an overheated horse. Mayhap the suggestion that she would never see and needed his help did it, she knew not. However, his words stopped her from going any further on this journey into passion.

'I cannot,' she said, pushing on his hand. 'I do not know you enough to trust you.'

His hand stilled, he stilled, and Sybilla waited for him to release her. Her body rebelled against this interruption and pulsed with heat in spite of her decision.

'I cannot,' she repeated.

He lifted his hand from her legs, allowing her garments to slide back down in place and helped her to stand on her own before letting go of her. Her legs shook and she held on to the table until she felt the chair being moved behind her. If she dropped a bit too hard into it, he did not speak of it.

'I bid you a good evening then, Lady Sybilla,' he said.

She heard him moving around the room, gathering things and then he paused at the door. Sybilla thought he would speak again, but the latch of the door lifted and he was gone. She remained seated, trying to recover her breath and expecting to hear the chattering of Gytha and Aldys as they approached, but only silence reigned.

As his wife, she had no right to refuse him her bed or her body, so Sybilla wondered why he'd given up on what was clearly his intent all along—to claim his marital rights to her. The bargain he offered, if indeed it was done in good faith, would never stand, for his rights as husband would never be questioned in matters such as these. Lord Soren could have taken her virginity right then, whether she willed it or not, and no one could have questioned his right to do so.

So, if he wanted her and he wanted to take her, why had he stopped? Why did he want her consent when he needed it not?

Her breathing had almost returned to normal when she heard voices coming down the corridor towards her chambers. The heat crept back into her cheeks as she thought of how she would explain what had happened when Gytha and Aldys asked her of it. And they would. She'd not yet thought of what words to say when they entered the room.

Though they stopped and must have been staring at the sight before them—the table, the meal consumed, two cups of wine, their dishevelled mistress… Oh! She'd forgotten her appearance! He'd pulled her hair free of the braid and it must be obvious what they were about from that and the veil that he'd tossed aside. They never spoke of it, only asked how she'd enjoyed her food.

Unable to talk about what had happened, she complained of pains in her head and found herself under the bedcovers shortly thereafter. Aldys sat with her for a short while, but left when Sybilla gave her leave to.

Exhausted from the events of the day and confused by the events of the evening, Sybilla expected to fall asleep instantly.

* * *

Hours later, long after the keep and manor had quieted for the night, she lay tossing and turning in her bed—her body pulsing with the strange excitement he'd caused deep within her and her mind trying to sort through the possible reasons for his bewildering offer.

If he desired her and intended to keep Alston, why did he offer her freedom from him?

Chapter Fifteen

Too restless to sleep and too aroused to even rest, Soren walked. A difficult thing to do at night, for the vision of just one eye limited how well he could see things in the dark. The moon lit his way and he was tempted to seek out the cold comfort offered by the stream, but decided to just walk.

He'd not planned to bed her this night, but when the opportunity presented itself and she seemed willing, he'd had to touch her. It was his undoing, for one touch, one taste of her skin, was not enough and drove him to seek more and more. Sybilla probably did not even realise how aroused she became in his arms. Her body answered his every touch, arching and heating, swelling and tightening…

He untied the leather hood and pulled it off. Ah, much cooler without it. Then he wiped the sweat from his forehead again. Reliving her reactions even in his thoughts was far too arousing.

And it brought back many memories about the man he used to be and the ease with which he could and did seduce women.

Before.

He stumbled then over a rock in his path that he did not see in the dim light thrown by the moon. Served him right to be trying this when so distracted by his innocent siren of a wife who had held back at the last possible moment from giving herself to him.

Though he could completely understand her lack of trust—after all, he had just threatened to destroy everything she had—he wanted it. He could not restore her sight, just as no one could restore his body to what it had been, but he thought that giving her back her usefulness would be a good thing.

Soren understood that she believed she had nothing to offer to her people now. He knew that she felt unable to do any task she'd done before in service to Alston and her father. She did not realise, as he had not at first, that her mind was the most important part of her and that her experience and knowledge was valuable, more so than whether she could sew or weave.

He rounded the south-west corner of the wall and stopped.

Weaving.

He remembered old, nearly blind women in the village where he grew up weaving almost without seeing the work before them, once someone had set up the warp threads in the colours needed. They had guided the weft threads with a shuttle back and forth, weaving cloth. Sybilla would never be able to weave large, intricately patterned tapestries, but she could work on cloth or simple designs. Smiling, he wondered where his men had discarded the broken loom when they took it from her chambers.

Would God further damn him for lying to the priest? For Soren had no intention of putting Sybilla aside if she remained blind. It was an answer to a prayer for him and he cared not if the Church or others considered it an impediment. He considered it a godsend, a blessing, in his otherwise cursed existence and he offered up a prayer nightly for it to continue.

Soren had not told her the whole truth of the matter between them and she might have sensed that withholding. He knew, though he would never admit it to anyone, that if her sight returned, she would never be able to look at him as anything other than the demonic-looking monster he resembled—torn skin stretched over badly healed bones, scars running across his head and down the length of his back and worse. He knew she would never want to remain married to him and he would never be able to tolerate the sight of horror in her gaze, so he would free her either way.

He had not lied to her about needing her help in Alston. What he truly offered her in return was not of necessity her freedom, but a chance to gain some confidence and experience at living blind in a place she knew before leaving here to live elsewhere. Just as he had had to relearn how to walk and see and fight and ride, she would need to do the same. What better place than Alston, where she probably knew every path and corner? But Soren held back from mentioning that because Sybilla was nearing the time when pity would break her spirit.

Soren knew it was coming because he'd lived it.

Taking responsibility for his actions meant he would give her the best chance at surviving the dark night that was coming ever closer for her.

He dearly wanted to talk his plan over with someone and wished Brice would arrive with the men who would serve under him and so he could talk with a friend. As much as he hated to think of it, he needed help in this endeavour. He needed someone he could trust.

Soren reached the gate for the fourth time and decided he had walked enough. He would check for the remnants of the loom in the donjon of the keep and then retire for the night. He had much to do in the morning.

Finding the broken frame, with its threads yet hanging with their small clay weights in place, pleased him. With no experience in working with wood or weaving, he could not tell if the loom could be repaired or if a new one must be built, but there were men here familiar with both and he would seek them out for their advice in the morning.

As he walked back to the kitchen, he noticed a couple talking in the shadows near the doorway to the yard. He recognised both of them immediately—Larenz and that she-dragon Aldys who served Sybilla.

Interesting…

Soren had not taken note with whom the old man kept company of the feminine kind; however, this would work out well for his plan. He needed someone he could trust and someone Sybilla would as well. He would speak to Larenz in the morn and gain his co-operation.

When he reached the small chamber he'd claimed as his own, Soren believed things might work out between him and Sybilla—he would gain a wife, at least a temporary one, and she would gain the chance to build her confidence before leaving Alston for a new life.

Or before accepting her blindness and staying with him.

After Sybilla's disturbed night, the rains and wind outside made her want to stay curled up in her bed for the day. The storms forced most to seek shelter inside, but she could hear the sound of men fighting in the yard in spite of the conditions. Every so often, Lord Soren's voice could be heard above the others, calling out commands or instructions to his men. When Gytha and Aldys arrived, she dismissed them and remained in bed, pleading the same head pains of last evening. Aldys returned every short while to make certain she was well, but even knowing she would do that did not spur Sybilla to get out of bed.

The men finished training and just in time, for the clouds began to pour unrelenting rain down by mid-morn and the thunder and lightning made outside a dangerous place to be. She had dragged herself out of bed and had managed to find the garments she needed to wear. The *syrce* was easy enough to get into, but the laces of the *cyrtel* would be impossible without help. Sybilla hoped Aldys would come back soon, for she was forced to sit with her outer gown open down her back until she did. She pulled a blanket from the bed and draped it over her shoulders to keep the chill away. As soon as she heard the door open and Aldys come in, Sybilla jumped up and turned her back to the door.

'Aldys, my laces, pray thee to hasten and tie them,'

she said, shivering as she dropped the blanket to expose the laces.

The hands that took the laces were not her maid's.

She began to pull away, but he grabbed her and steadied her on her feet in front of him. Lord Soren, she could tell now when he chuckled.

'Not Aldys, but I think I can conquer the laces of your…what do you call it, lady? Ah, *oui*, your *cyrtel*, as it is called here?' His hands took hold of the laces and began tightening them along their length. She could feel the heat in them and he touched her back more than once when he slipped his fingers under the gown to smooth the *syrce* under it.

Her traitorous body remembered his touch and she fought the rising heat in her blood as he worked behind her. How would it feel if he untied the laces and slid his hands inside and around to touch her breasts as he had last evening? If he pushed the *cyrtel* off her shoulders and pulled her against the hardness of his chest? If he—

'There, Sybilla. You are tied,' he reported as he stepped away.

Her cheeks must be flushed red and the tips of her breasts pushed against her clothing. Would he notice such things? Certainly he would! A man of his experience with women would know the signs of arousal and know success and seduction were at hand. No doubt he watched for them in every encounter when he had identified his prey. She took a breath and released it, trying to regain some control over her wayward reaction to even the nearness of him.

'My thanks, Lord Soren,' she said.

'Soren is my name, Sybilla. I would have you use it between us.'

So said the serpent to Eve in the Garden of Eden.

She changed the topic. 'I do not know where Aldys went off to,' she said, taking a few steps forwards, hopefully not into a wall.

'I sent her off on an errand for me,' he informed her. 'She should return shortly to you.'

They would be alone, then, until her maid returned. Sybilla turned around trying to judge from his position where she might be standing, but had lost her bearings when he touched her. He grasped her hand then and tugged.

'Here, here is your chair,' he said, pulling her a few paces and then placing her hand on the wooden arm. She sat down and tugged the blanket, still in her hands, over her.

'I would ask a boon of you, if you do not mind, Sybilla.'

He stood across the chamber now and she relaxed a bit. 'A boon, Lord…Soren?' It would take her some time to address him in such a familiar way.

'Your cold rains here wreak their havoc on my—injuries. May I use your chambers again for a bath?' he asked.

'Is your home warmer than England?' she asked, trying not to think of him in her chambers, naked. Instead, she realised that he'd never spoken of anything about his home to her, leaving her with only Gytha's gossip gleaned from Stephen.

'*Oui,*' he said. 'Aye. The sea breezes and the sun

warm the lands there. Bretagne is a beautiful place,' he explained.

'Alston and England are beautiful,' she added, feeling as though she needed to defend the honour of her land. 'But it does rain frequently.' It was true, but she had no knowledge or experience of places other than this one. She'd travelled only as far as Hexham once with her father, so she had little to compare it to.

'So, may I call for a bath?' he asked again.

'Aye, Lord…Soren. When do you wish it?'

The servants would need time to heat the water and set it up here. And she would need time to be elsewhere, she thought, developing a sudden urge to visit the kitchens and thank the cook for his efforts with last evening's meal.

'I had hoped your answer would be *oui*, for I sent Aldys with my request before coming here.'

She stood up, clutching the blanket to her, and nodded. She'd been counting her paces these last few days, much as Guermont did when he escorted her, and she knew that the door was six paces from the chair. Counting them, she reached it when she felt him approach behind her.

'You do not need to leave, Sybilla.'

'I will give you privacy, my lord,' she said, reaching out for the latch.

'I frightened you last evening and I apologise for that boldness,' he offered softly.

He did not scare her as much as her body's reaction to him did. That a complete stranger could touch her so intimately and her body would urge her on for more was beyond belief to her. Sybilla lifted the latch.

'Where will you go?' he asked, not moving from behind her, so close she could feel his breath on her face.

'I have not been to the hall in many days. I think I will visit with those there,' she said, trying to sound confident in her choice.

'Here, then, take my arm and let me escort you there,' he offered.

With the way she trembled, it was a good suggestion, for she suspected that she would tumble down the steps instead of walking down them. He lifted her hand onto his arm and pulled the door open. As they walked to the stairs, she noticed he was wet. And cold. They reached the steps and he waited as she found the rope there. He surprised her more by following Guermont's practice of taking each step by itself and counting off as they moved down them.

From the sounds as they approached, many had sought refuge from the storms in the hall. Because of the flurry of attacks in the area, Guermont had informed her Lord Soren had ordered those in the village to move into the manor. So, it was a busy place now, but it quieted as they walked in.

Other than his soldiers, she'd known everyone in Alston since her birth or theirs, but she felt as though among strangers. Not being able to see them made it all uncomfortable for her. Lord Soren guided her, whispering directions as they walked to the front of the hall and the main table that remained in place at all times.

'Bring the lady a chair,' he called out as they made their way forwards. She heard the scrambling of people and then Lord Soren brought them to a stop. He lifted her hand from his arm and positioned her so she could sit. Leaning over to adjust the blanket, he spoke softly to her.

'It is a score of paces forwards, then another to the right to reach the stairs,' he said. 'But I will send Guermont to you if you need to return to your chambers before I am finished.'

The heat struck at his words, and the flush of it filled her cheeks. He'd done it a-purpose, she knew he had. She waited for him to leave before allowing herself to be at ease there. Sybilla knew when he'd gone, for the people had been silent while he escorted her and now the usual noise of so many in one place began anew. It took but a few minutes before someone approached her. Sybilla spoke to every one of them, asking them about their family and their well-being. It seemed to go on for a long time before she realised where she was sitting.

Sliding her hands along the ornately carved wooden arms, she recognised it for what it was—the lord's chair. Then, as she sat in what used to be her father's chair, the weight of it all crashed down on her.

He was gone. Her father. Her brother. All whom she had loved and who had loved her were gone.

Now, when her people needed her most, she could do nothing for them. She could not even see them, she could not tell their condition. She would never again see their faces or watch the sun rise or set over Alston Keep.

They had tried to tell her and make her accept the inevitable, but she'd refused. Now, the reality of it settled in—there had been no change in her vision since the day it happened. No improvement. No sign of light. Nothing but darkness before and around her. It smothered her now and she felt her very breath being sucked from her.

Gasping for air, she stood abruptly, wanting to get away—from the truth, from the lies, from anyone and everyone, but she had nowhere to go. They called her name, trying to help her, but it changed into cries and sneers and insults, blaring at her from all sides. She stumbled forwards, counting her paces, catching herself, feeling them surrounding her.

She could not see!

Sybilla turned around and around and then again, searching for some light in her darkness, for a path to follow, but it was utter black everywhere she turned. She rubbed her eyes, trying to remove the layer that blocked her vision. Then even the blackness began to swirl around her.

She would never see again.

'Here, my lady,' someone said. 'Your chambers are this way.'

Sybilla tried to see who it was that offered aid, but she could not. His voice sounded familiar to her; however, she could not put a name to that voice no matter how much she searched her memory. Soon, he said the steps were before them. She dropped his arm and ran, tripping up the first two or three steps, before she grabbed hold of the guiding rope and dragged herself forwards. Her arms scraped along the stone wall, catching every jagged piece of surface and tearing her sleeves.

Her veil caught and was pulled off. Her hands slipped along the rope several times, burning her palms. But she ran. They called behind her and in front of her, but she could not see them. She could not see.

Out of breath, she stumbled across the landing at the top and fell hard into the wall. Scrambling to her feet, she ran once more, this time, now, seeking the one who'd caused this. He had blinded her and she would make him pay for it. Sybilla felt along the wall until she reached her door and flung it open, ignoring those who called her name from behind. They would stop her.

'Sybilla!' he called out as she ran in. Water splashed and sloshed. She heard it pouring on to the floor, but it did not matter. 'Stop!' he commanded, but she did not. The door slammed closed behind her.

She would never see again.

It pounded in her thoughts and even in her heart and she gasped for a breath. She sought the one responsible for this. He'd done it and even boasted of it. He had stolen her lands. He had stolen her sight. He had stolen her life.

'Sybilla,' he said, quietly now. 'Sybilla.'

The pain inside was so great that all she could do was react, launching herself towards his voice, hoping to hurt him as much as he'd hurt her.

Chapter Sixteen

He caught her just as she jumped at him, one foot out of the tub and the other still inside it. Somehow he managed to keep his balance and not let them both crash into the water. She was like a wild animal, fighting for its life, as she threw her body and her fists at him. Soren grabbed her hands and then she used her feet to kick at him.

'Sybilla,' he whispered, 'you must calm yourself.' Soren knew she did not hear him. In the middle of this panic and rage, she could not hear anything but what was screaming through her own thoughts. He knew. He'd lived through this.

He moved slowly, partly because she continued to fight and hit him, and partly to try to let her burn out this rage. Soren stepped out of the tub and walked them back away from it. She slowed with each step, her unintelligible screaming lessened and the fight began to drain from her. She gasped, as though not able to breathe. He made it to the bed and dragged her onto his lap. Ignoring her struggles, he placed a hand on her chest and one on her back and spoke quietly.

'Push out, Sybilla. Push against my hands with your breathing,' he urged. It took another minute or so before she did it, but he felt her lungs expanding. 'Good girl,' he said. He lessened the pressure, but did not remove his hands yet.

The door opened, but he waved them back with a nod of his head. He wanted no one in these chambers, for he was naked and he did not want Sybilla to be shamed by what she'd done once she came back to her senses. For though the blindness would remain, her dignity would suffer once she remembered, if she did, her behaviour. It could all be sorted out later.

He wanted to laugh at the irony of that moment, for only days or a sennight ago, he'd yet intended to make her suffer. Now, his heart, the one he thought cold and empty, even dead within him, ached as he watched this proud young woman go through this agony of soul and spirit.

'You did this to me,' she cried now. He noticed the blood dripping from her clenched fists as she raised them to pummel his chest. 'You...did...this...to...me.' He gathered both her hands into one of his and held her tightly against his body.

Words, his or hers, would not matter now. She needed time to let the anger and terror of facing a life of blindness seep away. It would take more than just this one episode, if she was anything like him, but this was the beginning. Like bursting a boil with a needle, this would relieve the worst of it, allowing the rest to ease its way out.

It ebbed and flowed over the next several hours—
each episode lasting less than the one before until she
collapsed against him like a child's doll that had lost all
its stuffing. Her breathing was shallow, her skin sweaty
and pale, but her heart beat strong in her chest. Easing
her from his lap, he laid her on the bed, pulled on his
clothes and went seeking a bowl and some linen cloths
to clean the scrapes and bruises he noticed on her hands,
her face and other places.

When he lifted the latch and eased the door open,
a veritable army jumped outside the door, with the old
dragon being first in line to attempt to enter. Soren shook
his head at them and then told them what he needed.
Aldys did not move from her place, but instead sent
Gytha off to gather the supplies and medicaments.

'My lord,' she began to argue when handing over the
bandages and unguent from Teyen's supply.

'Do not even think to naysay me in this, Aldys,' he
said quietly. 'I will see to your lady's injuries and will
call on you when she is able to have visitors.'

He watched her spine straighten with insubordination, but she kept her tongue behind her teeth. Wise. He
noticed and nodded at her before closing the door.

Carrying everything over to the bed, he pulled a small
table closer and arranged everything before touching her.
He poured some of the now-cooled water for his bath into
a bowl, mixed in the steaming water just brought and
then dipped a cloth into it. Easing open one fist then the
other, he cleaned away the blood and dirt from her torn
palms. She moaned and cried out in her sleep or faint,
but did not wake.

Soren moved around her, removing her garments so he

could clean her, first her hands, then he rolled her to one
side and unlaced the gown and tugged it over her head.
The *syrce*, or what was called a *chemise* by the women
of Normandy and Brittany, was looser and easy enough
to manoeuvre, so he let it remain. He cleaned the scrapes
on her arms and he applied some of Teyen's ointments
to the bruises. He winced when he lifted the chemise
and saw her knees. They would be sore for a long time
and she would be unable to kneel in prayer for a good
while.

It took nearly an hour or more to see to all her injuries
and then settle her in the bed. Peering around the chamber, he thought to sit by the bed in the chair, but decided
to lie at her side instead. Taller than most here and taller
than her by almost a foot, his height and weight would
not make it through the night in the chair anyway. Easing
the bedcovers over her, Soren moved next to her—close
enough to reach her if she needed, but far enough away
so that his body did not touch hers.

He had not slept well in weeks, nor in a bed for at least
a month, so the comfort and warmth of this one lulled
him to sleep within moments, or so it seemed to him. The
candles had burned down, leaving him in total darkness
and he realised how she must feel as he stumbled around
the chamber, before opening the door and using the light
of the torches burning in the corridor to guide his way
around. He lit an oil lamp and placed it on the table at
the bed's side, so he could see her and the chamber once
more.

Settled next to her again, he watched her sleep. She

moved not at all, but her breaths were the slow and deep and even ones of complete exhaustion. Soren joined her in slumber.

Soren woke only when the sounds of his men training in the yard echoed through the window in the chamber. He climbed from the bed and opened the shutter of the window to see that the sun was well up in the sky already.

He stretched his body this way and that, working out the tightness as he did each morning. The bath last evening had begun to ease it, but he'd not soaked long enough to make a difference. The worst of it was in his shoulder and neck. The blade of the axe had sunk deep into his flesh there, glancing off the bone and tracing a path of destruction down the back of his ribcage and on to his back and hip. Truly, he should be dead from it and he wondered once more why and how he had survived at all.

His stomach growled then, reminding him of his missed supper. He found his clean garments and dressed so that he could allow her servants into the room. First he put on his shirt, breeches and tunic and then he pulled the fabric cowl over his head. He would wear the leather hood under his armour and hauberk, but the cloth one was more comfortable if he was inside. He glanced at Sybilla again and decided he would remain close at hand.

Soren opened the door to find an entire entourage waiting there—house servants ready to tend to her room and remove the tub, his men to receive their orders for the day and hers to see to her needs. Aldys glared, Gytha trembled and Guermont and Stephen stared openly at the fact that he'd spent the night with Sybilla. Pulling the door open wider, he motioned to the servants to enter.

'Quietly,' he said to them as they moved past him and worked efficiently to empty the tub and take it from the chamber. Another laid a fire in the hearth and lit it. Yet another brought in an iron kettle and hung it from the hook in the hearth.

'Teyen said 'tis a tisane for the lady to drink when she wakes,' the man whispered as he left.

He expected a battle from the she-dragon, but none came. Instead Aldys carried in a tray and placed it on the table that had been moved aside for the tub. Uncovering the plate and bowl, she revealed a steaming porridge and a small loaf of cheese and one of bread. A cup and jug sat next to the food. When she'd revealed its contents, she nodded to him.

'To break your fast, Lord Soren,' she said quietly as she, too, left.

Within just minutes, the chamber had been cleaned, the fire tended and food brought in for him. Stunned by the quiet efficiency of her servants, Soren had a new appreciation for the lady's work. He knew she'd been in sole control of the manor since her…since Durward fell on Senlac field, but had never realised the extent of that responsibility until now. Although her battle tactics and strategies were sorely lacking, she'd managed the household extremely well, keeping all of her people clothed and fed during a terrible winter when many starved or worse. Then, she'd overseen the planting of new crops in the spring and had started a new, defensive wall built around the keep.

If he'd arrived a few weeks later than he had, he questioned whether his conquest would have been as easy as it had been.

Soren ate the food, downing every morsel and drinking every drop of ale. A fighting man learned early in his training to never let a meal go by wasted. On a march, it could be days before the next one, so you ate what you could when you could and prayed for another one soon. William's army had been held in Caen for months because of bad winds on the Channel and the hardest task was feeding all those men. Thousands needed to eat and many times not all did. The lesson was well learned, he thought as he placed the empty dish and bowl, cup and jug back on the tray. As he turned to take it to the door, he noticed her lips moving, though not making a sound.

Every part of her body hurt. Her skin ached. She dared not move to test out the extent of the pain, for even breathing sent waves of pain coursing through her. The only thing she could move were her lips and eyes. So she began offering up a prayer that the blindness had been a terrible nightmare and that when she opened her eyes, the day would greet her.

Sybilla gathered what little courage she had left within her and tested out her theory. The same unrelenting blackness greeted her once again and she felt the tears trickle from the corners of those unseeing eyes. The touch of a cloth to her face surprised her and she startled and then moaned at the pain even that caused.

''Tis I, Soren,' he said, revealing his presence and his identity to her. 'I have a tisane from the healer to ease your pain.'

His hand slipped behind her head and eased it up from

the pillow. As long as she let him move her, the pain was bearable. A few sips and he allowed her to rest back. She tried to speak, but her voice was gone. Sybilla lay quietly, unmoving for several minutes until the concoction began to spread through her and the severity of the pain began to dull.

'It should ease soon,' he offered softly as he moved around her, smoothing the bedcovers over her…her naked body.

She closed her eyes and wanted to die.

For so many reasons, she wanted to die right then.

'I tended your injuries and stayed through the night, Sybilla,' he explained as though he had heard the questions in her thoughts. 'Though Aldys is quite an old dragon of a woman, she could not have handled your rage.'

She laughed at that, or attempted to, but the tears flowed freely now and she could not lift her hand to wipe them away. Even moving her fingers made her palms feel as though their very skin was being torn off. But she cried not at the pain, she cried at the loss that she now understood would never be regained. A cloth touched her face, dabbing the tears from her skin.

His manner was distant, formal even, as he wiped and washed her face and urged her to drink again from the healer's brew. When its warmth spread into her limbs and took away more of her pain, he removed several bandages and smoothed on some cream before replacing the coverings. If he had seemed too caring, she would have lost control, but his seeming indifference allowed her to get through it.

In a short while, Sybilla felt herself being pulled down

into a deeper sleep. His voice, deep and calm, urged her to allow it and she did. She thought the pattern repeated several times, but could not be certain.

When she woke and the keep was quiet, she knew night had fallen. From the heat emanating from a source close to her, she suspected what he confirmed moments later.

Soren slept or lay beside her in her bed.

'How do you feel, Sybilla?' he asked quietly. 'Has the pain lessened?'

She gingerly moved a hand and then an arm, a foot, a leg and so on until she'd tested most of her body. She ached, some places worse than others, but the searing pain of some earlier time had been soothed. Sybilla tried to clear her throat to answer his questions and could not find her voice.

He cursed; she thought the words he whispered were foul Norman or Breton words, a suspicion confirmed when a hasty apology followed. She felt him roll away and climb out of the bed and then heard his path around the chamber until he turned, sitting at her side. Lord Soren slid his arm beneath her head and shoulders and he eased her up so she could sip from the cup he placed at her mouth. The watered wine soothed her dry throat and made it possible to answer him, though her voice sounded as scratchy as it felt.

'Not quite so bad, Lord Soren,' she said, almost whispering because it hurt less. She tried to brace herself up on her arms, but she slipped and her hand landed on a very hard, very naked male leg. A thigh, if she was not mistaken. She swallowed and tried to act as though she had not felt it, but she had.

Once again, he did not respond, but simply slipped off the bed and she heard him put the cup on the table. Then he climbed back in on the other side and eased closer to her. She waited for him to move nearer to her; however, he never did so, remaining instead just enough away that their bodies did not touch.

It mattered not, for she knew he was there.

The pattern repeated itself over the course of several more days, Soren at her side at all times of the day and the night, her maids permitted in her chambers only to see to her most personal needs and then gone as quickly and quietly as they'd come. She thought that Lord Soren must leave and see to his duties, but he was there whenever she woke. Then, one day—morning, she thought from the sounds outside and within the keep—the fog lifted and she felt more awake than she had in days.

Sybilla tried to move, slowly, easily, so as to not cause more pain and found that her body no longer screamed back with each attempt. As she rolled to her side to slide to the edge of the bed, she found a heavy weight holding her in place. Reaching down, she searched for it and found it.

A large arm and hand draped over her hips.

And only a thin sheet separated the two body parts—one of which was not hers.

Chapter Seventeen

'Good morrow, Sybilla.'

She'd had no doubt about the identity of the man, but his deep voice, made even deeper by sleep, greeted her pleasantly enough as though having a man in her bed was her usual custom. She shifted, trying to slide to the edge, but he held her in place.

'I would like to get up,' she began, reaching for the edge of the bedcovers and then realising she lay naked beneath them.

Sybilla felt him move, lifting his arm from her and getting out of the bed. Then he took her hand at the side of the bed.

'You have been abed for several days and Teyen said you will be unsteady the first time or two you get out of it.' Lord Soren put something in her hand and then let go. 'I thought you would want that first.'

A *syrce*. He helped her ease it over her head and shoulders, remarkably with little pain, and then took her hands in his and drew her to the bedside. Sybilla let her feet drop to the floor and let him help her to stand. Unfortunately Teyen was right, once more, and she began to wobble. She thought to sit back on the bed, but Lord Soren had other ideas, encircling her with his arms and holding her up…and tightly against him.

She noticed several things quickly. His body always seemed warm. His body, including a very prominent part of it, was always hard. And one more thing came to mind—he was completely naked. Though tempted to grab hold so she did not fall to the floor, she did not dare touch him…anywhere!

'Give yourself a moment to gain your balance, Sybilla,' he whispered, sliding his arms to hold her around her waist, which freed her arms now. 'Just stand and let me get the chair for you.'

He released his hold in increments and she did reach out for him once when the dizziness took over and threatened to spill her to the floor. He held her hand until she let go, never saying a word. Then, she heard the scrape of the chair as he dragged it to her. Once she was seated, he moved away and she heard him as he walked from one place to another and another. Then, when he guided her hand to his, she felt the fabric of his tunic on his arm and knew he'd dressed. He placed a cup in her hands and, when she winced, he explained.

'You burned your palms sliding too fast on the rope. Teyen left some ointment and said to keep them wrapped for a few more days.' She thought he now stood by the door, his voice was in that direction. 'I am going to allow the she-dragon in, so prepare yourself, Sybilla.'

She smiled at that, remembering now that he'd called

Aldys that several times now. And, truly, she could be quite a formidable force when she wanted or needed to be. The latch lifted and the door opened.

'My lord,' Aldys said in a stern voice.

'Aldys,' Soren replied, but his voice was tinged with laughter. 'Good day, Sybilla.'

Then he was gone, his heavy steps echoing down the corridor as he strode away.

Aldys helped her to get cleaned and dressed and soon she felt almost herself. Moving in this direction or that did yet cause some twinges, but Sybilla found that most of the pain had dissipated away. Aldys opened the shutters and the warmer breezes flowed into the chamber. Sybilla walked slowly to it and stood before it, feeling the sun on her face and wishing she could see its light.

Well, that was not going to happen. She knew in her heart and soul that her vision was gone. A long, empty life stretched out in front of her now.

The sound of laughter outside drew her attention. A game of some kind, mayhap. Or a contest? Some of the voices were familiar, while others carried the accented tones of the foreigners. A few called out in their native language, then stuttered over the English words. The thing that struck her most was the happiness in their voices. Clearly, her people had found some middle ground between them and their new lord and his men. They would be all right because he would protect them.

'My lady, the day is a fine one,' Aldys said, approaching her. 'Would you like to take a walk?'

She turned to Aldys, though she could not see her, and shook her head. 'Oh, what they must think of me now?' she whispered. 'A madwoman in their midst?'

'They saw their lady racked by grief and loss of an unimaginable kind,' Aldys answered softly. She took Sybilla's hand and patted it. 'They saw the woman who'd cared for them and their families through the winter and who'd stood up to the demon lord for them. Worry not, lady. They understand.'

The tears burned her eyes and her throat as she asked the question that plagued her the most. 'But what do I do now, Aldys? What do I do?'

'You live, my lady.'

So simple, those two words, but Sybilla could see only the impossibilities stretching out before her.

'I cannot see. I cannot carry out the simplest of duties or perform the easiest of tasks now. How can I live this way?'

'You have a quick mind, lady. You will learn. You will learn new ways to do old tasks. And those you cannot do, you assign to others,' Aldys finished with a laugh. 'Do you truly wish to help the butcher salt the meat?'

Sybilla smiled at that. The smells of that process, a necessary and vital one for their survival, made her stomach retch, but she did it because it was needed. Having someone else oversee it would be no hardship for her.

'But I will never be able to read again.'

'Aye, lady, 'tis true, but someone could read to you. I would be happy to do that,' Aldys offered. The woman did not seem like a she-dragon now. Sybilla smiled and nodded.

Never someone who shied away from the difficult situation or task, Sybilla wondered which things she could accomplish without her sight. Lord Soren, if his offer was an honest one, thought she could oversee the harvest and setting up stores for the winter. Had he meant that?

'Lord Soren offered to make this marriage a temporary one if I assisted him here over the next six months.'

Sybilla needed to talk over this strange offer with someone and it seemed right to do so with Aldys. She'd served her family and her mother for years and had seen much in that time. She'd not planned to blurt it out, but now she waited on Aldys's reaction to such a thing.

'I know, my lady.'

Of all the words she could have said, either supporting or opposing such an offer, Sybilla never expected those.

'You know of this?' she asked. Sybilla turned her head, looking around the room before remembering she could not see. 'Are we alone?'

'I sent that silly child off on some errands, lady. We can speak about this, if you wish it.' Aldys took her hand and led her to the chair. 'I—' A knock interrupted whatever she was about to say.

Sybilla waited while Aldys saw to it. So many questions raced through her mind over the matter that she was surprised when Aldys spoke from right next to her. She placed something on the table and slid it closer.

'Lord Soren ordered this sent to you and commanded that you finish it.' The she-dragon was back in her voice.

'What is it?' she asked, reaching her hands along the table to find it. A tray. A bowl. A plate. Then the aromas spread. Food. He'd sent her food.

'A porridge in this bowl. Some meat on the plate. 'Tis torn into small pieces already,' Aldys reported, the surprise evident in her tone. 'Eat while we talk, lady. You will need your strength.' Aldys spoke as though all plans were in place while Sybilla remained uncertain of what was to come.

When she dropped the first morsel she picked up, Sybilla knew she would stain her clothing. Holding out her arms, she asked Aldys to pull the sleeves up the way Lord Soren had and to give her a cloth napkin. Once her garments were protected, she began to feel each plate and eat from them, now ignoring any misplaced food. 'So when did he speak of this to you?' she asked.

'The second night after you...' Aldys paused and Sybilla nodded her understanding. After she'd lost her mind in the hall. 'He moved his belongings in and—'

Sybilla dropped the bowl. 'His clothing is here?' A wave of chills rushed through her. 'He moved into my chambers?'

Aldys placed the bowl and spoon back into her hands. 'Aye, lady. When his men moved his trunk and other things here, he asked me to accompany him to the chapel. I thought it a strange thing, but his man Larenz was there as well.'

Aldys paused, but Sybilla had noticed a slight change in her voice when she mentioned this man Larenz. She nodded.

'He called it not a marriage contract, but an unmarriage contract when he told Father Medwyn of it. Keeping you as wife, blind or not, at your word. Offering a dowry if you seek the convent, offering to set up a household if not.'

'He told you these things?' Why? Why would he speak

of such private arrangements with her servant with the priest? 'What happened then?'

'Father Medwyn argued with him. Said the marriage could be annulled if you were blind, but there was no way to end it if there was no impediment. Lord Soren seemed convinced that you would end it either way and so he ordered the priest to write it down.'

She doubted that anyone could resist Lord Soren when he set his mind to something. 'He said that if you remained married to him for the next six months, the choice was yours and he would see to it.'

Sybilla sat back, leaving the food on the table. Stunned by such a thing and that he'd aired his intentions before the priest, his man and her maid… That was why he did it! She had not trusted him or his offer and so he made it a binding contract with her maid as witness so she would believe him. When she said nothing, Aldys continued.

'We waited while the priest wrote out two copies, complaining and even praying under his breath the whole time of it, and then the lord made his mark and ordered the priest to keep one and gave me the other.'

'You have it? Now?' she asked and then she realised the futility of it.

'It is safely stored, for you, if you have need of it,' she answered.

'He slept here these last nights?' she asked. The question came out of nowhere with no exact connection to their discussion, but in a way it did.

'Aye. 'Twas after I questioned him about his plans—'

'You did not! Aldys, he could have you put out!'

'He smiled in his way and told me to come to the chapel. And that is when he had the document drawn up.'

Aldys was a she-dragon and on Sybilla's behalf! She suspected that a man like Lord Soren respected strength even in a woman.

'He has moved in then?' she asked again, understanding the true meaning of such an action now.

He was keeping her as wife, at least for the next six months, and intended to claim his marital rights to her. She shivered, remembering the feel of his mouth on her skin and the heat it created. If that was only the beginning of joining, what would the rest of it feel like?

'Aye, my lady.' Aldys placed a cup of wine in her hands and Sybilla drank it down.

Filled with nervous anticipation, she could eat no more. But, considering the way he'd cared for her these last days, the protection he'd offered by making up a contract, and the way her body reacted to him, it was not the dread of their first days. Sybilla knew she faced a life of blindness, but Lord Soren had offered her some measure of choice in how she lived it. No matter how this turned out, her people and Alston would be protected.

'Aldys? Would you help me learn to walk down the stairs?'

She heard Aldys's muffled reply and knew the maid was crying now. So much for being a she-dragon. Sybilla felt her own tears, but brushed them away. She had too many things to do this day to waste time crying like a babe. She pushed back from the table and stood, ready to take the first step in learning how to live without her sight.

An hour or two later and countless times of going down and back up the steps, Sybilla returned to her chambers, exhausted from all of it. Though she had not held on to Guermont's arm or on to Aldys's, she still feared falling. Yet, if she took each step carefully, holding on to the rope as a guide and support, she could make it down to the bottom without falling or screaming the way she had the first time.

By the time she gave in to her exhaustion, a crowd had gathered in the hall and had begun cheering her on. Calls for her to be strong and not to be afraid echoed around her in the stairwell as she pushed on to conquer them and her fear. Their cheering and support gave her courage to keep trying and their applause when she reached the bottom warmed her heart.

Sitting in her chambers, while the servants brought in a meal she knew was for two, Sybilla realised that this was only the first task she must learn. There was so much about herself and her limitations she needed to discover before she could make any other decisions. The stairs had only been the first.

Lord Soren would be the second.

Chapter Eighteen

It felt good to be outside and to have the sun shining after these last days, he thought. Soren made his way to the end of the new wall to meet with Stephen and Guermont and hear news from Brice. But, even as he left Sybilla behind, his thoughts seemed to return to her.

Had she discovered his trunk in her chambers? Did she object? Did she even know he'd slept at her side these last four nights? His body reminded him of it again. Soren had touched her, cleaning her and applying salves to the bruises and cuts, but he was a man and did not miss the creaminess of her skin or the fullness of her breasts. Or the curve of her hips. Or the pale triangle at the top of her thighs.

He shifted in his breeches, trying to ease the seem-ingly ever-present erection he lived with. Never in his life had he gone this long wanting and not having a woman. There had been times and reasons not to share pleasure, but he'd never held back when he wanted a particular woman and she was available to him.

Now, he was married, he wanted his wife and would not take her. He knew better than most what she was experiencing right now and he would not put another burden on her shoulders. Her words spewed in anger and panic were true, none the less—he had caused her blindness. His reawakening conscience reminded him that he planned on capitalising on it. Both of those things gave him enough reasons not to seduce her, even though he knew he could. Her body was ready, even if her mind was not.

The monster her father had created was once again at war with the man he used to be. He could not win, no matter the outcome. For if she remained blind, she would want to leave after their bargain was completed. If her sight, by some slight chance, returned, she would never want to remain married to him once she saw his true form. And if she learned the true depths of his vengeance—that he had killed her father on that day when Durward had destroyed him, she would hate him for all her days, blind or sighted.

How the hell had his life sunk to this? Vengeance was so much simpler.

Stephen called his name, gaining his attention, and Soren joined them. Brice's messenger had arrived and told them of the increased attacks by the rebels and that they seemed to be originating to the west. The Pennines, named by the ancient Romans when they controlled these lands, separated his lands from those in Cumbria and seemed to be the hiding place for Edmund's forces.

After neglecting his duties for these last days to see

to Sybilla's care, Soren decided to lead a small group of his men to search in the nearby hills for evidence of Edmund Haroldson or his rebels. They had plenty of daylight available and it would feel good to be carrying out the one duty William gave him in exchange for these lands…and her—find and destroy anyone not loyal to him, be they Saxon, Norman or whatever.

When he'd found the rolls of the manor, Soren noticed that some not known to be dead, but who belonged to the manor, were missing. Not many, but another two this week added made the total a noticeable one. His men and those who'd remained behind in Shildon until Brice arrived would give him enough bodies to keep the manor operating and safe, but he knew that allowing or ignoring the escape of those bound to him and the land would send a bad message and encourage others to follow. As long as Edmund was preaching his message of insurrection against William, there would be those willing to risk escape and the punishment if caught for the chance at some vague glory.

Harold Godwinson, who'd held these lands and more across the south, was dead and buried. Most of William's enemies had been neutralised or at least identified. William could not yet take on the king of the Scots, but he wanted the path to Scotland made difficult for those who would seek help from there. Soren needed to begin that in earnest.

He called for his horse, mounted and followed Stephen out of the gates and along the path that led to the hills. As they rode higher along the trails, he stopped and looked back and down on Alston. The keep appeared small from this distance, the outline of the wall barely visible. The fields spread out around it in a patchwork of colours and crops. To the north lay the land of the Scots. To the far east, Northumbria and the sea. To the west, Cumbria and the Irish Sea. But these below were his.

And no one would take them from him.

Hours later, the sun had set and they rode by the light of the full moon back to Alston. The smell of cooked food greeted his approach to the hall, as did Larenz with news of his wife.

'What did you find in the hills?' Larenz asked as they walked together from the yard after Soren handed his horse off to those overseeing the stables…including Raed, it seemed.

'Remains of several camps, though none large. Stephen will go back during the day to have a better look around. The ones we found were miles from here,' Soren reported.

'Do you think Edmund has arrived here? Will he make a stand here with the Scots at his back?'

Soren shrugged as they walked inside. 'His actions make no sense. He does not have the support of those on the Witan who yet live.' Most nobles of Harold's court had died on Senlac field. 'Their Atheling was chosen since he has the strongest claim,' Soren said. 'Even if Edmund can claim a blood connection to his father,' he added, exchanging a knowing glance with Larenz.

Edgar's claim was even stronger than William's, but as a boy of but fourteen, Edgar stood no chance against the Duke of Normandy and his war machine. As a son of Harold by his unsanctioned wife in the Danish manner, Edmund had no claim on the English throne. That had not stopped him from gathering together a small army in Wessex where his father's lands were and where they would prefer any of the Godwinsons to an outsider and marching northwards, creating chaos and killing along the way.

Edmund had nearly sold Giles's wife to a Welsh lord in exchange for money and men. Then he'd allied himself with Oremund of Shildon and tried to take control of Brice's lands in Thaxted. Now, he was using Alston as a pathway north. But Edmund would have to go through Soren to get there and Soren was determined to stop him.

'Is supper done, then?' Soren asked as he watched benches and pallets being placed in the hall for the coming night.

'Aye,' Larenz said, clapping him on the back. 'But Aldys says the lady saved yours for you before retiring for the night.' Larenz laughed then. 'One of the benefits of having a wife, eh?'

Soren felt a very physical disappointment, realising that Sybilla had sought her bed already. She must be exhausted on this, her first day out of bed in the last five.

'The lady caused quite a commotion just after you left, Soren.'

Soren turned and glared at the man. He was being goaded into something and Soren hated being goaded. 'Just tell me, old man.'

'The lady decided to master the steps on her own.'

Soren would have lost any meal he'd eaten in that moment. He thought his knees might have gone weak, for he stumbled before righting himself. Sybilla had been wobbly just standing next to her bed this morn and had no reason to think she could walk down the stairway unassisted. He had taken several paces in the direction of those stairs before Larenz grabbed him by the arm and pulled him to a stop.

'You would have been proud of her, Soren. As stubborn as you when faced with a challenge.'

'Did she fall?' he asked, afraid of the answer. He'd wanted her out of her chambers, but not…not…

'They cheered her on, her people did, once they saw her struggling with her fears. It made this old man's heart glad to witness it.'

'You watched it? Her?' Soren asked.

'I thought I should be here if she needed help. Aldys sent word to me before she left her chambers, so I was here watching. The lady would not give up. The people knew it, too.'

'Sybilla is asleep now?'

'Aye. Aldys put your food aside to stay warm and settled the lady in her bed before leaving her,' Larenz reported.

The old man and the she-dragon. It shocked him, but he'd seen stranger connections and couples. 'Any other news to report?'

'She said she'd like to try walking the yard on the morrow.'

Soren shook his head at Larenz's failed attempt at humour and walked to those same steps that Sybilla had faced. He could only imagine the terror she had felt—most likely the same he felt the first time he had to defend himself in battle after his recovery. A small skirmish, but it was Senlac field relived for him and he fully expected the death-blow at any moment.

She would survive this, he knew that now. If she'd regained her courage or had begun the process, she would be able to face whatever came at her in the future, with or without him. He reached the door and lifted the latch as quietly as he could.

A lamp had been left burning and he could see her in the bed in the corner. He closed the door and removed his hauberk, deciding he would need to leave that somewhere else the next time. Though flexible, it was a noisy thing to remove and he hoped he'd not disturbed her. Although, mayhap if she stirred… He hardened at the thought, making it difficult to remove his breeches, but he did. His tunic and hood followed.

There was a basin and a jug of water, so he poured some and washed his face and hands. Then, as he reached for the bottom of his shirt, he thought better of it. If their bodies touched in the night, he did not want her to feel the ridges of scarred flesh on his back. At least the linen of his shirt would prevent that. Soren walked to the side of the bed and watched her sleep.

Her hair lay spread around her head like a pale cloud. Other women braided their hair for bed, but she did not—it seemed she preferred to leave it loose. Soren noticed his palms sweating at the thought of stroking it with his fingers. He was so busy watching her expressions in sleep that he banged his leg into the table as he stepped nearer and cursed.

'Lord Soren?' she asked in a voice husky with sleep.

'Aye, Sybilla. Go back to sleep,' he said, hoping and praying she would…would not… *Merde!*

'Did you eat? Aldys said your meal is by the hearth to keep it warm.'

She began to sit up and only grabbed the covers at the last moment, but not soon enough to keep from gifting him with an arousing view of her breasts. Truly, in that moment, the only thing he wanted in his mouth was her tongue or one of those pert breasts. Heat poured through him, his heart raced and his blood surged through his body.

'Nay,' he said, trying to keep his voice even.

If she said the wrong thing, something that sounded vaguely welcoming, he would probably be between her thighs before she knew what had happened. He took in a couple of deep breaths and released them, trying to hold on to the scant control he felt slipping away.

'How are your injuries?' he asked. Good. Think about those bruises, he told himself. She had lain unconscious for nigh on four days, waking just this morn. What kind of perverse monster would bed a woman who was still recovering?

Soren felt the beads of sweat gathering on his upper lip from the effort not to touch her. He reached out for her several times, but always managed to draw back at the moment just before he touched her skin. Losing the battle within himself, he took a couple of paces away from the bedside.

'Whatever was in Teyen's brew helped. By later this afternoon, I felt well enough to conquer the stairs!' she told him. He knew this already, but to hear the enthusiasm in her voice, something that had been missing since he arrived here, pushed him closer to the point of no return. 'I did it, Soren,' she exclaimed, pushing her hair back over her shoulders and giving him a clear view of her graceful neck. 'I walked the stairs by myself!'

Had she just called him by name? He rubbed his forehead and tried to count to two score. Thankfully it had not been in that breathy voice with all its wonderful sexual undertones that spoke of passion and pleasure and desire. If she spoke to him with that voice, he would… he would…disgrace himself like an untried boy. Soren turned away, deciding that eating would be a good idea right now.

'Soren?' she said quietly. 'Lord Soren?' she repeated. Her voice was getting closer and closer to the one that would make him explode.

'Aye, Sybilla? I am going to eat.'

He found the pot left by the she-dragon and used a cloth from the table to lift it from the hearth. Lifting the lid of it, he found a stew with a crust over it. The aroma filled the chamber.

And her stomach growled loud enough for both of them to hear.

Sybilla laughed then, and he gripped the table to keep from going back to her and kissing her breathless.

'I confess, I did not eat much supper this evening.'

He gave in to the inevitable in that moment—and that was that he was destined to be tortured for the next six months by the woman he called wife. 'Come,' he said as he walked to the bed and took her hand. He grabbed the *syrce* hanging on the corner of the headboard and gave it to her.

Soon, they were both at the table and sharing the meal

he'd planned them to share earlier. He scooped out half of
the stew into one of the cups meant for the wine, crushed
up the crust into the gravy and gave her a spoon. Then
Soren ate out of the pot. He had never developed a refined
sense of taste, but he knew good food and he knew bad.
Alston's cook was good.

Either they were both very hungry or they were both
simply trying not to talk, for soon he noticed they both
scraped the bottom of their makeshift bowls. He placed
the cup that held the wine in her hands and guided it
to her mouth, holding it while she drank from it. He
lifted it back before she'd finished and so a drop of wine
remained perched on the edge of her lip, threatening to
spill on her *syrce* if she did not catch it. Soren had slid
to his knees next to her before he even knew it.

He caught it with his tongue just as it rolled down her
lip, and then he took her mouth as he'd been dreaming
of for days. With a hand on the chair at her back and the
other on the table, he did not touch her but for her mouth.
Soren would have stopped, but she sighed against his lips
and touched his arm. Slanting his face, he kissed her
again, deepening it to encourage another sigh from her.

And she gifted him with another, never moving away
from his mouth as he stole her breath. Soren slipped an
arm behind her and the other under her knees and lifted
her into his arms, carrying her to the bed without taking
his mouth from hers. When he felt the bedside with his
legs, he paused and did lift back from her then.

'Are you afraid?' he asked, just as he had before.
Somehow now, the thought of her being afraid of him
did not sit well with him.

She nodded, a quick one, and then her lips trembled.

'Can you trust me? Will you trust me?'

He would have sworn that she was gazing directly at him in that moment. Her sightless eyes seemed to look even into his soul. Sorèn held his breath, waiting for heaven or hell.

Chapter Nineteen

'I think I do trust you, Soren.'

Sybilla was not afraid, she was terrified. Remembering his size and his fierceness, she prayed he would not tear her asunder if he lost control of his passion. All of the gossip overheard came flooding back to her and she shivered in his arms. Mayhap if she could see him, it would not be scary, but having no way of knowing what he would do added to her fears.

'I will have a care,' he whispered to her.

And that was the answer, she thought. This man, though sworn to destroy her, had instead seen to her welfare, caring for her through the day and night. He could have taken what he now asked for, inflicting himself on her flesh, but he waited and he asked.

Sybilla nodded her consent, expecting him to throw her on the bed and take her. Instead, he kissed again as he laid her down before him. She did not know what to do, what he expected of her now, so she asked.

'What should I do?'

He laughed then, a rich, deep, full laugh that was both appealing and wicked at the same time. It sent chills through her, but also caused a rush of heat to flood through her body with each beat of her heart.

'Let me pleasure you.'

Her body shook now at the seductive promise in those words and in his voice. Then he kissed her again and she let him, opening her mouth to accept his touch and to taste him. Sybilla felt her body opening and warming with each second that passed. When he tugged on the laces keeping her *syrce* closed at her neck, loosening and opening it widely, she gasped.

She wished she could see his face, to see if he was pleased by what he saw now. Her breasts were unremarkable, but larger than some of the other women in Alston. Did they please him?

He ran the back of his hand over her skin, first at her neck, then over her shoulder and on to her breast. Slow and steady, he skimmed over the tip of one and then down and down until he reached her belly. She could not breathe as he touched her so. Then he began anew on the other side, touching, teasing, caressing her until she gasped and arched against his hand.

He climbed over her then, not between her legs, but placing her between his. Then, with a murmured apology that did not sound regretful at all, he took the edges of her *syrce* and tore it open all the way. Cool air moved over her skin, raising gooseflesh, but not for long. His mouth replaced his hand on her skin and soon she was burning with a fever from inside and out.

Sybilla ached for something, something, some touch

or kiss he had not gifted her with yet, but she knew he
would. When she tried to reach up and touch his face,
he placed her hands on the bed. 'Let me,' he urged and
she allowed him his way.

Lord Soren moved over her, kissing and licking a path
over every inch of her skin. But when he took the tip
of her breast in his mouth—did he truly do that?—and
suckled on it, she thought she might have screamed. His
mouth was hot, his tongue rough as he rubbed across and
around the sensitive tip over and over until she trembled
with the pleasure of it. When he used his teeth, worrying
them over it and scraping it gently, she did scream.

His mouth swallowed the sounds, covering hers and
possessing it until she quieted. Then he moved back
down and tormented the other in the same way. Only that
wicked laugh met her pleas for more. All the while, something deep inside her began to tighten with every stroke
of his tongue or nip of his mouth. The place between
her legs, one she rarely noticed before his arrival and
attention, grew wet and throbbed as he moved his mouth
now down on to her belly. It ached and seemed to have
its own beat that matched the pace of her racing heart.

She felt him slide down away from her and thought
it might end soon, but he was not done. Her body wept,
the core of her readied for what she knew would happen
soon—he would pierce her maidenhead and spill his
seed. But no one had told her of the pleasure that could
exist between a husband and wife. He eased her legs apart
and used his hands to tease her thighs. She felt him open
her legs now and kneel between them and waited to feel
him push inside her.

Sybilla knew he was a large man—the difference in

their height gave her pause. Could this work between them? Could he fit inside her? But instead of his manhood, she felt his finger slip between her legs and ease into that place. The moan escaped before she could stop it.

'Easy, Sybilla,' he whispered. He moved to her side now and lifted one of her legs up to rest over his, leaving that private part of her open to his touch. He stroked down her leg and into the folds, now slick with her body's wetness. He placed his palm on the curls and pressed down, making something throb over and over. Then he curled his fingers and used them against something buried in that flesh to make her body explode under his touch.

She grabbed his arm then and arched against his long fingers, which he slipped inside her. Sybilla could only let her body react and it did—wave upon wave of pleasure crashed over her even as he relentlessly stroked her to more and more. She felt the spasms deep within that flesh tighten around his fingers and every muscle in her body contracted and shook with the power of these sensations.

She lost any sense of herself for a moment of time that seemed to go on and on. Only when she felt the tears trickling down her face and the tremors still echoing deep inside her body did she know she was conscious.

'What was that?' she asked, not understanding what had happened. Then that part of him moved against her hip, confusing her even more.

'That was pleasure,' he said, without taking his hand from its intimate caress. He kissed the tears from her cheeks.

She felt as though she had run for miles and miles. It took several minutes to catch her breath, even while small waves of pleasure rippled in her body and through her blood. Her breasts swelled and their tips tightened even still.

'Are we done? You have not—' She stopped then because he moved his fingers ever so slightly within her flesh.

'No, I have not,' he said. Then he moved his fingers again and she gasped.

'What are you doing?'

'More, Sybilla, I am doing more.'

And he did until she thought she could not take another kiss or caress and stroke of his tongue or his fingers anywhere on her body. He moved her body as he wanted, moving from her side to over her to behind her. Then when she could not scream again, when her body seemed to float on this cloud of euphoria and passion, he spread her legs and pushed inside her.

And at each instant when she thought it was too much, he stroked her again, easing his way in until she was filled with him. And when she thought it over, he withdrew and stroked against her swollen flesh until he found his way back in. He slid his arm beneath her, lifting and arching her up so he could suckle on her breasts. Unable to resist anything he did, Sybilla gave herself over to him and let him have his way with her until she had nothing left to give him.

Then, she felt him harden more and thicken within her and knew he would spill his seed now. At that last moment, as her body reached yet another peak she had not thought possible, he pulled back and she felt his hot seed spill beneath her. Unable to do anything or move anything, she lay in his arms replete and exhausted. He gathered her close and whispered one word in his language over and over.

Sybilla felt sleep claiming her and realised that he'd never removed his shirt.

The lady snored.

Soren smiled as he thought of all the other sounds she made tonight. The sound of her sighing was his favourite, especially when she was not even aware she did it. He eased the torn shift from her, wiped his seed from their skin and tossed it on the floor. Then, drawing the bedcovers up over them, Soren tried to sleep.

He would not, he knew, get any sleep this night, not with her pressed against his side and his cock ready to pleasure her again. The way he had taken her, pleasured her until she passed out, guaranteed she would not be ready again soon. Soren had always thought that a woman of experience offered more spirited bedplay, but after this night in Sybilla's bed, he had changed his mind on the matter.

A siren disguised as a virgin. That was his wife. An innocent, ignorant of the pleasures of the flesh, who took to it with an honest and genuine curiosity and sought to enjoy what he did rather than pretend to delicacy. When she'd responded to his first caresses so fully, he'd sworn to take his time, to draw it out as much as he could so that she did not feel cheated when the pleasure faded from the pain of having her maidenhead breached. From the way she cried out and urged him on, they had both received a full measure of satisfaction from their joining.

She mumbled then in her sleep and her body arched against him as though reliving the moment of release and he prayed for restraint…again. He wondered if she would wake the demure innocent embarrassed by what they'd done or if she would want to experience it again with him. There was so much more he could show her in the ways of loving—Soren only hoped she was interested. If not, he would honour her refusal, but not happily.

He drifted off to sleep at some time in the night and woke as he mostly did—hard and readied. And she slept on, unknowing his condition and his unsatisfied desire for her.

Soren thought about this unusual level of wanting a woman before. It had been months after he was struck down before he even had a sexual urge and then, looking as he did, 'twas easier to pay a few coins to a woman willing to oblige him with a few minutes of attention. In war there were always camp followers who appreciated the coins or trinkets he could pay.

But once he'd left the king's quarters for the north and Giles's lands and then Brice's, he stopped that, unwilling for them to know how bad it was for him. By then, the pitying looks and sidelong glances bothered him and he did nothing that would expose him to more of those.

Then, one look at her, standing up for her people, offering herself in their place, accepting his need for vengeance, and he was lost in wanting and needing her.

Soren felt better about their bargain now—he knew that his offer was giving her the time she needed to regain herself and to learn the skills she would need to live blind and it was helping him in a number of ways. A temporary arrangement and one that would be over before anyone got hurt or wanted something from the other that could never be. Once she left him, he would find some other comfortable arrangement, with some woman eager to please the lord of Alston and make no comments about him or claims on him.

With the rebels scattered and Harold dead, Alston would be at peace and his life would settle to something bearable.

So, if all that was sorted out and all his plans made, why could he swear he heard Gautier laughing in the dark of the night? And why did he wake not to the soft sighs he craved but to screams and the sounds of an attack out in the yard?

Chapter Twenty

Soren was dressed and heading down the stairs before he even thought about ordering Sybilla to stay in the keep. She was not new at this, she would know to stay inside, much as he'd ordered done when the Saxon lords approached that day. With Stephen calling out orders in the yard, Guermont directing the people into the keep, and his men moving into defensive positions along the wall, Soren knew she would know and went on about the business of protecting Alston from whomever had launched this attack.

He ran to the stables to make certain they were ready in case of flaming arrows and found everything in position there. Larenz had ordered Raed to protect the lady in the keep, which kept him out of the line of fire. Unable to get to the wall, Soren could not tell where the attack was coming from. Once the people were inside, he would be able to focus on what he did best—fighting. The only ones left to be secured were their prisoners and Soren could see some of them resisting his men's orders to get on the ground where they would not be moving targets or in the way of his men's aim either. Running to them, he heard his name being called.

'Soren! Lord Soren!' Gareth called out even as one of Soren's men hit him and knocked him to the ground. 'Unchain us. Let us fight,' he yelled. When he tried to gain his feet, he was knocked down again. 'These are my people, our people, too. Let us defend them.'

Soren was torn. He could use more good fighting men, but dared he trust these Saxons to fight against other Saxons? Would they help or hinder him and his men? Soren caught Larenz's gaze. With but a raised brow, he had Larenz's opinion of the situation, so Soren nodded to Stephen. Some of his men looked as though they would argue, but they had been through the war with him and knew better than to disagree during a battle. With little delay, the men were released, given swords and ordered to spread around the yard in case the gate and the wall were breached.

After being caught unaware, it took a short time for Soren to regroup and begin to fight back in an effective way. He ordered his best bowmen to the top of the keep to seek out where they were being attacked from. Then, as he feared and expected, the arrows sent over the walls were flaming and aimed at the wooden outbuildings. The freed prisoners began fighting the fires that sprang up by passing buckets of water from the well and several horse troughs to wherever it was needed.

He thought they were getting the situation under control when he heard a commotion begin near the door into the keep. Soren could not believe the sight before him.

Sybilla ran out into the yard and then stopped. Too far from the keep and not far enough to be grabbed by one of his men, she stood there in the middle ground, a clear target for anyone firing into the yard.

Holy Christ! he thought as he jumped to the ground from the wall, praying his ankles survived the landing. Then he yelled and ran, trying to come between her and the path of the arrows. At least his hauberk and helm would give him some protection, but she had neither. He was still yards and yards away from her when it happened.

The arrow came over his left shoulder and took her down.

Time seemed to slow to a crawl for him then, no matter how fast he tried to run to her, his steps sluggish and dragging. Everyone watched in horror as the sleeve of her gown burst into flames, but no one could reach her. Just as he heard her scream, someone collided with her, taking her down to the ground and beating at the flames. Sybilla's gown yet smouldered when he reached her, so he tore the burning sleeve from it and threw it aside. He plucked Raed from the ground and flung him towards the keep's door where Larenz managed to get to the boy and get him inside.

Soren scooped Sybilla into his arms and ran, using his body to shield her from any more arrows. Once inside the keep, he handed her off to Aldys and left. As he reached the wall again, Soren heard a familiar battle cry from the woods where the attack seemed centred. Brice's men had arrived. Warriors on horseback, they burst from the shadows, chasing an assortment of the attackers. They stood no chance if caught so they ran, not yet realising that they had no chance of escape from the skilled warriors.

Though Soren would have liked one captured alive, he also wanted them dead. Brice's men obliged him without even asking and then rode in pursuit of any who escaped through the woods or up into the hills. Soren remained inside the gates, wary of a secondary attack and helping to manage the fires and the damage wrought. Several men had been wounded and needed to be tended and moved inside.

The stables' and the chapel's wooden roofs seemed to have been spared while most of the storage barns' had burned. None of the horses had been injured. Once things outside were under control, Soren waited for Brice's return before heading inside.

There was another reason he hesitated. Soren thought his heart had stopped when he saw Sybilla standing out, a clear target, and he could not reach her in time. Then when she was felled by the arrow, he felt a fear unlike any he'd experienced before. Not even facing death himself felt like that.

And he would kill her himself for making him feel that terror.

Brice approached the gates and called out to Soren. The gates were opened to allow him and his men to enter and closed immediately. Until he was certain the area was clear, Soren would keep them closed. There were many questions about how this surprise attack had happened and he would not rest until he knew the answers and could prevent another such attack.

'Tell me you were not abed enjoying the favours of

your new wife when this happened,' Brice said, as he walked up to Soren.

He nodded at the others he knew and then turned his attention back to Soren, who waited for the inevitable. He did not acknowledge the question nor the rightness of his suspicions, but met Brice's gaze. For a moment neither one moved, then Brice stepped closer and grabbed Soren and hugged him.

''Tis where I would have been, if I'd been home,' he whispered and they laughed together. 'I sent one of my men ahead to let you know of our arrival and he told us of the attack. We thought we could help.'

Soren knew, and Brice must as well, that his arrival was the difference between losing much of what they'd only just rebuilt and probably more in casualties and injured. And though they might have fought off this wave, a second or third one would see them compromised and vulnerable.

'Is this all of your men?' Soren asked, peering across the yard at the newly arrived men who were already assisting where they could. He saw many renewing acquaintances with some of his men. Many had served together before and were friends or even family.

'Nay. I left ten more with the carts a few miles back,' Brice replied, nodding back at the road. 'Gillian insisted,' he explained, holding his hands up to deny accountability. 'You saw to reclaiming Shildon for her, us.'

Supplies, Soren imagined. Foodstuffs, fabric and more. All the things Gillian had asked him about before he set off on the orders of the bishop to aid Brice in retaking his wife's inherited lands from her half-brother's control.

'My thanks for whatever you bring, and my thanks

to your wife for sharing your bounty,' Soren said with a bow of his head, acknowledging the gifts. It would give them a measure of comfort and aid Sybilla's efforts to keep their stores filled.

Sybilla.

'There is a gift for your wife among the packages as well. Gillian worried that…'

Brice did not have to explain. They had expected to receive news that he'd killed her when they arrived, so the news that he had married her was a surprise to all who knew him and his plans.

'The gift may be premature,' Soren said, motioning for Brice to follow him into the keep. 'She may yet be dead by my hand.'

Brice laughed loudly and Soren did not doubt that he'd heard the story already from one of his men. They entered to find the keep and those inside almost calm and orderly. Now that the danger was past, most knew to go back to their normal duties, but a crowd yet milled around in the centre of the large room.

Soren knew who was at the centre and he made his way there, pushing those who did not move from his path. His hands were shaking by the time he found her, there, sitting on a chair. Her face had no colour in it, she was paler than death and she trembled, holding her hand over a place on her other arm that must have been burned by the arrow. She looked terrible and wonderful at the same time. Angered by his own response, Soren felt his control snap.

'What in hell did you think you were doing, Sybilla?' he yelled. Moving closer now that the crowd scattered, he continued, 'What were you thinking? Running into the yard during an attack?'

The words were out before he realised that she flinched as though he struck her with each word spoken. Her face blanched more and she pressed back against the chair as he walked towards her. Torn in that moment between taking her in his arms and admitting the terror he had experienced when she was hit right before him or strangling her for daring too much too soon, he settled for another order. 'Go to your chambers and await me there.'

Raed stood at her side, glaring—glaring!—at him as he ordered her gone. The boy had saved her life and prevented serious injury by his quick actions that day. Soren would excuse the mutinous expression this once and sent him off with Sybilla.

'Take the lady to her chambers, boy.'

Soren tried not to notice the way her hand shook when she placed it on Raed's shoulder, or the way she stumbled as she walked behind him on the way to the stairs. Complete and utter silence reigned as all present watched her leave. Another minute passed before anyone spoke. He'd thought it would be Brice who would rebuke him for such behaviour, or even Larenz, who could and would do it wordlessly and with only a pointed expression.

He had never expected it to be delivered by someone else—someone who never had learned to keep his mouth shut and who Soren had hoped to never see again.

'Well done, cousin,' Tristan le Breton called out from his place at the door. 'Very well done of you!'

Soren was coming to like a particular Saxon epithet and it worked well in situations like this one. He said it aloud, in fact, loud enough that everyone in the hall heard the word and then, content in knowing that Brice would handle anything that needed attention for him, he stormed up the stairs to find his wife.

Sybilla barely made it to her chambers. Even leaning heavily on Raed, each step was nearly impossible for her. He led her up the stairs and down the corridor to her room. She heard Aldys rushing up behind her and heard her gasp, probably as she saw the torn gown and burned flesh on her arm.

'Get her inside, lad,' she ordered. 'I will fetch supplies and see to her arm.'

The she-dragon was back, Sybilla thought as she fell onto the bed where Raed led her.

'My lady,' the boy whispered, 'he did not mean it.' He touched her hand and squeezed it. 'He was just afraid for you, like we all were. He—' Raed stopped and dropped her hand.

His reaction meant only one thing.

'Give me those and get out.'

She pushed herself back and up against the headboard of the bed as she heard his heavy footsteps come closer. Rubbing the tears from her eyes, she would have tried to explain. But to do that, she had to be able to explain why she'd done it and she could not. So, she sat in silence, waiting for whatever he'd come here to do to her in punishment for her rash, and foolish, act.

He dropped whatever he carried on the table at the bedside and she jumped at the sound of it. Lord Soren took her hand and, not knowing what to expect from him, she found herself shocked by the gentleness of his touch.

Lord Soren lifted her arm and peeled off the remnants of her *syrce*, easing it off the burned skin, but he muttered under his breath, and loud enough for her to hear, the whole time. 'Twas clear to her that he preferred his own tongue when angry and she was glad not to understand much of it. Every so often he used some English words with great vehemence—those she could understand and flinched at them.

Women, she understood. *Wives*, as well. Then *stupid*, *foolish*, *does not listen*, *orders*, *commands*, *disobeys*, *stupid* again, *invincible*, and he finished with something that seemed to compare her to a horse.

He never paused, tending to her injury or muttering, as he cleaned the burn, applied some unguent to it and wrapped a bandage around it. Only when he was tying it off and she winced did he slow his pace or stop cursing at her. Then he stopped and she waited.

'Why, Sybilla? What made you do such a thing?' he asked and it was the quiet tone that was her undoing.

'I...' She shook her head. How could she explain such a thing to him? 'I did not think, Lord Soren,' she began, shaking her head. 'I...'

How could she tell of her confusion? When the sounds of screaming woke them and he had left her chamber, calling out orders to everyone, she had just wanted to help. Aldys had dressed her quickly and they had made their way down to the main hall. Sybilla had intended to help with the children, and only went to the door when she heard Soren calling out orders to his men to release the prisoners.

How could she tell him the truth of the matter?

His finger slid beneath her chin and he lifted her face as though to meet his gaze.

'You what, Sybilla? You…?'

Now that she knew he would not mock her, she thought back to what had happened and answered him truthfully.

'I forgot,' she admitted. 'I forgot I could not see.'

She waited for him to laugh at such a thing. She waited for him to insult her for such a foolish *and* stupid thing to think or to say aloud. But he did neither. Instead, he astonished her.

'I'd barely risen from the sickbed when I was called on to defend myself in a skirmish,' he said. 'Out of habit, I drew my sword and waded into the worst of it, prepared to fight the way I had before.'

He laughed then and moved back away. She listened to his steps.

'I forgot I had not lifted my battle sword in months. I forgot that the muscles I needed to lift the sword had been cleaved nearly in pieces and were not healed yet. I forgot,' he said, but his words drifted off as though he thought of that skirmish and those wounds once more.

'What happened?' she asked, not able to stop her curiosity about him.

'Larenz saved my arse,' he replied, laughing again. 'And he taught me that I needed to learn basic things first before I could go back to what I had been.'

He understood because he had lived it. Strange that she'd never noticed the similarities in their lives before.

'Now, what did you hear that made you react in such haste that you forgot your blindness?' She felt his body as he sat next to her on the edge of the bed and she shifted her legs to accommodate him. When he placed his hand on her leg, she tried to imagine it was the normal custom between a man and his wife. They'd been intimate after all, his hand on her leg meant nothing.

'Did someone say something that drew your attention or caused you concern in that very moment?' he asked.

She forced her attention to his question and away from the way her leg heated and tingled under his hand. Away from the memory of how he had caressed her skin in that same spot just hours ago. Naked. In this very bed. Naked. Sybilla swallowed and tried to answer him.

'Sybilla?'

'I heard Gareth call to you. I was standing near to the door and it was yet open and I heard him ask you to release him.'

'Which I did. But that is not when you ran into the yard.'

She'd sworn not to betray her people, but telling him the truth would, to an extent, do exactly that. The only thing that safeguarded her promise was that she could not identify who said the words to her.

'In the confusion, someone rushed past me and claimed that they would rid me of my bastard Norman husband.'

'Breton.'

'Pardon?'

'I am your bastard Breton husband,' he explained.

Why did men seem to pick up on the absurd and obscure things and miss the main point she was trying to make? She'd run out to warn him that he was the target of this attack and had forgotten she could not see. Before she could point this out to him, he kissed her, fiercely and possessively, until she lost her breath. Her head spun by the time he lifted his mouth from hers, but she ached for more.

'Certainly I was the target. You were struck by accident, but the attack was against me. Killing you would do them no good, for I will simply bring a good Norman bride here and breed loyal Norman heirs.'

Which was exactly what he would do when she left in six months. But for now, she wanted to scream. He knew? Men!

'I am thankful that you wanted to tell me, but next time, think about the matter before placing yourself in danger like that.' All she could do was nod in agreement. It was difficult to believe she either would forget again or would need to warn him of danger.

'If you are comfortable now, I must go,' he said. His footsteps led to the door and she said his name. There was one matter she needed to ask him about before he left.

'Gareth and the others, Lord Soren? Will you put them back in chains now?' she asked, fearing the answer and fearing the repercussions of such an act with many outside Alston whom she knew watched this new Norman lord and how he treated his people.

'I will come to an agreement with them to serve me as their lord,' he explained.

'And you would accept their word in such a bond?' she asked. His sigh surprised her.

'Why must you judge me as the rest do?' he asked. But before she could explain about the news that had come to her from other villages and the rebels seeking new recruits, he explained his actions—something he'd not done before. 'I will accept their oaths and as long as they do not prove otherwise by their actions, they will be freed from their chains to live with their families.'

In truth, it was more than they could have expected from him.

'Now, rest a while here and let that salve do its work. I must go and thank Raed for his quick action and see to our guests.'

'Guests?' she squeaked. 'We have guests?' Had they heard his rebuke of her?

'Brice has arrived, which was good timing, and he brings gifts from his wife to us and to you,' he said. 'And my cousin accompanies him. Tristan le Breton, he is called.'

The undertones of his voice spoke of dislike.

'Is this Tristan a problem for you, Lord Soren?'

'An annoyance more than a problem, I think. But he is family, though a distant relation.' The latch on the door lifted. 'Sybilla, when you feel strong enough to show your face in the hall below, wear a contrite expression and let them believe I beat you. I have a reputation to uphold and a disobedient wife whom I have not disciplined will surely ruin it.'

He was teasing her and acknowledging what was said and believed about him, even by her. She settled back against the pillows and wondered about his comments. But no sooner had she relaxed back than the door opened once more.

'Sybilla?'

'Aye, Lord Soren?'

'Two matters before I go. The first is that I think you should concern yourself with learning and familiarising yourself with the inside of the keep before you venture to learn the outside. Organise this chamber, for example, to make it easier for you to move around it and find things.'

'An excellent suggestion, Lord Soren.' And it was. 'The second matter?'

He strode towards her, decisively and directly. Had it been earlier, she would have feared his intent. Now, she felt anticipation surge through her body and heat in her blood.

'I told you to call me by name and you consistently disobey me.' His mouth was hot against hers and his tongue tasted hers and teased her with memories of last night. 'Tonight I will teach you the cost of such disobedience.'

Her bones melted and she had to fight to remain sitting upright. She ached deep within at the sexual tone he used.

'You will?'

He kissed her then and his hands wandered over her body, touching, teasing, tempting her and giving her a reminder of how he could control her in ways she could not even conceive of yet.

'Tonight I will have you crying my name out and moaning it as I pleasure you until you beg me to take you. You will learn my name this night,' he promised.

He was as good as his word and he did as he said he would. Throughout that night, he made her cry out his name and moan it in the back of her throat, and scream it as he gave her pleasure and release countless times. And, as he'd warned or promised or threatened, he made her beg him using it—for more, for no more and for whatever he wanted to do to her.

By morning she had learned much about that other reputation he carried from before Hastings and she understood why women of all kinds would seek his bed night after night.

And when nightfall approached that next day, her body readied itself for more of him and even thinking of his name made her ache for what she knew he would do.

Chapter Twenty-One

Sybilla took Soren's advice and remained mostly inside the keep over those next few days. She marvelled that she could function during the days after spending her nights completely in the power of the passion he roused in her. She would find herself drifting off in the middle of speaking to her maids when something reminded her of what he'd done or said or *made her do*.

The only thing prohibited between them was that he did not allow her to touch him the way he touched her. She only felt his body when he moved over her or pressed against her from behind or when he pulled her close as they slept. But each time she reached out to caress his face, he brushed her hands away.

She had managed to brush her hand against his manhood once and he did not seem to mind that. And during one bout of pleasure she slipped her hands around and caressed his…bottom! Sybilla felt overheated and asked Gytha to seek out some cool water for her.

Aldys laughed, but it was a knowing laugh, one based on a common experience. Gytha was young enough to be innocent of the details about what truly happened between men and women, so Sybilla tried to spare her.

They'd spent most of the last two days rearranging the furniture of her chamber so that she could move more easily around it, as he'd suggested. He'd told her not to put anything in the corner nearest the door, for he had a surprise for her, but gave no word of what it was or when she would find out.

They established a sort of routine over these last days, since Lord Brice arrived. Though neither she nor Soren would eat with others, preferring to use the privacy of her chambers alone for that, they did sit at table in the hall and enjoy the company. Though Soren remained aloof and distant from the others, Sybilla liked it. None too happy over having some of his past exploits described to her by his friend and his cousin, still Soren did not put a stop to such talk.

She could hear things in people's voices that she never noticed before—fear, anger, even softer feelings. Even though they never expressed it, there was much of the latter between Larenz and Lord Brice and Soren when they spoke to each other. Clearly, they'd shared much of their lives with each other, so it felt right to her. Of course, they would deny such things if she pointed them out, so she did not, keeping them to herself and learning more and more about these men who had invaded her home and, she feared, her heart.

Tristan le Breton was different. Though Soren admitted to a family connection, this cousin seemed to revel in the fact that Soren no longer was as attractive as she'd heard he'd been. He claimed to have come north to seek a place in Soren's household, earning his place by serving as harpist and scribe, since he could read and write. There was tension between them over that, as well, for she'd learned that Soren, like many warriors of his kind, could not.

Sybilla could tell that Soren itched to throw Tristan out or send him back with Brice when he left, but something prevented him from doing so. One good thing had occurred—Tristan had offered to teach her to play the harp. He said she did not need to see the strings, only feel her way along them, so she looked forward to her first lesson.

Soren had growled under his breath when Tristan offered, but he'd not refused her his permission. Then he'd practically dragged her to their chambers and possessed her body in every way he could that night. She ached by morning from his vigorous attentions and felt a curious sensitive spot on her breast and another on the inside of her thigh in the morning when she washed. He'd just laughed when she asked him what they were. But it was that wicked laugh that made her shiver.

Now, she asked Aldys to take a walk with her, something Aldys liked because they always stopped to speak to Larenz. Sybilla could hear something going on between those two in their voices. Before they could leave, three men, from the sound of the different voices, carried something into the room. Aldys gasped at whatever it was.

'My lady!' she exclaimed.

'What is it, Aldys? Tell me, I pray thee!' She felt the woman take her hand and squeeze it and was not certain whether to be afraid or not.

Once the noise of moving something into the room finished, Aldys whispered a word that left Sybilla stunned.

'Loom.'

'A loom, Aldys? They brought a loom here?' she asked, her hands itching to feel it.

'Not a loom, my lady,' said one of the men still present. 'Lord Soren had your loom repaired. Only the one beam broke, some of the weights came loose and the threads needed to be sorted out. My wife straightened out the threads for you.'

Sybilla lost the ability to speak then. Her loom was her last connection to her father, the man who had struck him down. Why would he do such a thing for her? Would it not remind him of his bitter hatred and need for vengeance every time he saw it?

'Good day to you, lady,' the men called as they left.

Torn between going to it and being terrified of not being able to use it, Sybilla stayed where she was.

''Tis in the same place it used to stand, lady. Other than the new upright piece, it looks exactly the same.'

She tried to remember what she'd been working on the day Soren had arrived, but could not. She shook her head, unable to believe it was here.

'Come, here now,' Aldys said, guiding her to it. She held Sybilla's hands out and she ran them over the threads and the outline of the frame as Aldys named each piece. 'You were making a bedcovering when it…broke. The blue colour you liked so much when you saw—it.' Aldys finished the words, never realising until they were out the new reality—that Sybilla would never see that colour again.

'Does he think I can weave without being able to see the warp threads and the weft? How could I keep to the pattern?'

'Come now, lady,' Aldys admonished. 'You always claimed to be able to weave on this loom with your eyes closed. You used to do it half-asleep and with only the light from the hearth.' She lifted Sybilla's hands and placed them on the heddle rod. 'At least try it before you give up.'

Her hands shook and she dropped the shuttle three times before managing to get it between, over and under the warp threads and across the width of the loom once. She could only imagine how uneven her work was. Trying to keep the pattern in her mind, she counted as her fingers moved across the warp threads, and soon had completed three passes back and forth.

'How does it look, Aldys?' she asked. When she laughed, Sybilla took it as it was meant and shrugged. 'I will have to practise,' she promised. Aldys produced a sack filled with the yarn the dyers had made for her for this bedcovering from the closet where they stored the linens and other clothing.

Later, after trying for another hour or so, she convinced Aldys to help her find Soren so she could thank him, but soon discovered that he had left Alston and was not expected back until very late that night. She tried several more times to use the loom, but became frustrated when she remembered how easily she'd been able to weave both simple and intricate patterns for tapestries or clothing or linens.

Dinner was quiet for most of those she sat with had gone with Soren and had not yet returned. Tristan tried to convince her to let him teach her to play, but her thoughts were on the loom and the man who had restored it to her.

Sybilla went to bed alone, but could not sleep and ended up back in front of the loom, trying to feel for the lost pattern among the threads. It was much, much later when the door to her chambers opened and Soren returned.

The day had gone from bad to worse.

More attacks on outlying villages and the mill for Alston was burned. The miller and his family escaped, but the wheel that turned the millstone had been pushed from its support and the framework broken. Soren arranged for men to work on repairing it and left a small troop of well-armed, well-prepared soldiers guarding the workers and the mill.

Then word had come from one of Morcar's relatives to the east asking to meet with the new lord of Alston. Since they'd travelled east to the mill, Soren arranged to meet some miles between the Tyne River and the edge of Northumbria. It had taken most of the day to reach it. Having Brice at his back again felt good and for the first time in a long time, Soren felt a measure of control returning to his life.

The ride had given him time to think about something Larenz had told him that seemed ludicrous at the time, for he had just been recovering and the need for vengeance raced hot in his blood and kept him alive. The old man had said that living and living well would be the best vengeance against a man out to kill you. It made no sense to him then, but now, now that he had a taste of a life worth living, he was beginning to understand.

The problem was that he was beginning to want that life to include Sybilla. But he would stand by his bargain with her and give her her freedom at the end of six months.

Due to his actions, she'd become the only person in the world who could understand his trials, his challenges, because she was living them herself. In the supreme twist of irony, in trying to destroy her father and her, Soren had created the perfect woman for himself. And one he was destined to lose regardless of how it was to happen.

He found himself wondering about her reaction to the loom. Had it made her happy? Or would she regard it with sadness because of the connection it would always remind her of? Once he had met with this emissary, he could get back to Alston and find out.

They had met Beornwulf of Hexham at the designated place and Soren could not have been more shocked by the topic under discussion. Brice hid his surprise well, but just barely.

Beornwulf came to offer a marriage contract—one that would see him wed to the daughter of Morcar, who was currently in Normandy with William. When Soren pointed out that he was already married, Beornwulf lamented over the condition of Durward's daughter and how the marriage could be ended easily, allowing Soren to align himself with this powerful family of the north. When Soren did not immediately jump for the bait dangled before him—that there were easier ways to end a marriage to a blind woman that did not involve getting his king or bishop's permission—Beornwulf began to make the offer more attractive.

This was a trap of some kind and Soren would never consider falling in with it, but it was good to know your enemies and their plans. Without William's permission, Morcar would never regain the earldom of Mercia, so Soren and Brice suspected that this must be part of Morcar's plans to get himself back in William's good graces and back to his lands in the north.

It made sense in that light for Morcar to try to connect his family to a newly made nobleman who clearly had the king's support, but Soren had to fight the urge to take the man's head off at his unashamed boldness. Since Soren could not begin to maintain the necessary level of detachment to discuss the intricacies of such an offer, he asked Brice to remain behind to continue discussions with Beornwulf. Becoming outraged would not help matters and Soren was very close to that as he realised the implied threat to Sybilla's life.

His head spun from all the implications and possibilities for such an offer, but as he rode back towards Alston he could think of only one thing—could he convince her to stay? If she remained blind—pray God!—could he convince her to remain married to him? In spite of the horror of their beginning, in spite of what had brought them together, would she stay?

By the time he arrived home, had removed his hauberk and other armour and climbed the stairs to her chambers, it was well into the middle of the night.

Chapter Twenty-Two

He looked around the chamber, trying to enter quietly and not wake her. Soren loved the way she purred and stretched against him when he woke her in the night. He needed her to do that this night. The room was dark and only the light thrown by the torches in the hall lit his way…to an empty bed. Soren squinted into the dark, looking for her.

And found her.

'Sybilla? Why do you stand in the shadows there?'

'Light the lamp and close the door,' she whispered.

He did so and discovered that she stood by the loom in the corner, dressed in only the thinnest shift. It covered nothing and yet it did. He was hard in scant seconds.

'Why are you standing in the dark?' The words were out before he could stop them. If the callous question bothered her, it did not show on her expression. 'What are you doing?'

Soren walked to her side. The men had done a good

job repairing the loom and righting it as he'd asked. Even the threads hung evenly, all the clay weights in place as they should be.

'I have spent hours trying to weave.'

'And?' He looked at the last few lines woven and knew she'd not been successful. 'It will take you some time to learn to do this again.'

She reached out, spreading her hands and lightly gliding her fingers across the threads, almost as he'd seen Tristan do as he plucked the strings of his harp. She traced the horizontal and vertical lines held in place on the loom. And she shook her head, dropping her hands to her sides.

'I cannot see the pattern.'

He heard defeat in her voice and recognised the tone from countless times of voicing it himself when faced with the challenges of learning even simple tasks again after nearly dying. Two of the same kind, he thought as he moved behind her, remembering how Larenz had taught him to train his muscles again after the destruction. That had not involved holding an almost-naked woman in his arms, but this would.

Soren reached around her, lifting her hands and placing the shuttle in them. Then he guided her fingers over the threads.

'Feel the pattern of the threads, Sybilla. You know it, you wove it already.'

She leaned against him and he whispered to her.

'Think of it. See it where it matters—in your thoughts. Now find the pattern in the threads,' he repeated, letting his arms hold hers up and moving them across the surface of the loom. 'Tell me the pattern you see.'

'Every other, for one row. Then every second for another row and then every third.'

'Do it, Sybilla. Count the threads as you touch them, in your mind, hear the numbers you need. Let the shuttle draw the pattern,' he whispered.

She counted numbers softly, easing the wooden piece over the number of threads, then under the next, then over, row by row until she'd completed a half-dozen or so. He could see they were not perfect, but that did not matter. She was regaining her weaving and would have years to perfect it or to simply enjoy working on the loom.

Just as he had moved through every step of using his sword, over and over in his mind, until his body could do it. Then his muscles had followed his mind and he had regained the skills necessary for a knight. It took months of pain and hard work, but he'd been successful. Her pain would be of a different kind, but the work would be worth it in the end if it gave her back a taste of what she could do before he'd arrived at Alston's gate.

She completed another few rows without his urging or his hands moving hers, but he did not move from her. Her body moulded to his and her head rested against his chest. Then she placed the shuttle down and silence filled the chamber. He knew her question before she asked it.

'Why, Soren? Why did you give this back to me? Knowing who made it and what you must remember every time you look at it? Why?'

What could he say? How could he tell her that he did it because it made him feel like the man he was beginning to want to be? The one who had some good in him and did not live to hate. That helping her regain herself helped him to find his soul. How could he say those things when he was not yet certain he was ready to accept them as true? In spite of coming here for vengeance, he had found a way to seek redemption. So, instead of trying to hide behind his rage and his pain, he told her the truth and prayed she would not know how much he was coming to need her.

'It seemed the right thing to do, Sybilla.'

The words surprised him, for he had lived his life based on his looks without much care for anything more serious than finding women to swive and battles to fight. Then, without his looks, he lived on the need for vengeance. Now, she seemed to be his chance to find the real man buried deep within, the one who lived for more than hatred. 'It was the right thing to do for you.'

She turned in his arms then and lifted her face to him. He kissed her, moulding his mouth to hers, giving and seeking something more than simply pleasure this time. Soren bent down and lifted her into his arms, carrying her to the bed. Instead of laying her on it, he stood her on it. He tugged off his own garments, down to his shirt, and then pulled her shift over her head. Because of his height, this brought her breasts level with his head.

He guided her to lean her elbows on his shoulders and then he feasted on her breasts, teasing the nipples into tight buds and making her sigh and arch against his mouth. Soren held her steady with his hands on her waist, then traced a path down her chest and on to her belly until she writhed in his hold. Soren had pleasured her in many ways, save one, and his mouth watered now in anticipation of tasting her in that intimate way.

He guided her down onto the bed now, on her back,

and climbed between her legs. Instead of covering her with his body, he eased her legs apart, leaned down and lifted her legs over his shoulders. He kissed his way along the inside of her thighs as she gasped and sighed with each touch of his mouth. He did not think she realised his intent until the first touch of his tongue to the heated place between her legs.

Sybilla's body arched against his mouth, but she tried to pull back from it. From him.

'You must not,' she urged, even while her traitorous body opened to allow him access to her most private place.

'Oh, but I must, Sybilla,' he said and he laughed in that deep, sinful way he did whenever he was pleasuring her. 'Do you like it?'

He had licked her! He could not have. But he did it again and again until she gave up fighting it and moaned at the intensity of the waves of pleasure that spiralled through her with each touch. Somehow he found the centre of it, the place where everything she felt was focused, and suckled on it. She lost all thought then and could only feel… Feel the wondrous fire that moved through her blood. Feel the need for him that grew in her core. Feel the edges of her mind begin to fade as he forced her to the edge of the abyss and then over.

As she began to come apart, he lifted up and filled her, thrusting in so deeply and so hard that she keened out her release immediately. But he did not stop—relentless and unstoppable, he filled her emptiness with his body much as he'd filled her spirit. Over and over, thrusting and withdrawing, deeper and deeper, until he became part of her. She screamed out her release, praying his name again and again until she could not speak. Just when she could take no more, when she had no more to give, she felt his manhood harden more within her and knew his peak was close. He withdrew just as his seed spilled.

He held himself off her, trying to catch his breath as she recovered hers. She took the chance at that moment and reached up to touch his face. He moved back from her, out of her reach.

'Let me see your face the way I see the threads, Soren.'

When he did not come closer and did not answer, she whispered, 'I know your skin is damaged. I know you have scars. You do not have to hide them from me.'

The silence that met her words continued until he climbed off of her and slid from the bed. 'I cannot, Sybilla,' he said. 'I want to, but I cannot.'

She sensed that his admission was a bigger step between them than if he had let her, so she dropped her hands to the bed, giving up her quest to touch him. He helped her get under the covers and then climbed in next to her. Soon sleep came to claim her and Sybilla wondered if he would ever consider keeping her as his wife.

They fell into an easy pattern over the next weeks. Brice stayed on and Giles promised to arrive once Fayth gave birth. Sybilla's chambers became their refuge, where Soren could remain uncovered without fear of being seen and stared at and where Sybilla could continue to learn and relearn many skills.

Each evening began in the hall where everyone ate at

the end of the day. Tristan's attempts to belittle Soren's upbringing or past grew fewer now that Sybilla clearly was not interested in hearing such things. But, she did enjoy his talent with the harp.

When they retired to her chambers, they would eat and talk over the day's activities. Sybilla remembered her parents' habits and thought of the changes in both Soren and herself as they toiled together for Alston.

But the best part of each day was the time after night had fallen that found her wrapped in Soren's strong arms, her desires appeased and her body exhausted from his strenuous attentions.

Soren knew that her counsel to Guermont about the coming harvest and her mediation with the people eased many rough spots as Normans, Bretons and Saxons learned to exist together. And, as she lived more easily with him, the people did, too.

Troubles continued to escalate in Northumbria and rumbles of it spread into Alston. The people were not happy with William's choice of earl, no happier than they had been with Edwin or Tostig before him, so it seemed doubtful that any plan to bring Edwin back into power would move forwards at all.

Soren, may the Almighty forgive him, prayed every night that Sybilla would remain blind, knowing that blind he still had a chance to keep her with him. With everything between them, he could not find a way to ask her to stay, so he continued to show her that she could find some happiness with him and hoped she would decide on her own when the time came.

And he lived in fear that she would recover her sight. Or worse, realise how much of her life he'd been responsible for destroying. Either of those would end any chance of a future together. As autumn and the harvest arrived and knowing the winter would follow quickly, Soren knew that the rebels would have to make their move towards Scotland before the snows came. And, in his bones, he recognised that resolution of one kind or another was coming between him and Sybilla. He just hoped one or both of them would survive it.

Soren paused as he climbed the stairs. Those in the hall had grown silent after Sybilla had left and he heard the voices and conversations go back to their usual tones and volume once he did the same. Though her ease in his presence had lessened the tension between him and those he now controlled, it would take far more than their lady's approval for them to accept him.

As he reached the second floor and walked towards their chamber, he wondered if they ever would…or if she ever would. Shrugging off the wave of maudlin feelings, he lifted the latch and opened the door, never truly knowing what he should expect or what he would find within.

Or rather he could never believe what he found within.

Sybilla stood before the loom, her brow furrowed in concentration as her hands felt their way across the threads. She did not slow or stop, so he suspected that she had not even heard his entrance. He closed the door quietly, leaned against it and watched her.

She'd released her hair out of the tight confines of the netting and veils she wore outside this room and the length of it swayed even as her body did. He found her in this position day and night, at any or all hours, applying herself to relearning to weave. Sometimes clothed, sometimes not. Soren smiled at that and hardened, knowing how this encounter would end. Glancing at the bed, he noticed the path to it from the loom was cleared.

On one recent night, a chair had been left in the way and he only managed not to fall by the sheer strength of his will. Regaining his balance and holding her body to his as he carried her to the bed, he stumbled and landed on the chair, pushing himself deeper into her and moaning from the pleasure of it. Instead of startling or pushing herself free, Sybilla had simply tightened the grip of her legs around his hips and echoed his moan with one of her own. Watching her now, Soren finally allowed himself to accept what a marvel she was.

'Did you run up the stairs?' she asked in a soft voice. He'd been so lost in his thoughts he did not realise she'd stopped weaving and faced him. He drew in a deep breath and tried to calm the desire that controlled him.

'Nay,' he admitted. Let her know how much he craved her body, 'twas safer than letting her close to the truth of his need for her.

'Oh.' Her mouth formed the sound and he watched as a blush crept up her cheeks.

He wondered if her nipples had tightened at the thoughts of what could be between them. Her nipples responded to the slightest provocation. Soren stood away from the door and considered how to approach her when her stomach rumbled. Her soft laughter joined his own as another need made itself known.

'Do you never eat enough, Sybilla?'

She clutched her stomach and shrugged. 'Clearly not.'

Soren looked over at the hearth and saw a pot hanging there. A covered basket on the table held more. Knowing that their mutual pleasure would wait, he approached the table. 'Come. Eat. Your day must have been a busy one if you have not eaten yet.'

She turned back to the loom and placed the shuttle in the threads before making her way to the table. Soren noticed her mouth moving silently as she counted her steps along the way. She'd stopped a bit short, so he directed her.

'Another pace to the table,' he said.

Soren wondered at the ease with which he could speak to her here in the privacy of their chamber. He'd fought to keep himself from being too familiar with her, but he had no way to fight the effect she had on him. Determined to keep a distance between them, he had tried to remain aloof even during the nights in a shared bed. Someone should have warned him of the impossibility of it all.

Soren was learning the difference between a lover and a wife very quickly, even though he'd never planned to find either in Alston.

Sybilla reached the table and felt for the chair. Sitting in it, she waited while he brought the pot to the table. They'd learned that she could not yet carry things like a steaming pot of stew while trying to find her way around the chamber. Since she could not see the edges of her *syrce* and *cyrtel*, and had nearly set them ablaze more than once, it was safer, Aldys explained in clear tones, to allow someone else to bring such items to table.

Soren scooped some stew into bowls for each of them and handed Sybilla hers. She slid her hand across the surface and grasped the spoon there. He waited until she'd finished about half of her food before beginning his questions.

'Guermont said the harvest is going well and should be a successful one,' he began.

All she needed was for him to begin and she joined in the discussion, reviewing the day's activities and the plans for the next. Her mastery in overseeing this manor and keeping her people alive shone clear. Sybilla understood the management of crops and livestock, as well as how to get the villeins to work effectively in the fields, the manor and the mill. Alston would thrive under her hand.

But she would be gone soon, he remembered.

His mouth went dry and he grabbed for the cup of ale to wash down the food he'd been chewing. But he would be sending her away soon, in only a scant few months.

'Soren? Is aught wrong?' she asked.

'Nay,' he said a bit forcefully and then quieter, 'Nay. I but swallowed at the wrong time.'

As he had in the past, he searched for the anger that had always served him well when threatened. He searched deep inside for the hatred and the fury that would help him erase any softer feelings that came from their closeness.

And he could find none to use as protection against her.

Surely this time of ease between them was nothing more than that? They both knew the terms of their agreement and would abide by them. He could have accepted that if not for her next words. They completely tore apart any defences he'd built against her. Four simple words and he was lost, for so many reasons he could not even identify, but he knew in his soul.

'Take me to bed,' she whispered.

Soren did not question her about the change in topic or what she meant. He knew, for he felt it also. The heat between them had sparked when he entered the room and every minute, with every word, the delay in claiming her had added fuel to his need and desire for her. He pushed back from the table, lifted her into his arms and carried her to the bed.

Something was different between them this time. Oh, his passion spiked and he claimed her every way he could, thrusting deep and feeling her release as it pushed him to his own. He withdrew only at the last moment because being inside her felt…right somehow. No matter that he was a feared warrior. No matter that some still crossed themselves when they saw him. No matter that he'd sworn to take her life to repay the debt of her father.

In that moment, as their flesh joined, Soren knew she had managed to touch him in ways no one else ever had. He also knew to his marrow that if she left, it would destroy him. So his prayer as he drifted off to sleep some hours later became one for his own survival.

Sybilla lay awake, entangled in bedcovers and Soren, but did not wish to move and free herself. She felt the heat of a blush in her face every time she thought of how bold she had been this night. Though she had never refused him, she had never initiated bedplay before, always waiting for Soren to take the lead. And he had.

With vigour and inventiveness and forthright passion,

he'd led her down the path from virgin to lover. He had never apologised for the ways in which he pleasured her and never made demands of her that she was not willing to do. Tonight, though, something had changed.

She pushed her tangled hair away from her face and wished for the thousandth time that she could see him. No matter how skilled she was becoming in hearing tones in voices and noticing smells and tastes and the feel of things, not being able to see him, to watch his face as he touched her, to see the man called 'beautiful' and the damage rendered by her father left her feeling lost. She sighed and then smiled as he grasped her hand, pulling her closer as he turned to his side.

Did he even know he did that? Did he let down his guard in his sleep? Did his anger and need for vengeance ease when he was caught in rest?

She wanted to scream out her frustration, for without asking someone, she knew not the time or how many hours remained until morn. 'Twas in the latest part of the nights that she worried about her life, such as it was. Well, at least now she knew he did not mind her boldness and she planned to use it often. If he was going to put her aside, she would build enough memories to live on. Memories that would get her through the lonely, cold nights without him in her bed…or in her heart.

Mayhap the frustration gave her courage, for she lifted her hand, now freed from his, and reached out to him. Once her hand found him, his hip from what she could tell, she paused and waited for his reaction. When none came, she gently slid her fingers along his skin, tracing the line of his waist. He'd permitted her to touch below his waist, but never above it. Sybilla held her breath and let her fingers glide up his back.

A ridge of scarred skin began just inches above his waist. She traced it lightly, following it across his back and waiting for him to wake. She felt the moment he did and stilled, preparing for his anger. There was no way for her to claim the touch was accidental, so Sybilla spoke of it.

'Is it painful?' she whispered.

'Nay, Sybilla. Not all of it,' he answered without hesitation. 'Some of it feels nothing.'

When she would have asked another question of him, she felt him move away and his weight left the bed. The sound of him using the pot explained his absence, or did it? 'Twas almost as though he sought escape from her touch. Truly, he'd allowed her more in that one caress than she'd ever been permitted before.

Thinking he would avoid her further attentions, he surprised her by returning, arranging the bedcovers over them and pulling her into his embrace and against his chest. They lay quiet for several minutes, but her curiosity ran wild and she could not stop the questions from escaping.

'Tell me of the others,' she said. 'The other…bastards.'

He laughed and it rumbled beneath her ear. It also eased the tightness in her heart as he began to tell her of Giles and Brice and of Lord Simon, the legitimate son of their foster father in Brittany. Soon, tales of the escapades of the four flowed, describing boyhood to manhood and in between until she laughed and cried at some of the incidents described.

This nobleman Gautier had taken three common boys and turned them into extraordinary young men before his own death. He had given opportunities to these three that enabled them to face the challenges that life and war would toss at them. Knowing the ways of nobles here in England, she could not comprehend why he would have done so, but he had and this man was the result.

He did not refuse her questions; indeed, only when the sound of the cock crowing in the yard could be heard and his voice grown hoarse from speaking so much did he stop.

Something had changed between them. Something more than the need in her to learn about him. Something had changed within Soren and she hoped and prayed that it would continue.

And even though she remembered their agreement and knew he would put her aside, it was easier for her to hope for some future together than to face the bleak knowledge of one without him. The days had flowed quickly, filled with hard work and accomplished tasks, and the nights had raced by, filled with honest passion and shared stories. But Sybilla knew that this was simply a truce, time spent without too much thought of what should be or could be, but always with the truth standing between them.

So, as the harvest was gathered and news of rebels gathering in the hills and to the north grew more frequent, Sybilla offered prayers for herself and for Soren and for whatever they would face in the coming months.

Chapter Twenty-Three

Sybilla finished counting the last of the sacks of flour and tied the number of knots on the rope that hung on the wall next to them. Guermont had come up with this way for her to keep count and track of which supplies were stored and how many there were of any given kind. Harvest was done and they were almost ready for the cold of winter.

She was in the storeroom on the lower floor of the keep, waiting for Guermont to come back for her, when she moved too quickly and lost her balance. Banging up against a row of barrels, she put her hand out to stop herself from falling, but a moment too late to help. Though she did not think she hit her head, she lost consciousness for some time.

'Lady Sybilla? Lady Sybilla, can you hear me?'

She knew Teyen's voice and nodded, making her head

hurt even worse and making her stomach lurch from the dizziness.

'Do not move,' he instructed.

Too late. He should have said that first.

From the chuckles then, she knew she'd spoken those words aloud and others had heard her. 'Who is here?'

From the names listed by Teyen, it sounded as though everyone who lived in the keep, save Soren, was there watching her. At least he would not be witness to her clumsiness.

'Sybilla, are you well?' Soren had arrived as well.

She took a deep breath and tried to sit up. When that did not happen, she waved them out, hoping they would leave and she could lessen her humiliation. Now he would begin the lecture he'd perfected for those times when he thought she had tried to do too much, especially when he had already warned her of his opinion on the task at hand.

'Pray thee, all return to your tasks. I will be all right,' she begged. Not a sound, no one moved, no one left as she asked. The pounding in her head worsened and she thought mayhap some assistance would be the best thing after all. 'Soren…'

She did not have to ask; he was at her side in moments, easing his arms around and under her and lifting her up from the floor. Unfortunately, in spite of his gentle approach and care, each step he took made her head hurt more. By the time they reached their chambers, she wanted to cry.

Lying on the bed made things a bit better, as did the quietness, so she expected the pain to ease and everything to be all right, but it was not. Later she realised how much it felt like that first day all over again. Teyen saw to her, checking her head and finding no injury or bump. By resting, it hurt much less by nightfall.

Soren offered to sleep elsewhere so he would not disturb what rest she could get, but she knew from other nights spent without him in her bed that she would not sleep at all. He climbed in carefully, easing up behind her and surrounding her with his strength. Her sleep was fitful, partly because Teyen ordered it so and partly because of the nightmares that plagued her when she did fall asleep.

Swords cutting into bodies. Demons shrieking in the darkness. Someone tearing down Alston piece by piece and setting it aflame. Then more and more until she screamed. She woke to Soren whispering her name until she realised she was not sleeping or dreaming. The night was one of the longest in her life and she was glad when she heard the keep and yard coming to life.

After much arguing and being teased about needing a day of leisure, Sybilla was able to convince Soren to go about his duties. He apparently ordered everyone to check on her throughout the day, so from Aldys to Gytha, Guermont to Larenz and even young Raed, each visited her, asking about her head and telling her about the progress being made on readying the keep for winter. A heavy measure of guilt lay on her for remaining in bed, but the dizziness returned each time she tried to remain sitting.

When the symptoms continued into a second day, Aldys broached the possibility of being with child with her. She could feel herself blush as she stuttered out the explanation of how she knew she could not be with child, but Aldys seemed placated more by the fact that Sybilla's cycles had arrived regularly every month since they'd begun.

Mayhap it was another illness or ailment, she knew not, but she did feel better on the third morning, enough to sit up and even get out of bed. She had been thankful, for Soren had grown increasingly tense about the situation and she knew he was worried. When she woke from a nap later in the day, her head felt different somehow and the colours from her dreams seemed to remain inside her head.

Sybilla decided to try weaving a few rows, so she made her way over to the loom. It happened so slowly that she did not realise it at first, and then she could see shadows where everything had been black. Turning around, the brightness of the sun began to pierce through the shadows. She blinked and rubbed her eyes, believing she was dreaming while awake, but soon forms began to take shape and Sybilla recognised her bed and the loom in the corner. Then the colours filled in and the blue that she had loved when she first saw it on the yarn came into focus, clear and bright.

She trembled and shook and tears poured down as the possibility that she might see grew real. She needed to tell someone. She needed to tell Soren.

No! She needed to wait to see if this was happening or if she was imagining the change. If she called Aldys or Soren or anyone, even Teyen, and she was wrong… So she forced herself to sit in the chair and to wait a little while. Her stomach tumbled and her heart raced as she prayed over and over and over again that her vision was restored to her. That she would be able to see, be able to read again and to see the sunrise and the sunset. To see the people of Alston and do all the things that gave her joy and purpose.

To see Soren and to relieve him of one of the too-many burdens he carried on his shoulders. To see Raed and Guermont and the others and decide if the faces she had given them in her imagination were close to what they looked like.

She laughed then, feeling the excitement with each passing minute when her vision did not fade back into blackness. Giddy at this change, she decided that she would only wait for the next person who came to check on her before revealing it. She could not wait any longer—she wanted to run down the stairs and shout it in the yard.

Finally…finally…finally she heard soft footsteps approaching down the hall. She counted them as they moved ever closer to her door and to her revelation. Sybilla held her breath as the door opened and an incredibly tall man stepped inside. He turned back as though looking at something in the corridor and she was struck by his beauty.

Strong, masculine lines carved out a face that showed a handsome nose, strong brow and full mouth. His hair was black as coal and he wore it longer than most Normans she'd seen before, leaving it long enough to touch the edge of his tunic.

It had to be…

'Soren!' she said, catching him in the motion of

removing a cowl and a piece of leather from his face. She stood as he turned to face her, not yet realising that she could see him.

The other half of his face was as horrible as the first was beautiful. Torn asunder and put back together, the flesh pulled this way and that, giving him a garish twist to his lips. The scars… The scars…

'Dear God in Heaven!' she cried out, horrified at what she saw.

'You can see me?' he asked, turning from her, hiding that part of him from her sight. 'Your vision…'

'Oh, Soren,' she whispered, shaking her head.

He wanted to die in that moment more than at any time before.

Everything he ever feared seeing in her gaze was there: horror, disgust, fear and, the worst, pity. Part of him, the stupid, foolish part, had hoped she would be different than all the others. That she would look past the damage to the man she'd come to know these last weeks and months.

But, no, just as he knew would happen, she saw only the monster before her. His one chance had been destroyed. And for a moment, the man who had survived only for vengeance pushed his way out.

'So, now you see what your father did to me that day and why I had to kill him.'

'Soren, I pray thee—' she started, but he stopped her with a motion of his hand.

'I could accept it from strangers, from any of them, but not you, Sybilla. I thought we had some measure of trust between us, but I can see it all in your eyes now. The horror at this flesh. The pity.'

He struck out, needing to cause pain for the pain she was causing him. Now in a blind rage, he threw the last one, the worst one, at her. 'I only married you because you could not see me. And I prayed to God every night that you would remain blind. I wanted you blind, so that you could not look at me with disgust in your eyes.' Sybilla gasped, so he thought he might have hit his target.

She crumpled to her knees then, just as her maids arrived at the door. They had been yelling, so it was not surprising that others came, too.

Soren turned and walked out of her chambers, not bothering to put the cowl or patch back in place. Damn them all and damn her more!

He charged down the steps and out into the yard, the word of the miracle spreading even as he walked to the stables. His expression stopped anyone from saying anything to him. Saddling his horse, he mounted and rode out of the gates, not caring where he headed or why. He just needed to get away and try to erase the sight of finding all the things he feared most in her gaze.

Soren was so wrapped in his own pain that he never noticed the small boy watching him ride out of Alston or the disappointment on his face as he did.

All the joy she had felt as her sight returned fled in the face of Soren's revelations and his reactions.

When she'd looked on his face with the terrible damage, all she could think about was the horror that anyone had suffered in that way and lived through the terrible pain of it. Sybilla was horrified that someone she loved could have wrought such damage. In spite of Aldys and Larenz trying to explain the realities of the terrible battle at Hastings and in spite of any doubt that they tried to cast on her father's guilt, Sybilla understood why he had come seeking vengeance all those months ago.

And horrified at the shame and humiliation he suffered as a result of her father's actions. She'd lifted her hand to touch him, to try to ease the pain she knew he felt every day of his existence, and he had misread the action and the feelings behind it.

From there everything deteriorated.

Any sympathy, any understanding she might have tried to have was obliterated by his announcement that he'd killed her father. Sybilla realised that she'd never asked because she feared learning he had. And now, the thought that she had fallen in love with and given her body and heart to her father's murderer made her sick.

Had he really been the one or had he used that claim to hurt her more? He'd struck out in that moment when he'd misread her expression, but was it true?

Word spread first of her vision being restored and then the news of her reaction and his. Now Alston was like an armed camp and all the hostility of the first days was back. He slept elsewhere, ate elsewhere and would not speak to her. If he entered the hall and she was present at table, he left. Anything he had to tell her, he sent through intermediaries.

The thing that tore her apart was waiting for him to send her away. Her heart hurt as she waited for that final blow to land. As it turned out though Alston was more important than she was to him and all matters between them ceased to be of concern when Alston was in danger.

Because of that temporary truce, Sybilla now had to adjust to her life again. She put names and faces together and found that she had not imagined anyone to look as they did, except for Raed, whom Aldys had described well and mentioned that his name and hair did indeed match.

The distance he forced between them did not mean she did not care about him or watch him. Sybilla tried to reconcile all the different Sorens she'd known with the man who towered over his friends as well as the rest of her people. He now reminded her of the first time she'd seen him—sitting on his horse ready to attack, looking like the devil incarnate. The anger and rage was back, and the man who'd rebuilt her loom and who'd held her the night she faced the knowledge that she would be blind for the rest of her life was gone.

And she tried to imagine that he was the man who had shown her such pleasure. Somehow, he always seemed to be looking in her direction whenever she thought about their lovemaking. And she would blush, a certain sign to him about the direction of her thoughts.

The only thing that brought about a change was when Soren's searches found the rebels' camp and he, Brice and the newly arrived Lord Giles set their plan into motion to capture the leader. With her sight restored, and she was surprised to learn of it, he returned all her former responsibilities to her so that Guermont could join his fight force. She wondered what his friends thought of the situation between them.

Chapter Twenty-Four

'So, you suspect this Wilfrid of Brougham is helping Edmund recruit men?' Giles asked.

His friends understood that he needed to focus on the coming battles rather than the woman who had torn his heart apart with her betrayal. Soren shook his head in reply, forcing his thoughts back to the information they'd gathered. It was safer to think of killing than to think of *her.*

'Nay, I think it is Maurin de Caen. He acted as though his Norman heritage should persuade us he is not involved.'

Soren unrolled a map that Stephen had drawn during his search of the mountainous region between Alston and Maurin's lands to the west. 'There are so many places that could mask the presence of small groups of men,' he continued, pointing to several spots on the map. 'And none further apart than a few hours' march.'

'But why do they remain here in England at all when the border is so close?' Brice asked.

'I suspect you are the answer, Lord Thaxted.'

His body reacted just to her voice. He closed his eyes and tried to get his wayward thoughts and desire for her under control. Then, with a deep breath, he met her gaze.

They all turned and looked at Sybilla, who had crept up on them without them noticing her. Soren held on to the edge of the table, fighting the urge to drag her into his arms and kiss the breath from her. But then he would remember the expression on her face as she saw all of him in that moment and he could control the need.

'How am I the cause, lady?' Brice looked at her with open curiosity.

'The supplies and gold you brought. The rebels know and are going to try to take it.' She squinted and moved closer to the shadow of the building. Soren bit his tongue to stop from asking her if the bright light hurt her eyes. It must, for he'd seen her block the sun with her hand whenever she was in the yard.

Damn him for noticing!

Soren turned back to his friends as Giles looked at the map and then at her and back again.

'So, if the rebels saw us moving the carts with the gold and supplies, they might follow it in the hopes of re-supplying themselves and continuing their fight?' Though Giles was not asking Sybilla, she answered anyway.

'Lord Soren told me about Edmund Haroldson and his struggles to regain his father's lands and titles. He has lost his way in this and now only fights to fight again.'

'Lord Soren told you about Edmund?' Brice asked, glancing over at him as he said it. 'Interesting.' Soren glared at his friend, warning him off that path. 'Am I the only reason he does not head north?' he asked instead.

Sybilla glanced at Soren first before replying. 'Nay. Edmund has little support here in the north, other than one or two nobles who are hiding him. Once winter comes, he will use all his resources and have none to attract new followers. So he needs to make a stand now in order to keep the ones he has.'

'You know, it worked at Thaxted,' Brice said, looking at him and then Giles. 'We used a fake treasure to draw them out into the open.'

'Will Edmund be suspicious of it so soon?' Sybilla asked.

'Oremund is the one who was lured in, Edmund had no choice but to follow,' Soren explained, even though he'd vowed not to speak to her. Lucky for him and his weakening self-control, she stepped away from the table and their discussions after bringing up some good points. Brice nodded to her and she walked away, thankfully without another word to him.

And he watched every step she took.

'So you discussed military strategy with a woman?' Giles asked, drawing his attention back to the plans.

'She has a quick mind for details,' he said. His praise earned him several exchanged glances and questioning expressions. They did not even try to hide their curiosity.

'Soren, is there truly no chance of a reconciliation?' Giles asked. 'Clearly there is much to hold you together.'

'How would you feel if either of your wives looked on you with horror and pity? I saw it and I know I could not bear to see it when I wake in the morn and when I go to bed at night!'

He hated explaining. He hated that so many knew of the strife and the reason for it, but there was nothing to be done about that now. 'I asked for a temporary marriage and she agreed and is carrying out her part of the bargain. The harvest is mostly done and stored and Alston is ready for the coming winter. Once Edmund is no longer a threat here, I will release her from our marriage as I promised.'

They tried to argue with him, but he diverted their attention by calling in several of his men to discuss the plan to bait Edmund into a trap. Within hours, all the arrangements were made and news was let out both in the manor and in the nearby villages about the riches that Lord Brice would be transporting home.

They split up their men, leaving a good number here to protect the manor and the people and sent some out to 'beat the bushes' and stir up their quarry. Then they drove them right in between the three of them and when the battle was done and the bodies counted and identified, there could be no further claim by Edmund Haroldson in the north or anywhere in England.

'Has there been enough pain yet?'

Soren looked over his shoulder as Larenz walked to his side. He'd ridden to the hills and stood looking over all they'd—he'd—won by defeating the last wave of rebels and strengthening William's border with the Scots. He'd sought refuge in the distance and solitude of this high-perched place.

'There is always a cost for any gain, Larenz,' he said. 'You taught me that.'

'Of all the things you heard me say, that is the one you listened to?'

'It is true.'

Larenz let out a frustrated breath. 'You love her. She loves you. You are a fool. All of those things are true, as well,' he said, angrily.

He wanted to beat Soren to a pulp for messing this up, but he could understand why Soren had reacted the way he had, seeing things that might not have been there and hearing meanings to words the lady never meant.

'When you look over Alston, did you imagine it would be this way? You letting the woman you love walk away because you are afraid?'

Soren struck out, swinging his fist quickly, but Larenz expected it and stepped aside.

'I am honouring the agreement we had.'

'You saw what you wanted to see in her eyes, Soren, not what was there.'

'I imagined the horror, the hatred, the pity?'

'You convinced yourself she would feel those things. You convinced yourself she could not accept you and see past the flesh to the true man underneath. You never gave her a chance,' Larenz said. 'Then, just in case you might have been wrong, you made certain she would hate you by telling her you had killed her father.'

'I did kill him.' Soren's hands flexed as though holding his sword and reliving the moment. 'I stabbed him as I fell.'

'He was dead when he struck you, Soren. An arrow

in his back. He probably did not even realise that his axe hit you.'

Soren faced him, shaking his head in disbelief. 'I turned and swung my sword as I fell. I did kill him,' he argued, though his voice did not have the confidence it once carried. Mayhap he was beginning to question his memory of that day and the consequences. 'If he did not, why did you let me believe it?'

Larenz had seen it all, but was too far back to help get to Soren and defend his back. Now he revealed the truth to Soren that the warrior had been unable to face before now. Soren's face twisted in shock, but he knew Soren had suspected this truth for a long time.

'You had to believe it because only this gave you purpose and the strength you needed to live, but now it lies between you and the lady,' Larenz pointed to the real truth of the matter. 'And now you are strong enough to know and to accept that you did not kill him. What has happened here and between the two of you is your responsibility, not his.'

Larenz watched as Soren relived that day in his thoughts; only the gasps as the memories flooded him whispered in the space between them.

'You lived by your looks for so many years, even you believed that's all you were. The Beautiful Bastard! A man living from bed to bed and war to war.' He softened his tone. 'Then Durward took that from you and you lived on vengeance and hatred. And Sybilla took that from you and now you do not know what kind of man you are.'

Soren would not meet his gaze, but Larenz would have his say.

'I understand your fear. But do not give her up for fear.'

'She is beautiful, Larenz. She needs a man who she can gaze upon without disgust.'

Larenz backhanded him. 'You insult the lady with those words.'

Soren wiped the blood from his mouth. 'I cannot watch her tire of looking at this horror,' he said, pointing to his face. 'I cannot watch her fall in love with another. Someone who looks as I used to. Like my cousin Tristan. Someone who will lure her into their bed as I once did with other men's wives.'

'You do not trust her?'

Soren did not answer.

'To get trust you must give it. Did she never ask about your injuries? Did she never feel the scars?'

Silence met his question. 'You expected much from the lady but offered nothing in return.' Larenz shook his head and closed his eyes. 'You surprised her. You expected a young woman who had never seen the horrors of war to simply not react. Now that she understands, let her see you. Trust her.'

He could see Soren considering his words, but the fear of being rejected again was so strong. There was not much time.

'Did you ask her to stay? Did you ask her to tear up that contract and stay? Or did you tell her you were ending the marriage?' he demanded.

He knew he should not goad a dangerous, hurting man, but he needed to get through the pain. 'The lady leaves with Brice and Giles in the morn. Think about whether the risk of asking her is worth what you will become without her, what Alston will become without her. Whether emptiness and regrets will be enough for you to live on now that vengeance is gone.'

Larenz walked back to where he'd tied the horse and mounted. Gautier had claimed that Soren was the smartest of his four sons, but at times like this, Larenz doubted even his late brother's wisdom.

Soren remained without moving for some time after Larenz left, thinking on his words. His past experiences as a warrior, as the 'Beautiful Bastard', would not help him now. That shallow existence, from woman to woman and from fight to fight, with no thought of commitment or future, was over. But could he grab hold of the future and move forwards now? He kicked at a few stones at his feet and crushed them into the loosened dirt, letting Larenz's words and challenge sink in.

He'd been judged by his appearance, his good looks, tall muscular stature and sexual prowess for so long he'd forgotten many of Gautier's lessons. Or had tried to forget until *she* forced him to consider the values and truths of his life.

Sybilla had never seen that man, the one who caused women to swoon and some to fight over his attentions. The one who thought nothing of swiving another man's wife. Though he'd presented her with someone much darker and more dangerous, she'd brushed aside her fears and accepted him. *Certainement* it had not been easy for her, but Soren realised that their evenings alone in her chambers had been the turning point for her in getting over her fear of him.

He suspected that she might even have fallen a bit in

love with him when she could not see the monster that everyone else saw. And he also realised that he'd let a little of the man he wanted to be for her out during those intimate night encounters.

The wind blew against him and he turned his face into it, allowing it to cool his skin. His horse nickered as though reminding him of the time. Soren untied the reins from the tree and gathered them in his hand.

Though he understood the truth in Larenz's words, Soren felt the ripple of fear in his gut and in his heart as he considered his choices.

His life would be empty without Sybilla at his side.

His future bleak.

Worse, his heart would never recover and his soul would wither.

Climbing on to his horse, he glanced down at Alston once more and knew that he had no choice.

Alston was Sybilla and he could have neither without the other.

He did not want Alston if he did not have Sybilla.

Guiding his mount to the path, Soren gathered his courage and prepared himself to face the most terrifying moment of his life.

Chapter Twenty-Five

Sybilla stood by the gates as the last of the carts was secured. *He* had insisted that she take anything that remained of her family or her father, so she had. The loom had been dismantled and would be rebuilt when she found a place to live.

She'd finally finished the blue bedcover, but she could not bear to bring it with her. When she looked at it, she saw all the parts of her life—from the perfect before he arrived to the flawed section of her blindness, to the part they wove together, and then the last part she'd finished alone over the last weeks of turmoil and pain.

She'd left it behind for him to do with as he pleased.

Brice and Giles were saying their farewells to the men who'd served with them. This would be the last time the three were together for a while, for Giles had a new babe at home and Brice's wife was now carrying. Sybilla had accepted Giles's invitation to stay with them at Taerford for a while. Giles signalled that they were ready and

Sybilla looked around the only home she'd ever known for the last time.

She had the feeling that she'd forgotten something, so she went back into the keep for one last look. Brushing the tears from her eyes, she walked up the stairs to her chambers and looked around. Only the bed remained, with its blue cover in place. She could not help herself; she reached out and touched it. Closing her eyes, she let her hands glide over it, remembering hour upon hour of pleasure and love spent in it.

They might not have called it that. They did not even realise what they had between them in those times, but she knew it now and she would mourn its loss for the rest of her days. Separated or not, annulment or not, she had given herself, body and soul, to him and could never hope to forget it.

'I did not only pray that you would stay blind every night,' he said from the corner of the room.

She did not look up at him. She couldn't in that moment.

'I also prayed that I could find a way to make you stay.'

Soren walked towards her.

'But I did not have the courage to ask you,' he said, taking her hand and lifting it to his mouth. He placed a kiss in her palm. 'I did not have the courage to trust you when you asked me to.'

Sybilla dared not hope. She held her breath, praying for the chance to prove that she loved him.

Soren held her gaze as he unbuckled his belt and removed it. His tunic and breeches followed and all of his clothes until only his shirt remained. He was doing this in the light of day and she would see everything he'd tried to hide from her for so long. Then he closed his eye and waited.

His stomach lurched with the fear he denied having. He loved her. He had known it long before Larenz had forced him to see it and admit it. He just did not have the courage to accept it.

He'd spent so long hating, he had not recognised their love when it happened. It took the threat of losing it all and of losing her before he could come to her and risk his heart and his life. He held his breath as he pulled his shirt, the last barrier between them, over his head and stood naked before her.

He could not bear to look. He waited and waited for some reaction, some word, something.

The touch of her mouth on his back shocked him. She kissed the ridge of flesh where the axe had torn, following its path of destruction along his back on to his neck, then she pulled his head down and kissed his face and the place where his eye should be. He fell to his knees before her and held on to her, wrapping his arms around her.

'Stay with me,' he begged. The man he wanted to be for her pushed his way out, giving Soren the courage to reveal the truth of his love to her. 'Be my wife, be my future.'

She touched his head, caressing him and guiding him to stand. Soren did not release her as he stood.

'Always,' she whispered.

He bent over and lifted her into his arms, carrying her to the bed, their bed, and placing her on top of the now-finished bedcover. It represented their relationship from beginning until now and it felt right to make her his and to claim her body and heart on its surface.

Within moments, she lay naked in his embrace and he eased between her legs, filling her body and melding their flesh even as their hearts joined. And this time, for the first time, he did not withdraw as his seed spilled. As he poured himself into her, he hoped she understood the step he, they, were taking. The trust he was offering and accepting.

The love he was giving and accepting.

In that moment of complete satisfaction, of giving and receiving, he looked into her eyes and saw only love shining back at him. Soren knew he could become the man he needed to be for her.

'I will never let you go, Sybilla,' he swore to her.

And he never did.

Epilogue

Alston Manor
northern England
December AD 1067

The winds blew down from the Pennines and the snows came with them. Alston was blanketed with it for weeks before the day of Christ's Mass and would be for several months after it. It mattered not, for the people of Alston Manor were well prepared for the winter.

Life went on as it always did, even as earls and kings came and went and the new year approached, giving them the opportunity to look ahead at the life that spread out before them. Sybilla had a special present to mark the day of Christ's birth for her husband. Unsure of his reaction, she waited until night had fallen and they lay in their bed, their bodies satisfied and exhausted.

It had happened quickly—it seemed that as soon as they stopped trying to avoid the possibility of a child, she conceived. By counting back and thinking on the timing of this, Sybilla thought it might have even happened that first time when he pledged his love and future to her.

And she would tell him this night.

She would tell him now.

'Soren?' she said, testing to see if he was awake or asleep. 'When do you plan on visiting Brittany?'

'When do *we* visit Brittany?' he repeated and changed the words. 'Giles and Brice spoke of going in the summer, so that you can see the beautiful warm weather.'

'I know.' She laughed. 'Where it never rains and the sun shines every day.' In spite of numerous hot baths that now included massages to ease the tightness of his injuries, he still complained about the terrible weather in England.

'Are you dreaming of that warmth now?' He rubbed his body against hers, offering all the heat she could ever need.

'Nay.' She shook her head and prepared for his reaction. 'I was just thinking that I would like to give birth here at Alston rather than on a ship or on a road somewhere between here and there.'

His mouth dropped open and moved, but no sound came forth. Sybilla could not tell if that was good or bad until he yelled her name and began to laugh.

It warmed her heart to see this man, who'd suffered so much in this last year, finally have something to celebrate on this special day.

On the twenty-third day of July, in the Year of Our Lord 1068, Lady Sybilla of Alston presented her husband with a most beautiful baby girl. And so, the last of the bastard knights of Brittany found love and happiness far above what he had ever dreamt possible.

* * * * *

Author's Note

Although the 1066 invasion of Duke William of Normandy brought about huge changes in the politics and society of England, some of those changes were already underway. Normans had become an integral part of England during Edward the Confessor's reign, many gaining lands and titles long before the Conqueror set foot there. So, the Saxons had some experience with Norman ways before this major invasion force landed in Pevensey in October 1066.

Many Saxons held their lands after William's arrival—those who pledged their loyalty to the new ruler were permitted to retain them, but many were supplanted by those who'd fought for William. Important Norman nobles gained more property and often Saxon heiresses.

Thought ruthless and not hesitant about using force to implement his rule, William did not employ it fully after the Battle of Hastings until the revolt three years later in the north of England. Then, he unleashed his anger on those in what's still called the 'Harrowing of the North', destroying everything in his path and effectively wiping out what was left of the Saxon way of life.

In my story, one of Harold's sons, Edmund, appears as a leader of the rebels. 'My' Edmund is really a composite of several real people who lived in the aftermath of the Battle of Hastings and continued to fight the Normans as they moved from the south-east of England northwards and westwards to take control of the whole country.

It is believed that at least two of Harold's sons did survive—or avoid—the battle that killed their father and that they and their mother joined in the efforts of some of the others opposing the Normans. The earls of Mercia and Northumbria, Harold's brothers-by-marriage, switched sides several times during this conflict, were even taken to Normandy along with the designated Saxon heir-apparent, Edgar Atheling, and were later part of this struggle that led to William's 'Harrowing of the North'. So, any resemblance of 'my' Edmund to the real protagonists of history is intentional!

COMING NEXT MONTH FROM

HARLEQUIN®
HISTORICAL

Available March 29, 2011

- **THE BRIDE RAFFLE**
  by **Lisa Plumley**
  (Western)

- **DELECTABLY UNDONE!**
  by **Elizabeth Rolls, Michelle Willingham, Marguerite Kaye,
  Ashley Radcliff, Bronwyn Scott**
  (Anthology: Various time periods)
  *Five sensual short stories specially selected from
  Harlequin Historical Undone! digital program.*

- **WANTED: MAIL-ORDER MISTRESS**
  by **Deborah Hale**
  (Regency)
  Gentlemen of Fortune

- **HIGHLAND HEIRESS**
  by **Margaret Moore**
  (Regency)

HHCNM0311R

REQUEST YOUR FREE BOOKS!

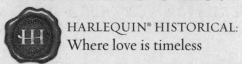

HARLEQUIN® HISTORICAL:
Where love is timeless

2 FREE NOVELS PLUS 2 **FREE GIFTS!**

YES! Please send me 2 FREE Harlequin® Historical novels and my 2 FREE gifts (gifts are worth about $10). After receiving them, if I don't wish to receive any more books, I can return the shipping statement marked "cancel." If I don't cancel, I will receive 6 brand-new novels every month and be billed just $4.94 per book in the U.S. or $5.49 per book in Canada. That's a savings of at least 18% off the cover price! It's quite a bargain! Shipping and handling is just 50¢ per book in the U.S. and 75¢ per book in Canada.* I understand that accepting the 2 free books and gifts places me under no obligation to buy anything. I can always return a shipment and cancel at any time. Even if I never buy another book from the Reader Service, the two free books and gifts are mine to keep forever.

246/349 HDN FC45

Name	(PLEASE PRINT)

Address	Apt. #

City	State/Prov.	Zip/Postal Code

Signature (if under 18, a parent or guardian must sign)

Mail to the **Reader Service:**
IN U.S.A.: P.O. Box 1867, Buffalo, NY 14240-1867
IN CANADA: P.O. Box 609, Fort Erie, Ontario L2A 5X3

Not valid for current subscribers to Harlequin Historical books.

Want to try two free books from another line?
Call 1-800-873-8635 or visit www.ReaderService.com.

* Terms and prices subject to change without notice. Prices do not include applicable taxes. N.Y. residents add applicable sales tax. Canadian residents will be charged applicable taxes. Offer not valid in Quebec. This offer is limited to one order per household. All orders subject to credit approval. Credit or debit balances in a customer's account(s) may be offset by any other outstanding balance owed by or to the customer. Please allow 4 to 6 weeks for delivery. Offer available while quantities last.

Your Privacy—The Reader Service is committed to protecting your privacy. Our Privacy Policy is available online at www.ReaderService.com or upon request from the Reader Service.

We make a portion of our mailing list available to reputable third parties that offer products we believe may interest you. If you prefer that we not exchange your name with third parties, or if you wish to clarify or modify your communication preferences, please visit us at www.ReaderService.com/consumerschoice or write to us at Reader Service Preference Service, P.O. Box 9062, Buffalo, NY 14269. Include your complete name and address.

HH11

Selene wanted nothing to do with the father of her son, Alex; but Aristedes had other plans...that included them.

Read on for an sneak peek from
THE SARANTOS SECRET BABY by Olivia Gates,
available April 2011, only from Harlequin Desire.

"You were right to turn my marriage offer down," Aristedes said.

And Selene found her voice at last, found the words that would not betray the blow he'd dealt her. "Thanks for letting me know. You didn't have to come all the way here though. You could have just let it go. I left yesterday with the understanding that this case is closed."

Before the hot needles behind her eyes could dissolve into an unforgivable display of stupidity and weakness, she began to close the door.

The door stopped against an immovable object. His flat palm.

"I can't accept that." His voice was low, leashed.

What did her tormentor mean now? Was he ending one game only to start another?

She raised eyes as bruised as her self-respect to his, found nothing there but solemnity and determination.

Before she could voice her confusion, he elaborated. "I never let anything go unless I'm certain it's unworkable. I realize I made you an unworkable offer, and that's why I'm withdrawing it. I'm here to offer something else. A workability study."

She leaned against the door, thankful for its support as partial shield. "Your son and I are not a business venture you can test for feasibility."

His gaze grew deeper, made her feel as if he was trying to delve into her mind, take control of it. "It's actually the her way around. I'm the one who would be tested."

She shook her head. "Why bother? I know—and *you* know—you're not workable. Not with me."

His spectacular eyebrows lowered over eyes she felt were emitting silver hypnosis. "You're right again. Neither you nor I have any reason to believe that isn't the truth. The only truth. It might be best for both you and Alex to never hear from me again, to forget I exist. But then again, maybe not. I'm only asking for the chance for both of us to find out for certain. You believe I'm unworkable in any personal relationship. I've lived my life based on that belief about myself. I never really had reason to question it. But I have one now. In fact, I have two."

Find out what happens in
THE SARANTOS SECRET BABY by Olivia Gates,
available April 2011, only from Harlequin Desire.

HARLEQUIN® HISTORICAL
Where love is timeless

USA TODAY
BESTSELLING AUTHOR
MARGARET MOORE
INTRODUCES
Highland Heiress

SUED FOR BREACH OF PROMISE!

No sooner does Lady Moira MacMurdaugh breathe a sigh
of relief for avoiding a disastrous marriage to Dunbrachie's
answer to Casanova than she is served with a lawsuit! By
the very man who saved her from a vicious dog attack, no
less: solicitor Gordon McHeath. Torn between loyalty for a
friend and this beautiful woman who stirs him to ridiculous
distraction, Gordon knows he can't have it both ways....

But when sinister forces threaten to upend Lady Moira's world,
Gordon simply can't stand idly by and watch her fall!

Available from Harlequin Historical
April 2011

A *Romance* FOR EVERY MOOD™

www.eHarlequin.com

HH29638